"You find me amusing, Brodie?"
Kristin demanded.

"No." Tiny laugh lines crinkled his eyes. "I find you delightful." He slid a fingertip around her rigid jaw. "And desirable."

He was close—too close. "I have no intention of sharing your bed," she warned.

"Mmm." He rested the finger̶ ̶ ̶ ̶ ̶ ̶ ulse point below her ̶ ̶ ̶ ̶ ̶ vited you to my b ̶ ̶ ̶ ̶ ̶ ll invite me to yours ̶ ̶ ̶

Her skin flan̶ ̶ ̶

She was furio̶ ̶ ̶ ̶ ̶ ̶ ̶ ̶ erself than with him. He could contr̶ ̶ her with a touch, a whispering caress, and he knew it. He was confident in his abiility to arouse, to excite. Even now she trembled.

With a maddening, lazy grin, Brodie continued his erotic assault on her senses. "When hell freezes, Kristin?" He brushed his lips across her ear and whispered, "Honey, it's getting mighty cold already."

Their eyes met, and she knew that snow was falling on the gates of Hades.

Dear Reader,

Got the February blues? Need a lift? You've done the right thing—you've picked up a Silhouette **Special Edition**. Among the guaranteed-to-cheer-you-up offerings this month is a particularly inspiring love story by Bay Matthews, *Summer's Promise*. The compelling portrait of a family torn apart by tragedy, then made whole again by the miraculous healing power of love, it's a very special kind of romance, a radical departure from "boy meets girl."

Whether they're traditional or innovative, written by your Silhouette favorites or by brand-new authors, we hope you'll find all six Silhouette **Special Edition** novels each month to be heartwarming, soul-satisfying reading.

Author Bay Matthews says: "I believe we all read romances to recapture the breathless, sometimes bittersweet feelings of falling in love. As well as fulfilling that promise to the reader, Silhouette **Special Edition** features exciting plots grounded in the psychological and emotional makeup of the characters. **Special Edition** allows me to stretch the boundaries of romance, to create realistic people and explore their minds, their souls and the entire spectrum of emotions ruling them. As a writer *and* reader, to me, that's special."

Let us know what's special to *you*—all the authors and editors of Silhouette **Special Edition** aim to please.

Warmest wishes,

Leslie Kazanjian

Senior Editor
Silhouette Books
300 East 42nd Street
New York, N.Y. 10017

DIANA WHITNEY

Cast a Tall Shadow

Silhouette Special Edition

Published by Silhouette Books New York

America's Publisher of Contemporary Romance

To Pat Warren, a real-life heroine
who is my teacher, my mentor and my friend

SILHOUETTE BOOKS
300 East 42nd St., New York, N.Y. 10017

ISBN: 0-373-09508-2

First Silhouette Books printing February 1989

Printed in the U.S.A.

DIANA WHITNEY

says she loves "fat babies and warm puppies, mountain streams and Southern California sunshine, camping, hiking and gold prospecting. Not to mention strong, romantic heroes!" She married her own real-life hero fifteen years ago. With his encouragement, she left her longtime career as a municipal finance director and pursued the dream that had haunted her since childhood—writing. To Diana, writing is a joy, the ultimate satisfaction. Reading, too, is her passion, from spine-tingling thrillers to sweeping sagas, but nothing can compare to the magic and wonder of romance.

Underlined places are fictitious.

Chapter One

The ancients believed that worthy men in pursuit of a righteous love, stood tall on the pillar of their deeds, casting shadows on the sun.

The wing gate shuddered to a close, trapping a bellowing, indignant calf in the crowded holding pen.

With weary frustration, Nathan Brodie lifted his Stetson, wiped a sweaty forearm across his brow, and surveyed the chaos of men and beasts surging through the branding corral. The whistles and shouts of the ranch hands began to ebb, replaced by disgruntled snorts and mournful bawls of the reimprisoned cattle.

These sounds were a stark contrast to the wailing sirens and screeching tires of city streets. A different world, Brodie mused. A different life.

He spoke to the spindly man slouched beside him. "Is that the last of the runaways, Gus?"

Gus grunted. "Danged if it ain't, and no thanks to them mule-headed, smart-mouthed whelps you keep rammin' down my throat."

Brodie's jaw clamped. Aware that his cantankerous foreman was essentially right, he swallowed the urge to defend his young wards. The three teenaged boys for whom Brodie had accepted court-appointed guardianship had been a constant source of irritation for Gus. Their inexperience and youthful exuberance continually hampered ranch operations.

Cattle, however, were not Brodie's priority. The New Wave Ranch existed to provide poverty's children with a safe haven, away from the violence of the inner city. Gus knew the ranch's purpose as well, and Brodie knew the acid-tongued cowpoke was honestly concerned about the boys' welfare. Brodie lowered his glance, assessing the man before him.

With tiny, dust-reddened eyes Gus glared up, puckered his lips and stroked his stubbled chin with misshapen fingers. "Whatcha' gonna do this time?" Gus's voice, thin and high-pitched, snapped like a dry twig. "Tap a knuckle and send 'em to bed without supper? Or maybe you're just gonna ask 'em to pretty-please shut the gate while they're breakin' ranch rules." Gus pinched his lips and punctuated this statement with a stream of tobacco juice.

Brodie smiled. Gus was a spindle-legged, son-of-a-tree toad and had tried Brodie's patience more than once. A deep, long-term friendship with Gus Krieger gave the weathered cowpoke leave to speak his mind, a privilege invoked frequently and with a zesty irreverence no other man on the ranch would dare imitate.

"You're getting testy in your old age, Gus," Brodie said. "Seems to me you were a bit more tolerant when I was their age."

When Brodie had met Gus twenty years ago on Dar Garrett's Montana spread, Brodie had been an arrogant and sullen runaway escaping the barrios of East Los Angeles.

"Hmmph. There was only one of you, if'n I recall. There's three of them and danged if each one of 'em don't stretch a man's patience. You was a pain in the butt, too. Never did fig-

ure why old Dar'd take you in, scraggly pup that you was." Gus
eyed Brodie shrewdly. "Got to admit you polished up nice.
Wouldn't've figured as much, what with your mean temper and
all."

"You're the one that cured my temper," Brodie said with a
soft chuckle. "Once I crawled out of that pig wallow you threw
me in, I learned to keep my mouth shut." Brodie sounded
wistful. "I'd been so sure I could whip you, too."

"Whup me?" Gus was indignant. "Couldn't then, boy, and
you can't now. Anytime you think different, I'll be plumb
pleased to oblige."

Brodie laughed and clamped a firm hand on Gus's shoulder. "I can still get your goat. I always did love to see you with
your shorts in a knot, but you know I couldn't run this place
without you."

Gus was partially placated. "That's a fact."

Yes, it certainly was, Brodie agreed silently. That long-ago
journey at age fifteen had been a turning point for Brodie. It
had demonstrated more eloquently than any textbook an alternative to the violence and despair of the ghetto's asphalt
cage.

Brodie glanced across the checkerboard of enclosed pens toward two sullen adolescents slumped on a fence rail. "You
know, Gus, you *did* make a pretty good point yesterday, telling those two their roping technique left a bit to be desired."

Gus expelled a derisive snort and muttered a sharp exple-
tive. "What I told them ornery pups is that they couldn't lasso
a fence post with a Hula-Hoop." His leathery forehead creased.
"What I *didn't* tell the dang fools was to leave the gate open
whilst they worried some poor dogie by flinging loops at it."

Stifling a smile, Brodie replaced his hat, tugging it firmly
over a mass of curling brown hair. "Maybe," he acknowledged. "But it seems to me they were just looking to do what
you told them." He slanted a glance at Gus. "Maybe even
trying to make you proud of them."

The older man sputtered, then mumbled a partially unintelligible, but obviously uncomplimentary response. He snatched

off his own ragged headgear and, in a fit of pique, smacked the gatepost with it.

"Blast your hide, Brodie. Didn't we just lose the whole dang morning roundin' up loose cows? Them extra drovers don't give a fig whether they're wranglin' runaways or doin' the branding we hired 'em for, they get paid by the hour, and thanks to them two—" Gus jerked his head in the direction of the somber, fence-sitting duo "—they got at least an extra half-day's pay comin'."

Reflexively, Brodie began to massage the back of his neck, a shadow of concern crossing his face. Gus was right. This stunt would cost plenty and what he didn't need at this moment was one more problem. Then, as a distant billow of dust caught his eye, he realized with leaden certainty that one more problem was exactly what he had.

The automobile veered closer, heaving over the rocky ground, then shuddering to a stop at the crest of a small rise about fifty feet away. Brodie watched a slender woman emerge. She seemed hesitant, straightening to survey the surroundings as a skittish ground squirrel might rise on its haunches to sniff danger.

Brodie cursed her ill-timed arrival.

A full day early, but there she was, Ms. Whatever-the-heck-her-name-is, Chief Bureaucrat and Obstructionist from the Los Angeles County Social Service Agency. Swell. This was just what he needed to cap off a totally dismal, cow-pucky day.

After eight years as a probation officer, Brodie was intimately acquainted with the preponderance of red tape associated with an unwieldy, ineffective juvenile system. Still, he bristled at anything that even remotely smacked of government interference and this woman's presence was like a canker on his soul. New Wave itself was located in Mariposa County, but the boys had come from Los Angeles and were wards of that county's juvenile justice system.

Brodie's muscles bunched with the unconscious clenching of his fists. He had no doubt whatsoever that this woman's prime directive was to create as much turmoil in his operation as the power of her position would allow.

Gus also regarded the woman's arrival as somewhat inopportune, sourly mumbling, "Ain't that a kick in the rump?" before he ambled away.

The warm spring air was heavy, polluted by dust and a fetid animal smell. Kristin Price stood immutable beside the rental car and felt her skin frost at the sight: a horde of huge, hoofed beasts that snorted, slobbered and swarmed as far as the eye could see. The ground seemed to undulate with the constant motion of hundreds of the massive brutes.

Why, in the name of heaven, had she allowed herself to accept this assignment? How could she, who panicked at the sight of a leashed poodle, possibly maintain even a mere shred of sanity while the flesh-and-blood embodiments of her childhood nightmares surrounded her?

Shoulders squared, chin lifted, she held herself erect and rigid. She knew perfectly well why she was here.

Scanning the dust-choked scene, her gaze stopped on the figure of a tall, broad-shouldered man standing spread-legged and staid, arms tensely folded, expression grim.

Apparently, he knew why she was here, as well.

Dressed in faded denims, he sported a cowboy hat and his shirt sleeves were rolled nearly to his elbows, revealing well-formed, sinewy forearms. He was grimy, disheveled and, in most respects, very much like all the other men hustling through the compound.

There was something about him, though, a self-assured, commanding presence that alerted her that this was probably the man she'd been seeking—Nathan Brodie, owner of the ranch and court-appointed guardian of three adolescent wards. According to the thick files nestled in her briefcase, all three of them were problem kids.

Kristin saw that the man seemed to be watching her intently, but he made no move in her direction. Her stomach twisted with the realization that he expected her to meet him on his own turf, within breathing distance of an entire herd of those wretched, bellowing beasts.

She took a deep breath and studied her options. The animals were contained, she noted, and however flimsy the splintered wooden rails appeared to her, the cattle seemed to respect the barrier.

Intellectually, she was aware that cattle, as a species, were mentally incapable of conspiring to leap the fence en masse just to trample her and bite her face. They were vegetarians, after all. They ate grass, not people.

That rational thought, however, did little to keep her flesh from slithering and her heartbeat from thundering like the rhythmic thud of a thousand hooves. They were still animals. Big ones, and to Kristin, all animals were unpredictable and dangerous.

Fixing her stare on the man's taut frame, she willed her brain to ignore the extraneous. She had a job to do and with rigid determination, Kristin marched down the hill.

Brodie regarded the woman who strode toward him over the rocky ground as though she wore combat boots instead of high heels. Her hair was blond, very light in color, and as she closed the distance between them, he saw that its well-scissored layers were brushed forward to dust her cheekbones like silky feathers. She wore tailored business attire, Brodie noticed. A power suit, as though she wanted no dispute over her control.

When she banked and halted a few feet in front of him, her gaze was still moored firmly on his face. Her eyes were silvery gray and displayed such unexpected intensity that his innards flinched and coiled.

He saw her lips part slightly, as though to speak, but she didn't. Instead, she tilted her head to one side and scrutinized Brodie with undisguised curiosity. Her gaze seemed as tangible as a touch. When she finally spoke, her voice was low and husky. A throaty whisper. He shivered.

"I'm looking for Nathan Brodie," Kristin said. "Have I found him?"

Kristin was affected by the power of that craggy, square-jawed face. Her throat felt suddenly dry, parched as rope. She saw Brodie appraise her, noticed that his deep-set eyes were a cool, ocean blue.

In reply to her question, Brodie managed a curt nod. "You have." His tone was sharper than he'd intended, but he was annoyed by his reaction to this woman. Bureaucrats weren't supposed to be sexy. He didn't need this complication.

"I'm Kristin Price, Mr. Brodie," she said with a tight smile. "I assume you were expecting me."

"Tomorrow. Not today."

"Oh. Well, I apologize if my arrival is inconvenient. I understood that you were told only to expect me some time this week." She attempted a friendlier demeanor and extended her hand. "Anyway, I'm pleased to meet you, Mr. Brodie. I've heard quite a lot about you and your ranch."

Brodie stared down at the slim hand as though it were an alien life form, then took it. Her skin was soft, her grip was firm.

"I'd expected someone a bit more . . . experienced," he said.

She seemed amused. "I think you'll find my experience quite adequate to satisfy your needs, Mr. Brodie." Her head tipped as she returned his scrutiny. "You don't exactly fit my image of a hard-bitten, ex-probation officer, either."

"What image is that?"

She laughed huskily. "You know, shadows under the eyes, a day's growth of whiskers, reeking of tobacco and liquor."

Brodie's eyebrows hitched. "Sorry to disappoint you."

"I'm not disappointed."

He smiled—a slow, very male smile. "Neither am I."

Incredible eyes, Brodie thought, the color of a winter sky. Combined with her pale hair and light skin, she exuded a silvery, moonlit aura that was both exotic and mysterious.

Wavering beneath the intensity of Brodie's gaze, Kristin realized her skin was becoming uncomfortably warm and a bit prickly. She'd had her share of admiring glances, but this man seemed to disarm her very soul. A soft breeze carried his earthy, masculine scent and she felt imprisoned by some strange magnetic force. Her breathing shallowed, her mouth dried. Why did he have to be so attractive? She didn't need this complication.

Reluctantly, she dragged her eyes away, swallowed hard and tried to regroup. She was startled by activity on the far side of the pen which excited the cattle and initiated a new round of noisy bellows.

Brodie, noting Kristin's reaction, began to walk away from the pens toward a twisted oak that stood alone in the barren roundup area. Kristin gratefully moved beside him, synchronizing with his easy gait.

"How long is this bureaucratic bull going to take?" Brodie asked. He'd tried to lighten up, to take the nervous edge off his voice, but was unsuccessful.

When they reached the tree, Kristin watched Brodie lean against the trunk. He casually bent one knee and propped a boot against the fat root that was snaking into the soil. When he pushed up the brim of his hat, a trickle of mahogany curls escaped to bounce against his forehead.

Kristin regarded the hard, chiseled man with some trepidation. She wouldn't back away from trouble, but she had enough to deal with on this assignment and had hoped for a more amicable relationship. She could understand a certain amount of concern on Mr. Brodie's part. She was, after all, charged to report on the efficiency of the operation and her analysis would play a major role in determining the future, if any, of his project.

Still, he seemed to be guarded, a bit more hostile than she would expect. Unless, of course, he had something to hide. If he did, Kristin had no doubt whatsoever that it would soon be exposed.

The number of young ranch residents could expand to well over a dozen in the near future. If her report was favorable, that is. The number could also plunge instantly to zero. She had the power to transfer all the boys and revoke the ranch's foster home status with the slash of her signature. She'd used that authority more than once. In fact, she'd garnered a well-earned reputation for padlocking more unworthy foster homes than any investigator on staff.

Kristin knew from bitter experience that intricate maneuvers were sometimes used by those interested in abusing the system and the kids to satisfy their own perversity and greed. Most people who accepted the enormous responsibility of caring for these confused, lonely children did so with a true sense of love and commitment. For those with less pure motives, Kristin had no patience, and no mercy.

She prided herself on being thorough. Very thorough.

Kristin cleared her throat. "My assignment is rather open-ended, Mr. Brodie, although I expect it will require from two to four weeks." She gave him her sweetest smile before adding, "If we don't run into any problems."

Brodie's forehead creased. "Just what kind of problems are you expecting, Ms. Price?"

"I'm not expecting any at all." She arched a brow in question. "Are you?"

Brodie's face darkened and he turned away. He was silent for several minutes, and when he finally faced her again, his eyes were hollow. "What I expect or don't expect is not the issue. Let's talk about what you're looking for."

Kristin eyed him coolly. So the man wanted to be evasive, she told herself. "My function is to assure compliance with those regulations pertaining to court-appointed guardianship." She noted a slight convulsive twitch in Brodie's cheek. "It's my understanding that you currently have custody of three adolescents, all of whom have relatives available to care for them. Is that correct?"

"Basically."

"It's also my understanding that these juveniles have rather lengthy records of petty crime and socially unacceptable behavior." Kristin paused, awaiting confirmation.

"Yes. 'Hard-core salvageables,' I believe the system calls them." Brodie didn't try to cover the sarcastic tinge of his voice, but Kristin appeared to ignore it. Instead, she surprised him by pursing her lips and giving him a thoughtful, searching expression.

"You know, your idea...this ranch...is being hailed as a creative alternative to the current foster home system. It's seen as having a great deal of positive potential," she said.

Shifting uncomfortably at the unexpected praise, Brodie made a brief, neutral sound and jammed his hands into the pockets of his jeans.

"At any rate, I'll be interviewing the boys, reviewing the operation, analyzing options...." A playful smile danced across her lips. "All the normal bureaucratic bull."

Eyes widening slightly in surprise, Brodie finally returned her smile with a subtle twitch. He cursed himself for being so belligerent, and still didn't completely understand his own reaction. Certainly, he held an intense dislike for a bulky and impersonal juvenile system. He'd experienced firsthand that, in such a sprawling bureaucracy, paperwork came first and people came second.

Still, this woman held the purse strings and with them, the future of the ranch. Even if the ranch eventually became self-supporting, as he had every reason to believe it would, without the blessing of the courts and other agencies, he would never have access to the kids who really needed the New Wave experience.

He had to "mellow out," as the boys would say.

Brodie forced a starched smile. "I suppose you'll also want to spend some time with the boys," he said. "We can arrange to accommodate..."

The words died in his throat as he saw Kristin blanch. He followed her wide-eyed stare, looking over his shoulder to see Merle Deever, one of his full-time ranch hands, trotting toward them on a bay gelding. Deever reined the horse at the edge of the oak and the animal wheezed and snuffled, mincing sideways anxiously.

Kristin stood rigid, staring at the monstrous brute as it rolled its eyes, nostrils flaring, lips curling to reveal enormous yellowed teeth.

Brodie recognized her anxiety and wondered about it. He also noted that she stood her ground, ramrod straight and at attention, like the ashen ghost of a spit-and-polish soldier. Brodie half expected to see her offer the steed a smart salute.

Deever appeared unaware of the distress his mount was causing, acknowledging Kristin with a deft touch to the brim of his hat and a curt nod.

"Begging your pardon, ma'am," he said politely, then shifted in the saddle and turned toward Brodie. "Boss, Gus wants to know if we should begin cutting. Says we can brand maybe twenty-five head by dark if we start now.''

Automatically, Brodie squinted at the sun's position. "Yeah, better get started. We've squandered enough of the day.''

Deever nodded in grim agreement.

"I'm going to take Ms. Price back to the house and see that she gets settled in," Brodie said. "Tell Gus I'll be back in half an hour or so."

"Right," replied Deever. With a garbled clucking sound, he snapped the reins sharply and turned his mount around. The big bay galloped toward the corral.

Brodie cupped his hands around his mouth. "Hey, Merle!"

Deever jerked the horse to a halt and pivoted smartly.

"Tell Gus to keep those teenaged rodeo rejects out of the branding corral, hear?" Brodie was vehement. "I don't care if he has to hog-tie them and hang them in the hay barn, just keep them away. I'll deal with them when I get back."

Deever indicated the message had been received and understood, then spun the horse and disappeared behind the crowded clutter of pens.

Returning his attention to the rigid woman in front of him, Brodie saw that her face was still colorless and she'd knotted her hands together in a vain attempt to still their trembling.

She's not just nervous around horses, he realized. *She's scared spitless of them. Two to four weeks? She'll be lucky if she makes it to the end of the day.*

The thought should have been immensely satisfying to Brodie. Somehow, it wasn't.

Kristin cleared her throat, moistened her dry lips with the tip of her tongue and willed her voice to be firm and clear. "It's not necessary for you to escort me back to the house, Mr. Brodie," she said, irritated by her quavering tone. "It appears your...ah...men need you here, and..."

Her voice trailed off as the movement of several mounted riders caught her attention. They were perhaps thirty yards away, but Kristin's gaze was riveted on the horses.

Everywhere. No fences, no barriers. They were everywhere—brown horses, black horses, spotted horses—everywhere.

Oh, God.

A warm hand closed firmly on her shoulder, startling her and tearing her attention away from the animals. She looked up and saw Brodie's expression. He knows, she thought irritably. He knows and he thinks it's funny. Terrific, just terrific.

His smile was meant to offer encouragement, but Kristin saw only amusement and was humiliated.

He squeezed her shoulder, then skimmed his hand down her spine to the small of her back and guided her toward the car. It was a brief, silent walk. As he held the door open, he told her, "I wasn't born with any great love of horses myself. It kind of grows on you."

"So does fungus," she replied crisply. "I avoid that, too."

Brodie's chuckle was deep and rich. "I never looked at it quite that way before," he admitted.

As Kristin slid into the driver's seat, a spiraling breeze puffed her hair, ruffling the silken wisps to expose thin, silvery scars carving ragged angles from cheekbone to temple. They were pale, subtle, not detracting from her fragile beauty.

And she *was* beautiful, Brodie acknowledged. With a translucent ivory complexion, full cushiony lips and those startling silver-sparked gray eyes, she was very, very beautiful.

Brodie noted her hair had been styled to camouflage the imperfections, but she appeared unperturbed, as though she were totally unconcerned whether the threadlike flaws were exposed or not. And why should she be? he thought grimly. She probably knew perfectly well what effect she had on men.

Closing the car door, Brodie said, "If you'll give me a lift to the house, I'll see that you get settled in." Kristin nodded. When Brodie slid into the seat, his presence filled the car with an aura of pure masculine power. Kristin took a quick breath, then let it out slowly and wondered if he realized the potent effect he had on women.

The stubborn engine grunted and coughed before droning into action. Kristin swerved the vehicle, carefully guiding it past larger rocks and bushes partially obstructing the dirt road that led from the roundup area to the ranch.

There was a small hill beyond the rise on which Kristin had parked, and as soon as they crested it, she saw that the landscape began to change from the bare, rocky ground, sterilized by years of constant trampling. The oak grew thicker, taller, with a profusion of tender new leaves, and even at this low elevation, various species of pine pocketed the stands. Fragile wildflowers swayed on the light breeze. A melodic warble filled the air, then another, as though the birds were serenading the glorious spring day.

Valleyed in the cradle of rolling hills, Kristin saw a scattering of whitewashed buildings. The cluster contained stables, the main house, a large barnlike structure and an elongated, rectangular building which resembled a bunkhouse.

Kristin realized it had been less than a quarter mile to the house, well within walking distance for one not wearing three-inch heels. She'd deliberately chosen business wear to establish her professional credibility, but she couldn't wait to change into more casual attire.

The house was a two-story wooden frame structure and as Kristin pulled the car in front, she noticed that the entire area seemed unfinished, barren, and she absently wondered what was missing.

Her mental meandering ceased with the slam of a car door. The vehicle bounced slightly and she saw Brodie at the back hefting luggage from the trunk.

She swung her door open and stepped out just as Brodie heaved a compact, but weighty case. With a brief, questioning look, he swung it carelessly toward the ground.

Reacting instantly, Kristin snatched it, yanking the object out of his grasp and hugging it as though it were a living thing.

Brodie raised an eyebrow in question. "What the devil is in there, gold bars?"

"My trusty typewriter." She stroked the vinyl cover.

"You travel with your typewriter?" Brodie asked curiously. "Sounds like you have some heavy-duty writing planned."

"Yes, actually I do."

Continuing to unload her luggage, Brodie asked, "Writing a book?"

"Umm . . . sort of. I have a manuscript in progress and hope to draft a few chapters while I'm here."

Thudding the final piece of luggage to the ground, Brodie dusted his hands and slammed the trunk lid. He angled an amused glance in her direction as he plucked one suitcase with each hand. "If you're going to be famous some day, this place will be a tourist attraction," he said with a teasing grin. "It might even become a historical monument."

She smothered a smile. "My work isn't exactly aimed for mass marketing appeal."

Brodie grinned a lazy, heart-stopping grin that had Kristin's breath catching in her throat. First he scorched her with smoldering intensity, then he disarmed her with boyish charm. Fascinating.

A high-pitched squeal of distress erupted from the barn. Kristin and Brodie both snapped toward the sound and froze. It sounded like a child, a terrified child. It was followed by a second, more fervid cry.

Brodie's long legs ate the distance from house to barn in seconds, while Kristin stumbled a few steps before kicking off her heels and racing after him.

The barn's large double doors stood open like a great gaping mouth in the sagging wooden structure. Kristin reached the doorway, blinking into the dimness. She heard ragged, irregular gasps emanating from one side of the barn and Brodie's soft, soothing voice on the other side. She also heard an unfamiliar rustling, like something moving on the hay-covered floor.

Brodie's voice was low. "Be still now, Todd. It can't reach you there."

As Kristin's eyes adjusted, she saw Brodie's powerful outline in the dim shadows. Then he moved quickly, fast and fluid, and snatched a flat-edged spade from its hanger.

In the triangular spray of light slanting from the open doors, Kristin saw a smaller form standing rigidly against a lopsided stack of hay bales. Half the boy's face was illuminated, revealing one wide, rounded eye focused raptly on the floor at a spot several feet away.

Kristin started toward the frightened youngster.

"Stop!" Brodie's command was issued in a low hiss. "Don't move."

Kristin froze midstride.

The unfamiliar rustling became louder. It was closer, more agitated.

Like the flash of a dagger, the spade sliced between Kristin and the boy, axing the straw covering, biting the wooden floor boards. Something glinted and thrashed like a bullwhip.

Thrusting his hand into the dense hay bed, Brodie seemed to wrestle a thick, humped cord before he finally held up the twitching, headless body of a rattlesnake. Kristin stiffened.

Air rushed from the boy's lungs in a relieved, whooshing gush. "Thanks, man," he said, then quickly added, "I wasn't scared of that snake-dude or nothing. Just wasn't...expecting it, that's all."

Expressionless, Brodie took a step toward the door and flung the snake. It skidded across the dirt like a fat rope. He used the flattened spade to scoop up the still-poisonous head, then carried it outside to lay beside the rattler's quivering torso.

Returning to the darkened interior, Brodie stood in front of the youngster. His voice was deceptively calm. "A bit forgetful today?"

Todd shifted under Brodie's even, unwavering gaze. "I checked, Brodie...honest. I did a full snake search before I started shifting bales." Todd could no longer meet Brodie's stare. "Might've missed a spot," he mumbled.

Brodie's eyes narrowed and the boy was seized by a minor coughing spasm. Finally, Todd's hands flew up in a gesture of defeat. "Okay, okay," he sighed. "So I forgot, you know?" He lifted his small chin defiantly. "So what?"

With a dark, hard glint in his slitted eyes, Brodie leaned forward until his face was inches from Todd's, and his voice was as harsh as his expression. "So *that*," he bit out, snapping his head in the direction of the snake's mutilated body.

Brodie straightened. Todd relented.

"Got it?" Brodie asked quietly.

Todd nodded. "Got it," he mumbled.

The boy's freckle-dusted, slightly snubbed nose and large round eyes gave him a vulnerable, childlike appearance. Kristin tried to remember details from her files. Todd Waring, she recalled, was the youngest of Brodie's charges. His mother was deceased, his father was an unemployed alcoholic.

"You're thirteen, aren't you, Todd?" she asked.

Startled, Todd stared at Kristin as though she had just materialized before his eyes.

"Yeah," he replied, suddenly wary.

"This is Ms. Price," Brodie said. "She's from the social service agency."

The boy's mouth tightened as he raked a broom-straight thatch of ragged hair. His eyes narrowed but the lowered lids didn't hide a shocking flash of coldness, jaded and brittle, inconsistent with the softness of his face. Then it was gone, replaced by youthful innocence. The episode was so brief, Kristin wondered if she had imagined it.

Todd muttered a rather neutral "Hi," then turned to Brodie. "Can I go now?"

Thrusting the spade at the boy, Brodie said, "Bury the head behind the barn. Three feet deep, no less."

Nodding again, the boy took the flat-headed shovel and slouched toward the door.

"Brodie?" Todd said.

"Umm?"

"Can I have the rest of it?"

Brodie seemed to cogitate the question, then smiled. "I guess so. Just get your tail back and finish in here before supper."

Todd was immediately delirious with excitement. "Sure thing, Brodie. Whatever you say," he chirped, then disappeared with his prize.

Kristin was still somewhat stunned by the entire episode. "Why on earth does he want a snake corpse?" she asked.

With a wry grin, Brodie replied, "He'll peel it, wrap the skin around his hat, then strut around a bit."

"Oh."

Shards of straw scratched at the soles of Kristin's feet as she walked, able now to visually absorb her surroundings. It wasn't a particularly large barn, perhaps the size of a three-car garage. The barn's twenty-foot height was divided by a partial loft made accessible by a rickety wooden ladder. Hoes, shovels and other tools dangled along the walls, as did bits, bridles and other items of tack.

There was no unpleasant manure odor and the area was obviously used as a tack room and for hay storage rather than as animal housing. The air was musty, thick with the scent of sweet green hay and most of the barn was littered with stacks of huge, bundled bales.

Carefully picking her way on the splintered floor, Kristin approached one bale that was propped, semivertically, against another. She pushed at it with her foot, then wedged her palm under the baling wire and pulled. The sharp band stung her palm, and the bale didn't budge.

"It weighs a ton," she pronounced.

"Not quite," Brodie said, sauntering to her side and swinging the bale into place with a smooth, arcing movement. "About eighty, ninety pounds, maybe."

Kristin was shocked. "And you expect a thirteen-year-old boy to stack these things?"

Brodie shrugged. "It's his job."

"But what if a bale fell on him? He could be badly injured." She made a sharp sound of annoyance. "Well, this is just too dangerous."

"Dangerous?" Brodie looked incredulous. "*Hay* is dangerous?"

Kristin shifted uncomfortably. Put that way, it did sound a little silly. Still . . .

Impatience colored Brodie's tone, but his voice was low and even. "In the barrios, these kids can get shot just walking down the street. I'd say that's a sight more dangerous than a few squares of hay." He made a derisive sound. "There's plenty of work around here, and everyone does his share. *Everyone.*"

Without a backward glance, Brodie strode out of the barn.

Well, she may have overreacted a bit, Kristin silently acknowledged, but that did seem a large chore for such a young boy. And yes, there would be a lot of work to an operation like this. Labor would probably take the biggest bite out of its operating budget, too. In fact, if labor costs could be significantly reduced, this ranch would probably increase its profit margin by a hefty percentage.

Brodie didn't seem the type to use kids and abuse the system, but as a foster child herself, she'd seen the faces of human duplicity before.

As an investigator, she trusted facts, not instincts.

Free labor provided by the dozen or more strong-backed teenagers Brodie was requesting just might make the difference between red ink and black on a small ranch like the New Wave. Could that be the reason Brodie was anxious to accept the responsibility of so many more youngsters?

Kristin was strangely disheartened at the thought, but she had a job to do and, as always, she would be efficient, methodical and very thorough.

And, as always, she would uncover the facts.

Chapter Two

By the time Kristin returned to the house, the abandoned stack of luggage had disappeared and Brodie was leaving. Clearing three wooden porch steps with one stretch of his lean legs, he pulled up directly in front of her.

"Your things are upstairs, first door on the right," he told her. "I've got to get back. If you need anything, ask Oaf."

Kristin's eyes expanded. Oaf?

Cryptic instructions issued, Brodie spun smartly and headed toward the hill bordering the roundup field. Assaulted by a strange sense of loss at his departure, Kristin suddenly felt isolated and alone.

"Wait!"

He turned and regarded her with intense interest.

There was a magnetic potency in Brodie's eyes that seemed to erase the contents of her brain leaving a void under her scalp. Kristin licked her lips, wondering what possessed her to blurt that pathetic entreaty. She had sounded almost desperate, even to her own ears.

But there he was, waiting, expecting something profound and relatively intelligent to flow from her parched mouth.

"I...uh, wanted to thank you for your assistance," she said, with prim formality. "And I...wondered when I could get started."

His eyes veiled. "Anytime you want. It's your show."

"Yes, well, I'd like to meet the other boys, of course, and I'll need access to your records."

Brodie tipped his head forward and seemed to be concentrating on the toes of his own scuffed boots. He took a slow step toward her, then met her eyes.

"Jess and Ernie are up at the corral. We're branding the rest of today and probably most of tomorrow." Brodie paused, poked at the brim of his hat and ignored her request for records. "You'll meet them at supper tonight. Of course, if that's not soon enough, you're welcome to come on up the hill."

His eyes held amused challenge. *Sure,* they seemed to taunt, *if you've got the guts to face a few cows and horses.*

He didn't say it, but Kristin was certain that was exactly what he was thinking and she stiffened, defying his gaze with a hard stare.

"Thank you, Mr. Brodie." Her voice was cool. "Perhaps I'll do that."

He nodded. "Brodie," he said, "just Brodie. Anything else, Ms. Price?" He spoke with exaggerated courtesy, staring pointedly at her left hand and finding it unadorned.

"No, thank you." Kristin dismissed him by spinning and marching into the house as though she knew exactly where she was going.

Brodie watched her rigid retreat. Spunky, he thought. A bit highhanded for his taste, though he had to admire her gumption. But there was something else about the woman, something powerful, riveting.

And Lord, what a body.

His mind replayed the roll of her hips as she'd mounted the porch steps. A man would have to be brain dead not to notice that tautly rounded derriere and sleek curve of leg. He'd also noticed that she wasn't wearing a wedding ring and Brodie wondered why such an obviously attractive woman remained unaccounted for. He also wondered why he was so pleased that she wasn't.

From the guest-room window, Kristin could observe snippets of roundup field activity. Rolling hills were dusted with green and dotted with clusters of gnarled oak. By summer, those same lush hills would be sunbroiled to shades of amber and tawny gold.

She unlatched the wooden frame to open the window and was rewarded by a fresh breeze billowing the curtains. The air smelled different here, she mused, sweet and clean.

Kristin closed her eyes, picturing the view from the bedroom of her Santa Monica condominium. The ocean. Tangy air, stinging salt spray and a vast, timeless sea undulating against the shore, thrusting and withdrawing like a lover's passion.

Home. She missed it already.

"Can it, kiddo," she muttered, reminding herself that she had a job to do. "Remember what pays the bills."

With that self-admonishment, Kristin broke her reverie and busied herself unpacking. She noted with surprise and pleasure that the room contained a desk, and she quickly put it to use, setting up her typewriter and arranging her writing supplies. Pulling a fat manila envelope from her suitcase, she fingered it reverently.

Her manuscript. The book that would unscrew the cap on the agency's inadequacies and let all the ugly little flaws spill out.

It would expose the ineptitude of the system she had observed over the years, the carelessness that allowed cruel, sick people access to frightened, innocent children. It would reveal abuse by the greedy, using the foster home program to supplement their own finances. It would uncover the ploys, the lies, the deceptions and it would unravel the very fabric of a corrupt system, allowing it to be rewoven with clean, honest thread.

Assuming, of course, that the details of her manuscript remained under wraps long enough to complete her research. Exposure at this point could mean the end of her career.

She slid the envelope into the top desk drawer.

Now what? Kristin paced nervously. Certainly, she couldn't hole up in her bedroom and expect to conduct a decent investigation. Obviously, she'd have to explore the ranch, get a feel for its atmosphere and its daily activities.

She flinched at the thought of those "daily activities." When she accepted this assignment, she'd known it would be rough; she just hadn't realized *how* rough. Through the years, Kristin had gone to incredible lengths to avoid confronting her fears and now she had allowed herself to be literally surrounded by them.

Why? she asked herself. For what purpose? No one knew of her secret terrors and, in the city, she could have lived to a ripe old age without ever being forced to face her weakness.

Or learning to control it.

That was the heart of it, Kristin realized. Control. She had something to prove, something to overcome. Here at New Wave, she would finally learn to control her hidden fears. She would have to.

Her glance skimmed to the window, then beyond, and she flinched at the memory of Brodie's wry amusement.

You're welcome to come on up the hill.

So, she chided herself, Mr. Macho didn't think she could hack it. Well, he was in for a surprise.

She could—and would—confront this little problem. It would take more than a few slobbering animals to send Kristin Price screaming and wailing back to the city. By the time she left New Wave, she would know every cow by name, how much Brodie spent on underwear and whether he brushed his teeth sideways or up-and-down.

Properly inspired, she slipped into a pair of jeans, pulled a loose T-shirt over her head and strode out the door. She hit the bottom of the stairs at a fast gallop, skidding to a stop in the sudden shadow of a huge, looming form. Her heart launched one loud, echoing thud, then seemed to momentarily cease functioning.

The man was massive.

Kristin tilted her head backwards, her eyes seeking the summit of his seven-foot bulk. A completely bald head shone as though waxed and two ridiculously small blue eyes stared down from a face the size of a dinner plate. A ruffled cotton apron was fastened around his mammoth torso.

In a small, faint voice Kristin croaked, "Oaf?"

Oaf grunted. "Ja." His tiny eyes narrowed to slits. "You needing something now?" he asked. His voice, soft and lilting with a pleasant Scandinavian accent, was as paradoxical to his appearance as was the ruffled apron.

Kristin relaxed slightly and cleared her throat. "No, thank you. Everything is just fine."

Satisfied, Oaf grunted once more and plodded slowly away.

Unnerved, Kristin wobbled out the door and down the porch steps. Everything around here was so...unexpected. Lethal reptiles lurked in the hay barn, bald behemoths were decked in frills. So far, nothing about the ranch fit into the neat, compartmentalized categories she had mentally conjured.

Passing the barn, she saw the rattlesnake skin stretched and tacked to a rough wooden plank, drying in the sun. Apparently Todd had wasted little time in mounting his trophy, she mused.

She cast a thoughtful glance at her grimy rented car and considered driving to the corral. If there was a stampede or something equally vile, she could dive into the vehicle and take refuge.

Kristin discarded the option as a portrait of Brodie's grinning face danced into her mind. It was only a ten-minute walk, for Pete's sake. She could just imagine how much he'd love to see her bulwark in the car and come roaring up the hill like an armor-plated sissy.

With a deep breath, she forced her leaden legs onward and upward, seriously contemplating whether she should switch careers and do something truly meaningful with her life, like becoming a go-go dancer.

Cresting the hill, she inspected the bustle of activity around the branding corral and shuddered. Everything on the roundup field—men, cattle, horses—was covered with a thick pall of billowing dust that emanated from each of a thousand hoofed feet.

And so much noise. This was not your average, run-of-the-mill, kid-shrieking, car-honking, tire-squealing cacophony of the city. No, indeed. This was a whistling, snorting, bellowing, grunting, stomping pandemonium of men and beasts.

Kristin loathed it.

Preference notwithstanding, she had to go down there and immerse herself in the nitty-gritty of the ranch, absorb the realities of the range, so to speak. She took two steps forward, then sat on the rocky dirt and hugged her knees.

Later, she told herself. She would absorb later. Now she'd just watch, from a nice, safe distance, and wallow in weakness.

Brodie strode to the center of the corral. Two drovers were wrestling with several hundred pounds of irritated calf, trying to ground it for the branding and vaccination process. The puller, or heel man, had hooked his loop and held the rope taut, stretching one of the animal's rear legs parallel to the ground. The mugger, however, had lost his grip, allowing the calf to struggle to its three unfettered feet, where it bawled and bucked in a vain attempt to free itself.

Gus barked orders and issued profane epithets with equal frequency. The mugger finally gathered a grip on the unfortunate animal's skull, twisting until the cow collapsed on its side and lay pinned.

"Fools," Gus muttered as Brodie approached. "Nothin' but a bunch of city-bred, weekend cowboys. Couldn't flip a kitten with a forklift." With that pronouncement, Gus began to scribble in his trusty tally book, then snarled at the iron drover, who apparently wasn't retrieving branding apparatus from the propane-fueled fire with appeasing speed.

Within moments, a loud hiss was followed by an indignant bovine bellow and a white puff of smoke. The air was filled with the pungent scent of burnt hide, and the deed was done.

"How many more?" Brodie asked.

"Forty head, mebbe." Gus snorted. "Might as well be a million, the way these boneheads work."

Brodie's eyes scanned above Gus's head, toward the far end of the field. "You're too hard on them, Gus," he said. "We're nearly back on schedule."

Gus made a neutral sound, then stiffened as some activity caught his eye. "Hey! Dang your hide, boy, you tryin' to tear that cow's ear off?" Gus shoved the thin tally book in the back pocket of his worn jeans and muttered toward the hapless cowboy. "Didn't no one teach you how to tag a cow?"

As Gus veered away, Brodie walked toward the fence. He saw Kristin talking with Jess and Ernie down by the holding pens.

She had finally made it. He'd been watching her for over an hour, since he first spied her sitting on the rise curled into a tight little ball. A while later, he'd seen her under the oak tree, arms wrapped around herself, kicking at pebbles, looking forlorn and thoroughly frustrated.

Now she was down to the cattle pens, within five feet of the fence. She could have driven to Mariposa in the time it had taken her to move fifty yards, but Brodie gave her credit for persistence and, considering her fear of animals, a bit of grudging respect.

He swung over the railing and proceeded casually toward the holding pens. When he could hear fragments of conversation, he stopped, leaning nonchalantly against the wooden slats.

"... when spring break is over," Ernie was saying.

Brodie couldn't hear Kristin's reply. He moved closer and hunched against the fence. Kristin was laughing, soft, low and throaty. He couldn't hear anything else and felt frustrated and guilty, like some kind of voyeur. Finally, he straightened and strode openly toward them.

Ernie, perched on the top rail of the holding pen, spotted Brodie first. He presented him with a gap-toothed grin and his usual greeting. "Hey, man."

Kristin whirled, and Brodie felt a surge of annoyance as her glowing flush of laughter faded into a wary mask. She tipped her head toward him in acknowledgement, but didn't say a word.

"Don't let me break anything up." Brodie's gruffness was not unnoticed. Ernie sobered instantly.

Kristin regarded Brodie curiously, then turned back to her conversation, addressing Ernie. "So after three months, how do you think the school here compares with your old one?"

Ernie shifted restlessly and shrugged. He was not a particularly handsome boy. His nose was too long, his Adam's apple too predominant. Kristin thought his rather rugged look showed promise of future appeal, but now, with that mop of dark curls topping a pencil-thin, angular face, he looked as though he should be shooing crows in a cornfield.

"You know," Ernie mumbled. "School's school."

"What about extracurricular activities?" Kristin inquired. "Do you like sports?"

The question brought a guffaw from Ernie and a snort from the dark, somber boy standing beside him.

"Ain't no time for that stuff," Ernie told her.

"Why not?"

"Work."

"What work?" As was her habit when annoyed, Kristin carefully enunciated each syllable.

Ernie shrugged again, uncomfortable at the turn of the conversation and Brodie's intense stare. He mumbled something unintelligible and inspected a tear in the knee of his blue jeans.

Exasperated, Kristin turned toward the dark-haired boy propped loosely against the fence. Jess Espinoza returned Kristin's gaze without flinching. His eyes were dark and angry. Whereas Ernie was outgoing, eager to please, Jess seemed aloof, sullen and self-contained.

Jess's appearance reflected his individualism—he hadn't switched to western, ranch-style attire as the other boys had. Instead, he retained the uniform of the barrio—black denims and black sleeveless T-shirt. A red paisley handkerchief had been rolled and tied as a headband.

"Well?" Kristin maintained unblinking eye contact. "Would you like to tell me just what keeps you so busy you can't participate in after-school activities?"

Jess's answer was slow and deliberate. "Look around, lady."

"I see."

Oh, yes. Work. A ranch like this has a lot of work. *Everyone does his share.* Kristin decided to take the matter up with Brodie. Later.

Making a conscious effort to soften her expression, Kristin asked, "What about you, Jess? How do you like your new school?"

Jess didn't take his eyes off Kristin's face and answered succinctly. "School sucks."

"Oh." Kristin smiled sweetly. "And does this school suck more or less than your old one?" Her conversational tone never wavered. Attempts to shock her weren't new, and usually weren't successful.

Jess gave a careless shrug. He'd been rolling a small twig in his palm and now flicked it into the dirt.

"Don't know. Haven't been to school since I was ten." He threw Brodie a meaningful glare. "Until now."

Several silent moments stretched out as Kristin thought over the implications of Jess's response. Finally, as though he could no longer endure the tension, Ernie blurted, "Can't we go to work now? The branding's almost done, Brodie. You promised we could help."

Brodie ignored Kristin's startled gaze. He squinted at Ernie. "Did I miss something?" he asked quietly. "Is the day over?"

Ernie folded his thin arms across his chest and his bony shoulders sank into a rejected slouch. "Aw, Brodie. Man, we said we wouldn't do that no more—"

Jess interrupted the other boy's whining complaint with a sharp warning. "Back off, dude. The man's got an attitude." As Ernie slumped and sulked, Jess stiffened defiantly, adding for emphasis, "What the hell do we care about a couple of freaking cows? Let's go."

The dark-haired boy swaggered past Kristin, who could only watch in stunned confusion as Ernie slid from the fence and followed, curl-studded head lowered to avoid her gaze.

They'd gotten less than ten feet when Brodie's voice, quiet and deadly, stopped them in their tracks.

"I think you boys have forgotten your manners," he told them. The clench of teeth etched his tone with a steely rasp.

Ernie whirled as though shot. "Sorry, Brodie," he mumbled, then gulped, peering at Kristin from under partially lowered eyelids. "Nice to meet you, ma'am," he intoned, then his eyes darted quickly to Brodie for confirmation.

Brodie responded with a curt nod, and Ernie stepped back, obviously relieved.

Chin high, Jess examined first Brodie, then Kristin with lazy indifference. His mouth twisted into a mocking half smile. "Yeah," he said, more to Brodie than Kristin. "It's been a real trip."

Kristin felt, rather than saw Brodie's chest expand and muscles bunch. Jess was insolent, rude and arrogant, but she was beginning to feel very, very sorry for the boy. Instinctively she realized that if Brodie was ever pushed beyond the limit of his temper... well, the result would be too horrible to contemplate.

Apparently, Jess wasn't ready to contemplate that result at the moment, either. He finally blinked under Brodie's scorching stare and turned toward Kristin.

"Nice to meet you, Ms. Price," he told her, politely but without enthusiasm, then skimmed a brief glance toward Brodie before strolling away with Ernie slouching behind like a whipped puppy.

"Well." Kristin cleared her throat. "Quite a pair."

Brodie looked grim. "Actually, this hasn't been one of their better days," he said.

"So that wasn't a true test of their natural personalities?"

"Oh, that was their 'natural personalities,' all right," Brodie said. "Just a bit exaggerated, that's all."

Interested, Kristin tilted her head and studied Brodie's face. It was hard, sharply angled and... well, craggy. The expression was so trite it pained her, but looking at the chiseled features, she decided that no description seemed more appropriate.

He was also, Kristin decided, incredibly attractive.

If you liked the rugged type, she mentally amended, which, of course, she emphatically did not.

No, sirree. No more macho mentality for Kristin Michaels Price. Thanks to her ex-husband, she'd had quite enough, and was fed up to her earlobes with the entire masculine charade.

As she scrutinized Brodie, she suddenly became aware that he was returning the examination and to her horror, she began to flush at the force of his stare. His eyes had darkened to a deep, almost velvety indigo, and something strange... almost frightening, was smoldering below the midnight-blue surface.

He blinked, breaking the spell, erasing the thin glimpse of soul and replacing it with calm neutrality.

Slightly rattled at her own fluttering pulse, Kristin fidgeted restlessly, then began a mindless meander toward the branding corral. Brodie fell into place beside her.

"Tell me about the boys," she said.

"You've got files on them."

"Of course, but files are just words. Tell me about the people."

Brodie slanted a glance at her solemn expression. She meant that, he decided. A bureaucrat who realizes that paper isn't people. Maybe there was hope for the world.

"Okay," he said finally. "Most of what you saw is what you get. Ernie's like a lap dog and he wants everybody to pet him, approve of him." Brodie stopped walking and slipped his hands into the pockets of his jeans. "He's also a little chameleon."

Kristin smiled. "How so?"

"He changes personality depending on who he's around. Wants to please everybody. That..." he jerked his thumb toward where the boys had been standing "... was his 'Jess' personality, tough, smart-mouthed."

"He did seem to smooth out when you showed up," Kristin observed.

With a dry laugh, Brodie bent to pluck a smooth pebble from the dirt, then began massaging it in his big palm. "That's because I give off a stronger background color than Jess." With a mischievous grin, he added, "Besides, I'm bigger."

"What about Jess?"

"Jess is hard-core, a tough little street punk who's had one hell of a rough time. He's got a real warped view of what life's all about, and what his role in it should be." Brodie's mouth flattened. "His weakness is cars—other people's cars, to be precise. Gus once caught him hot-wiring a hay thrasher."

"You're joking."

"Nope." Actually, the incident had amused Brodie, though he'd been careful not to let Jess know that. "Jess said he was just keeping his skills sharp."

Kristin absorbed that. "Does he have any redeeming factors?"

"He sure does," Brodie said vehemently. "That kid'll stand up to a rabid grizzly for his friends. He's loyal and, believe it or not, completely honest. You may not like what he says or the way he says it, but he won't lie."

The pebble skidded across the dirt, bouncing once. When Brodie spoke again, his voice had softened. "You know, that boy has an IQ of over 130." He looked at Kristin, his expression a mixture of wonder and sadness. "A mind like that, and he had to quit school in the fifth grade to support his family." Brodie's expression hardened as he thought back, remembering another special boy. He remembered Martin Alvarez's laughing brown eyes, his brilliant mind, his determination to beat the system of poverty and make something of himself. Martin had been desperate to escape the barrio. Two years ago, Martin had done just that. Brodie was still haunted by the memory.

Kristin was touched by the emotion flickering across Brodie's face. His pain seemed so genuine and he appeared to have a depth of feeling for these boys. Her voice was huskier than usual. "And Todd? He seems like such a cherub, so out of place with boys like Ernie and Jess."

"Looks can be deceiving. Todd lies like a rug and would sell his mother for five bucks and a pack of cigarettes."

Kristin was shocked. "I don't believe it! How can you speak about that child like that?"

"Because it's true."

Kristin was hot. "Still, if you feel that way about the boy it's bound to show in the way you treat him. I can't believe..." She winced as a cowboy spurred his mount, passing at a full gallop.

Brodie noticed her hand involuntarily clutch at her throat and her breathing become uneven. "Ever fall off a horse?" he asked.

"What?" Kristin's head snapped around as though she had forgotten he was there. "Oh... well, once actually."

With a knowing nod, Brodie said, "You should have gotten right back on it."

Kristin scoffed at the notion. "Not this kid. I didn't want to get on the beast in the first place."

"Why did you?"

She shrugged. "It was the only way to get to work. My foster parents didn't want me to lose my job and the truck was broken." She managed a wan smile. "The rest, as they say, is history."

"Must have been a bad fall."

"Bad enough."

Oh yes, she thought and cringed. She still couldn't remember details of the accident which had given her nightmares for eighteen years. They were terrifying dreams in which she heard an animal growl, felt the horse's panic. Then the ground was rushing up, slamming into her back. The horrible sound of low, rumbling snarls... and teeth. A lot of them. In her face.

Brodie saw her skin turn ashen and wondered what demons she had mentally summoned. "How old were you?"

"Ten."

"Ten?" Brodie was shocked. "Your parents sent you off to work when you were only ten years old?"

"Foster parents," she corrected. "They needed the money."

Brodie saw her chin lift, her shoulders straighten. There was pain in her eyes, and vulnerability. His heart ached for her.

He spoke softly, unconsciously wrapping his hand around her shoulder. "You're doing just fine."

The warmth of his palm sent shimmering heat waves down her spine. The sensation was so pleasant, so stimulating, so unexpected that she was instantly alert, instantly cautious.

Kristin stepped away quickly, too quickly, and attempted to redirect the conversation. Her eyes shifted, searching. She pointed to the corral. "What are they doing?"

Brodie followed her gaze. "Branding new calves and some unmarked yearlings."

A short, wiry man had just slung his lasso at the flailing legs of a calf on the run and had looped one of its hocks. The cowboy jerked the rope and sat down, bracing his boot heels in the dirt while another man grabbed the struggling cow's head.

"That's the mugger," Brodie explained. "It's his job to throw the calf so it can be branded."

The mugger grasped the calf's jaw with his left hand, yanked up, and twisted the poor animal's neck until it lost its balance and toppled. Then the cowboy spilled onto its shoulder, pinning it to the ground.

Brodie spoke again. "Now, Jake there, he's the one with the rope, he'll pull the leg straight so Matt can lay the iron smoothly on the calf's flank."

But the demonstration went awry. When Jake jerked the rope, the loop slipped completely over the animal's hoof, leaving all four legs free and kicking wildly. The momentum shifted and the mugger fought desperately to keep the calf from standing, as Jake, from his sitting position, attempted to recapture the errant hoof.

Kristin knew the exact moment that tragedy would strike. The mugger lost his footing, somersaulted over the calf's shoulder and landed flat on his back, winded and gasping. Hooves flew as the panicked calf tried to right itself, and Kristin's stomach twisted, wrenching at the sickening thud as a hornlike heel collided with Jake's forehead.

Oh God, thought Kristin, he's dead. The creature has killed him.

The terror she'd been fighting to contain surged to the surface and enveloped her with icy fingers. For a fleeting moment, she wanted only to turn and run, leaving the crumpled figure and this awful place far behind, fleeing until she reached the safety of her own snug little home.

Brodie flashed over the rail, reaching the limp form at the same moment as Gus. Jake's bloodied head lolled as Brodie gently eased him onto his back.

The liberated calf had loped toward the nearest holding pen and was bawling for entry. Kristin wasn't looking at the calf, or the horses mincing and snuffling at the far side of the corral. A deeper instinct had surfaced. Someone was hurt. She had to help.

Scaling the fence, she dashed toward the wounded cowboy. She heard the squat man with a chin full of gray stubble issuing a string of curses and loudly berating everything and everybody.

Kristin knelt beside Brodie and placed two shaking fingers against the unconscious man's throat. Thank heavens, she thought. The pulse was strong.

Jake moaned, and began to thrash.

"Ssshhh," Kristin soothed, using the tail of her oversize T-shirt to wipe the blood from his face. "You're going to be fine, just fine. Relax, now."

Although her voice broke and trembled, it seemed to have a calming effect, and Jake visibly relaxed. Kristin continued her ministrations, alternately soothing and wiping until two pale blue eyes blinked painfully and squinted up at her.

"Afternoon, miss," Jake mumbled.

"Hi, cowboy," she said, smiling with relief. "Bet you've got a devil of a headache."

"Yes'm," Jake agreed.

The gray-stubbled man suddenly exploded. "Tarnation, if that don't just beat it. Now what'n the devil are we goin' to do for a puller, I'd like to know."

Kristin glared at Gus, and the foreman continued his colorful tirade. She would have offered a rather explicit opinion of his language, but she felt Jake shift beneath her hands and realized that Brodie was helping the man to his feet.

"Are you hurt anywhere else, Jake?" Brodie inquired.

Jake, with one arm around Brodie's shoulders, started to shake his head, then winced at the pain and settled for holding it steady with his free hand. "Don't think so," he told Brodie.

"Think?" Gus hollered. "If you knew how to think, you wouldn't be standing there bleedin' all over my clean corral."

Kristin was indignant. "Now listen here—"

"Merle!" Brodie interrupted, motioning to the lanky man on horseback. Deever slipped from the saddle and loped to Brodie's side. "Put Jake in the truck and take him down to the house."

"Sure thing, boss," said Deever, grasping the wobbly cowboy.

Jake turned doleful eyes toward Brodie. "I'll be okay tomorrow. We'll finish them cows."

Gus snorted, obviously unimpressed.

"Oaf'll take a look at you," Brodie said, "then we'll see."

Jake gave a stoic nod and Deever ushered him away.

"Might as well bottle it for the day," Brodie told Gus. "We'll pick up tomorrow."

"We'll pick up, all right," Gus said, "but I don't rightly know what we're a'gonna do with it."

Gus ambled off mumbling, "Dang fool weekenders."

Kristin watched him, tension exploding as she bristled and whirled on Brodie.

"Who in the world is that awful man?" she demanded, enunciating clearly.

That opened Brodie's eyes. "Who, Gus? He's my foreman."

"He is positively crude," she announced.

Brodie seemed thoughtful. "Yes, I guess he is."

Kristin paced, adrenalin coursing through her veins, turning fear to fury. "I simply cannot believe that anyone with a shred of humanity could have stood there cursing at that poor man." She squared, hands on hips. "Why did you allow it?"

"Allow?" Brodie's eyes narrowed. "I don't *allow* my men to talk. They've a God-given right to speak if they've a mind to." Brodie took a deep breath and softened his tone. "Look, I know Gus gets a bit riled, but I guarantee he'll be the one bringing Jake's supper to the bunkhouse tonight."

"That doesn't justify such insensitive behavior."

She whirled and headed for the fence, passing within five feet of a very large chestnut stallion and apparently, in her anger, oblivious to that fact.

Brodie caught her in two steps. "Wait a minute. I don't have to justify Gus's behavior to you. He's a good man."

"He's coarse and crude and an absolutely *lousy* role model for three impressionable young boys."

She shouldn't have said that, Kristin realized. It was rude and tactless, but her nerves seemed to have frayed and snapped. She knew she had to get away, regain control. She scrambled to the top of the fence rail, pinned to it when Brodie grabbed her arm.

"Lousy role model?" Brodie was incredulous. "You've got the gall to sit there on your bureaucratic bottom and tell *me* that Gus Krieger is a lousy role model?"

She stiffened, staring at the hand clamped on her arm until Brodie released his grip. Kristin dropped to the other side of the fence, dusted herself lightly then marched toward the rise.

As soon as Brodie managed to rehinge his gaping jaw, he followed and planted himself in front of her. "Am I to believe that you find pimps and pushers to be more appropriate role models?" His voice was low and lethal.

"I won't dignify that with an answer." She spun to walk around him, but he cut her off.

"What is it? What's really eating at you?"

She looked him square in the eye. "All right. If I hadn't been here today, it might have been Ernie or Jess lying bloody in the dirt."

Brodie's chin dropped. "Where did you get that cockamamy notion?"

Kristin stiffened, her voice as rigid as her spine. "Tell me, Mr. Brodie, just what was the promise you broke, the one Ernie was so disappointed about?"

An expression of shock mingled with comprehension flashed across Brodie's face and Kristin pressed her advantage. "Isn't it true that if I hadn't shown up unexpectedly, it would've been one of them out there break dancing with a steer?"

Brodie's teeth were clamped as though welded, his eyes glinted with dark fury and strong fists twisted into rock-hard knots. "Do you honestly think I'd deliberately put any of those boys in jeopardy?" A tiny muscle twitched fitfully below his cheekbone. "Why did you even bother to come here, since you'd already made up your mind about the place?"

Anger drained from Kristin, replaced by astonishment. "I haven't made up my mind about anything. I'm here to do a complete and thorough investigation of the facilities."

"Are you, now?" Brodie's eyes narrowed. "Then when are you going to stop jumping to conclusions and do it?"

Without waiting for a response, he whirled stiffly and strode away.

Kristin watched his angry departure as her heart sank like a lead anchor. Never, in her entire professional career, had anyone accused her of being anything less than objective and thorough in the performance of her duties, but Brodie had done just that. He'd accused her of jumping to conclusions. He'd been insolent and downright nasty.

And he had been absolutely right.

Chapter Three

Brodie's words were as chilling as a bucket of ice water in the face. Kristin stood as though rooted to the rocky ground and watched Brodie arc himself onto the chestnut stallion, fusing with the saddle as though it were merely a part of his own body.

As Gus pulled the gate open, the mount leaped forward, knotting its powerful muscles and barely clearing the corral before shifting to a flat-out run. Brodie leaned low across the horse's neck, his expression grim as he rode toward the house. The sleek thrust of the animal skimmed the surface, skittering pebbles and puffs of sand the only evidence of hooves touching earth.

Kristin began to tremble violently. She fought her mind for control. It was over, she told herself. For now.

Kristin stumbled unsteadily across the uneven terrain sorting her own reactions to the events of a very confusing, very frightening day.

Already, she regretted her part in the unpleasant altercation with Brodie. She'd overreacted again and knew her own phobia was coloring her judgment, but good grief! In five hours she had seen a boy cornered by a rattler and a man's skull dented by a calf.

Kristin felt strongly about her responsibility and had grave concerns about the boys' safety as well as Brodie's motives in using them for such obviously dangerous work. And she certainly believed every word she'd uttered about that reprehensible Gus person. A crude, vile man, but she realized that it hadn't been the time or the place to so vehemently express her views.

Kristin kicked at a hapless stone the way she would've liked to kick herself. What was happening to her? It simply wasn't like her to lose control and blow an investigation. Her first impression was that New Wave was nothing more than a dude ranch for delinquents, but first impressions don't count. Evidence counts.

Unconsciously twisting a platinum strand of hair, Kristin realized that she would simply have to gather some semblance of objectivity to her inquiry. If she couldn't, she would have to remove herself from the assignment. That would be a crippling blow, not only to her career, but her ego as well.

When Kristin finally reached the house, she noticed that the ranch's battered blue pickup was missing. Her gaze swung to the action around the stable area, a hundred yards or so from the main house, as drovers and ranch hands groomed and settled the sweating horses, as tired from their gruelling day as were the men.

The house seemed strangely quiet after the bustling activity in the roundup area and she wondered about Jake. Perhaps he'd been taken directly to the bunkhouse.

A clunking cupboard followed by the metallic clang of bustling pots drew her attention. She tracked the sound into a huge, cavernous kitchen. The area, sprayed by daylight from windowed walls, was larger than most living rooms and housed a long, rectangular table flanked by matching oak benches.

Oaf, dredged with flour, towered over the counter smoothing thick dough with a rolling pin which seemed miniature compared to the manipulation of massive hands. The utensil's handles were too small for Oaf's giant palms so he pinched them between thumb and forefinger and spun the wooden tube across the springy surface.

As though he felt her presence, Oaf swiveled his big head and Kristin reflexively stepped back. At the sight of her bloodied T-shirt, his brow wrinkled with concern.

"Ja? You are hurt?" Oaf quickly wiped his hands on the apron and took a step toward her.

Kristin cleared her throat. "No, I'm fine," she said, tugging at the hem of her shirt to survey the damage. "This is poor Jake's blood." She looked up. "Is he here?"

Oaf shook his head. "Brodie takes him to town," he told her. "For pictures of his head."

"X rays?"

Oaf nodded. "Ja. X ray pictures." His little eyes narrowed as he scrutinized Kristin's worried expression. "Jake is good. Cowboys have..." Oaf screwed his face, trying to conjure the proper description. He brightened. "Fat heads," he finished proudly.

Kristin smiled. "They certainly do."

"Ja," Oaf said happily as he turned back to his dough.

Suddenly Kristin felt incredibly tired. The day had taken its toll, mentally and physically and she wanted nothing so much as a steaming shower. She managed to drag her quivering legs upstairs to her room where she promptly stretched across the soft mattress.

But Brodie's image floated into her mind, his scent flooding the secret recesses of her memory. The man frightened her, the man excited her. He had merely to look at her and she felt the potency of his gaze fluttering below her navel. She wondered what kind of a lover Brodie would be...and wished she had the courage to find out.

Kristin awoke with a start, groggy and disoriented. The room was dim and a small clock on the dresser announced that she'd slept for over two hours. Great, she thought with disgust. She spends her nights battling insomnia, but drops off in the middle of the afternoon like a napping toddler.

Painfully, she sat up, moaning aloud at the sight of her filthy clothes. She needed that shower. Now. Hastily grabbing her robe and a bottle of shampoo, she headed down the hall to the bathroom.

Twenty minutes later she emerged, clean, relaxed and somewhat refreshed. Head bent, she was still toweling her damp hair when she rammed into a large, hard object blocking the hallway. The force of impact bounced her backward and a pair of strong hands clamped a steadying grip on her shoulders.

Startled, she yanked at the towel and stared up at Brodie's sober expression. As his gaze traveled downward, Kristin flushed to realize she was clad only in a thigh-length terry bathrobe, barely secured by its loose sash.

A slow, potent scrutiny wafted like a scorching desert wind, burning her skin beneath the roughened folds of cloth. Brodie's expression was hard, inscrutable, his eyes glinting hot as molten steel.

Suddenly, she felt exposed, vulnerable.

Brodie heard her soft gasp. Her throat was exposed by the loose drape of her robe and he saw that she wore a single pearl dangling on a gold chain. His eyes followed a drop of water as it disappeared into the shadowed valley between her breasts.

Kristin clutched the towel to her chest and Brodie noticed a slight tremor touch her fingers. His own hands, still gripping her soft shoulders, seemed to tighten of their own accord, drawing her closer.

The atmosphere was suddenly thick, charged, like the heaviness before a summer storm. Sultry and palpable, the air became a living thing.

A hushed cry fluttered in her throat as she stumbled against him. He caught her. Brodie's stare fixed on her cushiony lips, moist and inviting, shimmering like pink petals. He was buffeted by an almost overwhelming urge, aching to dip into the velvety softness.

Kristin was awash with sensation. What was happening? Why was she fused against this man like solder on steel? Why couldn't she move?

Why didn't she want to?

The fresh scent of soap mingled with his musky, all-male essence, enveloped her. She felt dizzy. Words clogged, helpless in a mouth that seemed coated with cotton. Her tongue darted out to moisten her stiff lips.

The sensuous movement buckled Brodie's elbows until she was anchored against him. He silently cursed the intrusive barrier of wadded towel still knotted in her fingers.

Frantic warning alarms buzzed behind his brain. *Stop!* they screamed silently, *or kiss the ranch goodbye.*

His arms snapped rigid, the sharp realignment setting Kristin roughly away. As though releasing a treasure, each finger loosened its death grip.

"Are you all right?" His voice was ragged.

So was hers. "Yes, I'm fine."

She was *not* fine. She was, to put it mildly, horrified.

Half dressed, she'd nearly flattened the poor man in his own hallway and when he'd politely steadied her, she had launched herself against him like a sexually deprived spinster. She'd actually wanted him to kiss her. *Wanted?* Good grief, she'd done everything except climb up his chest and glue her lips to his mouth.

Obviously, she'd been celibate too long.

Pink with embarrassment, Kristin absently fiddled with a wet strand shrouding her cheek and mentally regrouped. Presenting herself as an ally was acceptable; drooling on his shirt was not.

Conscious of Brodie's burning gaze, she nervously grappled for an intelligent comment, some flippant witticism to demonstrate that she was totally unaffected by their brief encounter.

"I took a shower," she announced, then cringed. From someone who seriously resembled a drenched rodent, that was not a particularly startling revelation.

"I'd noticed."

"I . . . uh, hope you don't mind," she continued, struggling as words which once flowed effortlessly from brain to mouth now dropped like leaden pellets on the back of a useless tongue.

Brodie's somber expression cracked slightly, a small flame of amusement lighting his eyes. "No, I don't mind at all," he said. "Since you'll be here a while, I think we'd all appreciate it."

Surprised, her quick intake of breath melted into a throaty chuckle, shredding the thick veil of tension.

"How's Jake?"

"He'll live," Brodie said, "but he won't be happy about it for a day or so. No fracture, but he's got a hefty concussion. They're keeping him at the hospital overnight."

"He took a terrible blow," Kristin said. "I'm relieved to know he'll be okay." She tilted her head and peered up. "I imagine this creates a bit of a problem for you."

Brodie shrugged. "We'll get by."

"But he won't be able to work for several days," she persisted. "How will you cover his job?"

If Brodie knew what she was digging for, he didn't bite. He kept his face impassive and answered calmly. "Jake was hourly help, hired for the roundup and branding. Tomorrow would've been his last day here anyway."

"Oh? How many men work here full time?"

"Only four ranch hands and Gus."

Kristin thought she noted a tightening of Brodie's shoulders at the mention of his foreman and again berated herself for losing control earlier.

"I wanted to apologize for my... behavior this afternoon," she said slowly. "Obviously, I couldn't possibly know your foreman as well as you and my remarks were, well, inappropriate."

Brodie's eyes narrowed. "Yes, they were," he agreed.

"With the accident and everything..." her voice trailed off, and she conjured a sincere smile. "Perhaps we could just forget the entire incident, chalk it up to a rotten day?"

Regarding her with disquieting intensity, Brodie's smile was tinged with caution. "It has been that," he said.

Kristin was confused. "Has been what?"

"A rotten day."

"Oh."

Brodie straightened and stepped sideways. "If you'll excuse me, Ms. Price, I'd better get cleaned up myself."

"Kristin," she replied quickly. Allies should be on a first name basis. "Please call me Kristin."

His cheeks crinkled. Deep grooves bracketed his mouth, altering his expression from hard and forbidding to sensuous, sexy and downright inviting.

"All right, then, Kristin," he said, with a flash of white teeth. "Dinner's in an hour." He swept a glance across her bathrobe. "Clothing is optional, but customary."

He disappeared into the still-steamy bathroom, utterly determined to wring ice cubes from the shower head.

Kristin discreetly eased into the privacy of her room to prepare for dinner and another encounter with the enigmatic Nathan Brodie. Perhaps by then she would regain some capacity for intelligent speech and at least a small shred of self-respect.

The man's presence seemed to jeopardize both.

Raucous shouts and guffaws echoed from the kitchen rehashing the day's events. There was some good-natured teasing for some sort of misstep by Jess and Ernie earlier in the day. Tidbits of conversation drifted to the stairway as Kristin hesitantly answered the insistent clamor of the dinner bell.

"I dunno, Ernie," said an unfamiliar male voice. "Looks to me like you got good form, but you just ain't supposed to hit 'em in the face with the dang rope."

"Well," drawled a second voice, "he'll have his chance to practice tomorrow. Heard tell Gus's going to let Ernie take on Jake's job."

Gus's indignant snort was distinctive even to Kristin. "When pigs fly," he responded, loudly enough to be heard over the new rumble of laughter.

From the doorway, Kristin saw the entire kitchen was alive with cowboys, some already seated at the long oak table, others lounging lazily against the walls. A lanky, mustached wrangler ruffled Ernie's hair, laughing at the boy's obvious embarrassment. Brodie and Gus hunched at one end of the table conversing in low, serious tones as they scratched on a sheet of yellow lined paper.

Oaf set plates of steaming meat amid the huge bowls of fluffy mashed potatoes, biscuits and gravy already covering the vinyl tablecloth. He grinned down at Kristin.

The din subsided to a lull as each man in turn noticed her presence, shifted uncomfortably, then quietly took his place at the table.

It was Brodie who finally ended the awkward hush. He sat at the end of the table and, pointing to the place at his left, said, "Sit here, Kristin." A man already seated in the appointed spot moved down to make room.

The meal, which began in strained silence, soon buzzed quietly with individual conversations which, Kristin suspected, were considerably less animated because of her presence. She was aware of covert glances and an occasional sharp reprimand of "Ssshhh" when descriptions got a bit colorful.

Despite obvious discomfort with her company, it was quickly apparent that appetites weren't adversely affected and every edible substance in sight was consumed in record time. As the men attacked huge slabs of pie, Brodie snagged their attention.

"Listen up, boys," he said, then paused as conversation trickled to a halt. "Since we're a man short for the final day of branding, there've been some shifts in job assignments. Gus is going to fill you in."

Gus stood, eyed the motley crew, then began to rattle off a list of unfamiliar ranch terms, a language as foreign to Kristin as a Lithuanian dialect. Her ears perked, however, at the sound of Todd's name.

"You got your wish, boy," Gus told Todd. "You'll be helping with the shoot." He scowled. "Just don't go stabbin' no one, hear?"

Todd's cherubic face shone with excitement. "I won't, Gus, honest. I'll do it real good." He grinned across at Jess, who was smiling almost indulgently at the boy's enthusiasm.

Kristin, however, was not excited; she was stunned. Shoot? Who, or what, was going to get shot?

Brodie had been watching her reactions and perceived the problem. He leaned closer until, his mouth inches from her ear, he noted her subtle stiffening at the intimacy of his movement. A fresh, floral scent wafted from her hair. For a moment, his mind went blank, coherent thought fleeing behind an impetuous itch to burrow into the silvery silk strands feathering her shoulders.

He mentally shook himself, regathering his original intent and explained that a "shoot" was the vaccination process.

"After branding, each calf is vaccinated against blackleg, brucellosis . . . a host of diseases," he told her.

"Why Todd?" Kristin whispered.

Brodie's voice was low, and Kristin concentrated on separating his words from Gus's irascible warbling in the background. "Todd loves working with the animals. I wish he could relate to people as well."

Gus's voice echoed louder. "Ernie, you'll be workin' with Deever. Figured you could use the practice," he added with a scoff, inciting a new round of jovial laughter.

Kristin was confused by the inference. She'd felt out of place all her life, it seemed, but she had never felt more alien to her surroundings.

Ernie, however, seemed delighted by the turn of events. He swiveled on the hard bench, peering behind the backs of the two men separating him from Merle Deever. Deever winked at him.

"Bring your rope, kid," Merle told Ernie, a comment that broke up the entire table.

"Jess'll work tally with me," Gus concluded. "That about does it."

"Who's gonna be the puller?" someone asked, accompanied by a chorus of head nods and mumbles.

Gus cocked a mean eye at the questioner. "Well, since you couldn't pull straw from a haystack, what business is it of yours, I'd like to know?"

"Just wondering, that's all," came the repentant response.

"Since you're so all-fired curious, I'll tell you. Guess you boneheads don't know your boss just used to be a champion steer wrassler." Gus's rheumy eyes fell on Brodie.

The room was filled with a palpable hush.

Brodie, surprised and obviously embarrassed by Gus's revelation, glared at the roomful of grinning men. "Any of you got a problem with that?" he challenged.

"No sir, boss," Deever said, his respectful tone lit by amusement. "Ain't likely to get much done, though, everyone wanting to see a champion's technique and all."

Brodie flung a napkin on his plate and pushed back the seat. "A couple more words from you, Merle, and you'll be the one eating cow heels for breakfast," Brodie warned, but his mouth twitched slightly and Kristin realized he was not particularly upset by the ribbing.

As Brodie stood, half the men at the table followed suit and the kitchen again became a din of babel and clinking dishes. Kristin saw Brodie's eye contact with Gus and noticed the quick tilt of his head. Gus nodded, stood and both men left the room.

Ranch hands and drovers began to drift toward the back door which led directly from the kitchen to the yard. The sun hung heavily on the Mariposa foothills, half hidden behind their shadowed bulk, and most of the men were ambling directly toward the bunkhouse some seventy feet west of the main house.

The three boys were engaged in a lively discussion with one of the men, and Kristin, hoping for a chance to get better acquainted, called to them.

It was obvious from the slump of shoulders that they were not as anxious to acquaint themselves with her. Ernie, eyes wide in his thin face, spoke. "Yes'm, Ms. Price?" he said politely.

All three hovered in the doorway, one cautious, one defiant, one somber—none moving in her direction.

If the mountain won't come to Mohammed, she thought and waltzed toward them. "Mind if I walk with you?" she asked.

The question was met with a series of shrugs before the teenagers turned and went out the door. Kristin followed quickly and, deciding to take the bull by the horns, addressed herself first to Jess. He had definite leadership qualities and it was obvious the boys respected him. If she could get Jess to trust her, the others would follow his example.

"Assisting the foreman with the tally sounds like a pretty important job," she said. "Gus must have a lot of faith in you."

Jess cut her with a look, but said nothing.

"What does the, er, tally person do?" she persisted.

"Counts cows."

Succinct, but an answer nonetheless and Kristin chalked it up as a small victory. Ernie, however, was anxious to show off his expertise.

"It's more than that," he said, puffing his chest. "Tally-man is like the boss, the foreman. Jess'll even be in charge of tagging. He gets to give orders to all the other dudes."

Jess didn't appear to appreciate Ernie's lavish praise. "Put a lid on it, man," he warned.

"That really does sound important," Kristin said, meeting Jess's black stare. "Is that why you were all so pleased at your assignments?"

"Beats shoveling horseshit," Jess noted, then sauntered the final ten feet into the bunkhouse with Ernie in tow.

Well, Kristin thought dryly, that was a roaring success.

Todd veered off toward the stable and Kristin called after him. He skidded to a stop, and she could almost hear the dejected sigh.

"Wait a minute," she said. "Where are you headed in such a hurry?"

"Got to check on Martha," he said, obviously pained at the interruption.

Kristin's curiosity was piqued. "Martha who?" She was interested in anyone who could eliminate her unwelcome role as the only female on the ranch. The answer, however, was a bit of a letdown.

"Martha's my mare," Todd replied. "She's in foal."

Kristin's eyes glazed at the term, and Todd was not particularly sympathetic at her lack of knowledge on the subject.

"That means she's going to have a baby," he explained with exaggerated patience. "You know, a little horse?"

"Ah, thank you, Todd. I get the drift."

"Anyway," he continued with more enthusiasm, "Brodie says I can have the foal, too." His small chin lifted proudly. "I even get to help when it comes."

"Really? Well, Brodie did tell me you were very good with the animals."

Todd was pleased by the praise, but modesty wasn't one of his major virtues. "I am."

"Have you thought about a career working with animals?" Kristin inquired.

"Career?" he repeated, bewildered. Then he shook his head slowly. "What kind of career could *I* have?"

"There are lots of things I know you'd be just wonderful at, Todd."

"Like what?"

"Like zookeeper, animal trainer, why you could even become a veterinarian if you wanted."

Todd's face lit. "A vet? Man, that'd be so rad."

Kristin laughed. "I take it the idea appeals to you?"

"Oh yeah. Geez, I got to ask Brodie about that."

Instantly, Kristin was irritated that Todd's first reaction would be to run ask Brodie's approval on what career to pursue. Considering the magnitude of his influence with the boys, it was extremely important that his advice and encouragement be appropriate.

"Uh...Ms. Price?"

"Hmm? Oh, I'm sorry, Todd. What is it?"

"Can I go now? I gotta see to Martha. She might even be foaling right now." His round face twisted with concern.

"Sure, Todd. We'll talk later."

Before she'd finished her sentence, the boy had whirled and was running toward the stables, and Martha.

Brodie massaged his stiff neck and watched Gus pace the room in front of the desk. A waning, early evening pall cast the small office in gray, and Brodie squinted at the blurred ledger before flicking on the desk lamp. He leaned back in the old swivel chair, wincing as a flap of torn vinyl scratched his shoulder.

"You might as well accept it." Brodie delivered his message in the same soothing tone he used with the boys. "She's here and there's nothing we can do about it."

"Well, I still don't like it," Gus sputtered. "We ran forty thousand acres and ten thousand head of prime angus in Montana and we didn't need some damn fool government woman dolin' out the money to do it."

"This isn't Montana," Brodie pointed out, irritated. "We've got eight hundred head, not ten thousand, and you darn well know that we've got to appease the county or they'll take the boys and dump them in some juvenile detention center." Brodie's expression narrowed. "Right now, she *is* the government and I want you to treat her like she was Princess Di, got it? No more of your blasphemous bull while she's around."

Gus flattened his bony hands on the desk and stretched over the scratched surface. "How're you gonna keep her out of them books, I'd like to know?"

"I'm not," Brodie said tightly. "She's already asked for them."

Gus expelled a disgusted snort. "Well, after she gets her hands on 'em, you'll have a sight more problems than her not likin' the sound of my voice."

"Maybe not." Brodie's lips coiled into a wry smile as he snapped the red-covered ledger closed. "She's got a right to ranch records, but these..." He tapped the book. "These could be considered personal."

"Ain't nothin' personal to a woman." Gus squinted across the desk. "What about the rest of it?"

Jaw squared and twitching, Brodie snapped, "I'll handle it."

Gus straightened, tugging his ragged Stetson until it sat low on his brow.

"Yeah, you do that," he said, then strutted to the office door like a cocky bantam rooster. He opened it slightly, then turned back, fixing Brodie with an owllike stare. "You just do that," he repeated, "then I'll mop up your mess like I always done. But you mind what I say, boy. She's trouble, that one. Trouble."

At the same moment Gus emphasized the final word, he flung open the door and looked into Kristin's stunned face.

Gus didn't blink. "Evenin', ma'am," he intoned, then ambled out of the house.

It took all of Brodie's self-control to maintain an impassive expression as he silently cursed the Fates and wondered how much of their conversation she'd overheard. The tight line of her mouth told him she'd sure as the devil heard something.

Stretching stiff lips across his teeth in the semblance of a smile, Brodie made a supreme effort toward nonchalance, ignoring the fact that his gut spasmed at the sight of her.

Obviously, his physical reaction was merely caused by the tense situation and had nothing whatsoever to do with the silver glow of her eyes, or the way that knit shirt clung to her rounded form.

She was a government paper pusher. She was the enemy.

Standing politely, Brodie motioned to the chair across from his desk. She accepted the seat, then scrutinized him with wordless intensity. Folding into his own chair, Brodie met her gaze, locked with it and absorbed it until he felt almost drawn into a mind meld.

The trance shattered at the sound of her voice.

"Tell me about New Wave," she said in that wonderful, husky tone.

"What do your files say?"

"They say it's a working cattle ranch and you've owned it for nearly two years." She tilted her head, eyeing him shrewdly. "They also say you've got contacts in high places."

Brodie feigned innocence. "What makes you think so?"

"Because," she said slowly, "the L.A. County Social Service Agency just doesn't yank three troubled teenagers out of a very organized system and hand them over to your average, run-of-the-mill cow jockey. I like to know the history of those who will have responsibility for these kids, so I did a bit of investigating on my own."

Knowing Kristin was alert to the slightest change in expression, Brodie kept his face totally impassive.

"Your Probation Department personnel records have been red-tagged and that makes me curious," she added. His shoulders tensed and she noted with some satisfaction the crack appearing in Brodie's implacable demeanor. Pausing to await a response, Kristin saw a brief, wary glint in Brodie's eyes.

That hit a nerve, she thought and decided to delve into the subject a bit deeper.

"A red-tagged file is one that's been closed to any review." Kristin was certain her explanation was unnecessary. Brodie's jaw was twitching convulsively. She smiled sweetly. "It's very unusual for a probation officer to have his files sealed after leaving the department. Any idea why yours were?"

His mouth flattened, nostrils flaring slightly as his eyes flashed in warning.

Bingo, she told herself as she tried not to shrink under the strength of Brodie's darkening, ominous expression.

With slow deliberation, Brodie picked up the red ledger and slid it into the top desk drawer. He shut the drawer smartly, locked it, then stared at the vacant desk top for several seconds before speaking. "My personal history has nothing to do with New Wave. I'll answer any questions about the ranch or the boys."

Kristin decided to let it go for now. "I'd like to know why you wanted the boys. Did you know them from somewhere, had you worked with them before?"

"No, but I've worked with dozens just like them."

"Just like them?"

"Hard kids, brought up without a childhood—poor, neglected, sometimes abused. They're raised in a battle zone."

"But these boys have families," she insisted. "They have homes, brothers, sisters and except for Todd, both parents are available. Why have you taken responsibility for them?" Kristin was leaning forward, the movement of her hands echoing a depth of feeling for the subject. "There are so many kids who have no family, no one to care for them. Why these particular kids?"

"Because I understand them," he said quietly, "and they were all on their way to a future filled with metal bars and slamming gates." A deep sadness filled his eyes. "I was born where they were born, raised on the same streets. I fought the same battles, learned the same lessons, was headed for the same concrete hotel."

With a sigh, Brodie pushed away from the desk, standing so suddenly the rickety chair shuddered to remain upright. He walked to the window and stared into the darkness, remembering.

Two years had passed since the night Maria Alvarez had sobbed as she'd held the bleeding, dying body of her last son. Brodie had been shattered, his disillusionment complete.

Burned out and used up, Brodie had bought this small cattle ranch couched in the shadow of the California Sierras to refresh his spirit and renew his faith in life itself. In the earthy labor of the land, a vision formed, fuzzy at first, then focusing with increasing clarity. To loosen the ghetto's grip, he would have to create a new environment away from the chaos of the inner city. New Wave Ranch became the fruit of that vision.

Certainly, it hadn't been easy, and days like today instilled niggling doubts about the wisdom of the entire operation.

Kristin watched Brodie carefully, touched by his despondent expression. Still, she was confused. He'd offered pieces of the puzzle, mere tidbits that whetted her appetite for the entire picture. But there were too many holes, too many missing fragments.

"I don't understand," she told him honestly. "As a probation officer, you could have helped dozens of youngsters. Isolated out here, you're so . . . so limited."

Brodie's voice turned bitter. "No one can help them in the barrios. They're surrounded with pimps, pushers, gang wars and violence." He whirled, facing her with a hollow, haunted appearance. "I'm just one man. I'd wind one thread of steel into their moral fiber, then send them back to the streets and in twenty-four hours it'd be nothing more than a rusted, corroded wire. You can't keep polishing silver and throwing it into a vat of acid without it tarnishing."

"So you decided to get as many as you could away from that environment?"

She made it sound so simple, Brodie thought sadly. How could she know how bitter the taste of a failure when the future of young lives rested in the balance? How could she know the guilt of escaping, only to be haunted by the memories of children still imprisoned by the cruel environment? He'd left Montana and returned to Los Angeles as a juvenile probation officer. He was determined to make a difference, determined to show those kids, as he had been shown, that life exists outside the inner city. A good life, a better life.

But show-and-tell doesn't work with hardened adolescents incarcerated in a youth gang atmosphere where kindergarten is boot camp and survival demands battlefield strategy. It's a war, as real and as deadly as any armed revolution, and Brodie found himself the lone pacifist in a combat zone of urban carnage.

When Dar Garrett had died, the Circle L was snapped up by some conglomerate and Brodie coaxed Gus out of retirement to take charge of New Wave's cattle operations. Perhaps, in some small way, through Gus and the ranch, Brodie could recreate the environment that had so dramatically altered his own life.

Raking fingers through his thick hair, Brodie managed a tired smile. Kristin couldn't know, he realized. She could never truly understand that it was more, so much more, than just removing them from a violent environment. So he simply said, "That's the plan."

Again, the man had thrown her a curve. This was not what she'd expected. He was either totally sincere or deserved an Academy Award for his performance, and Kristin wasn't at all certain what to believe.

Skepticism colored her tone. "And you honestly think transplanting them from the city to the country is going to set them on the straight and narrow?"

He shrugged. "It worked for me."

She was still skeptical. "You're saying someone bundled you off to a cattle ranch and there, among cowpies and campfires, turned you from delinquent to upstanding citizen?"

"That's fairly close," he said. "I ran away from home when I was fifteen and ended up in Montana. I was a sullen, tough-mouthed know-it-all—" he paused, smiling to himself, "—pretty much like Jess, actually."

Kristin watched Brodie's face soften. Tired, tense creases seemed to melt as he reminisced. A pang coiled her stomach, a deep sense of tenderness which urged her to brush the way-ward lock from his brow, smoothing and crooning. His shad-owed cheek would feel rough against her skin and her palm actually itched at the vision.

Stunned, she reeled the sensation back, admonishing herself that this wasn't the appropriate time for misplaced mother in-stincts to surface.

It's just that Kristin didn't feel the least bit motherly. She could actually see Brodie in her mind's eye as a sullen adoles-cent, picture herself holding him, comforting him. Then it be-came Brodie holding her, demanding with a lover's touch until she acquiesced and turned pliable, welding her willing body to his hard frame. The graphic illusion flickered in her brain like a technicolor filmstrip, absorbing her consciousness until she was living it, experiencing it. It seemed so real.

"Kristin?"

She jumped, startled, certain her face revealed every erotic image from her obviously depraved mind. Good Lord, what was happening to her?

Brodie regarded her curiously, and Kristin felt herself flame with guilt, stammering like a schoolgirl. "I—I'm sorry..." She cleared her throat forcefully. "I didn't quite hear you."

"I said that I wanted to set the same kind of example for these boys."

"The same kind of example?" Kristin felt like a little lost echo.

"Yes. He showed me simple decency and caring, what life could be like outside the ghetto."

"Ah... who?"

Annoyed, Brodie's brows melted together. "Am I missing something, or have I been talking to a wall for the past five minutes?"

Kristin coughed, certain she was a vivid shade of scarlet by now and desperately praying she didn't begin to fluoresce.

"Of course not," she said as firmly as her nerves would permit. "You were depicting yourself as the original bad seed and discussing the person who single-handedly shaped you, for better or worse, into the man you are today." She met his dark stare with a virtuous smile. "I simply didn't catch the person's name."

Her smile froze to her teeth when Brodie repeated the man's name, and Kristin realized that the one person Nathan Brodie regarded as literally saving his life was Gus Krieger. No wonder he was so blinded to the vulgar little man's behavior.

She stood so quickly that Brodie appeared startled.

"I have some paperwork to complete," she said, motioning limply toward Brodie's desk, "and I don't want to hold you up any further."

Kristin spun and headed toward the door. When she reached it, she paused.

"You never told me why your file has been sealed," she said.

Brodie's response was terse. "If you had a need to know, you already would." He dismissed her with a curt good-night.

As Kristin returned to her room, she attempted to mentally organize the odd assortment of information gleaned throughout the day. *She's trouble, that one.* Kristin's lips pursed and she wondered just what kind of trouble the old man was expecting from her. What was Gus afraid of? And Brodie, well, Nathan Brodie was a complex man with a mysterious, red-tagged past, a past that piqued her interest as much as the man himself.

Kristin, however, had a few contacts in high places herself. She also had a lot of questions and no intention of stepping one foot off the New Wave Ranch until she had a lot of matching answers.

Something just didn't sit right with her, but she was certain of one fact: whatever the result of her investigation, it would obviously become a splendid addition to her book.

Assaulted with a strange uneasiness, Kristin sensed something was wrong, out of place in the meticulously organized

Chapter Four

Couldn't you find out anything, Bob?'' Kristin tightened her fingers around the telephone receiver. She was frustrated and disappointed.

"Sorry, kid, no can do," came Bob Sherwood's muffled reply. "I even had Mr. Bowers make a few calls, and if the administrative director of the agency can't get to Brodie's file, there's no way a mere peon like myself can break the code." Sherwood paused, then added, "Looks like the order came down from the court system."

Kristin massaged her forehead and sighed. Bob Sherwood was no peon in the County Social Services Agency. He was the director of the entire Juvenile Investigation Division and her boss to boot. If he had gone all the way to Bowers and still failed to unlock the mysterious red-tagged file, and if there was a court order involved . . . well, a lesser person might concede defeat. Kristin, however, was determined merely to regroup.

There had to be a way. She just hadn't thought of it yet.

"Thanks anyway, Bob," she said. "I know you did everything you could."

"Yeah, well, wish I could've done more. How's the rest of it going?"

"Oh, it's coming along, but for the past four days all I've done is dissect ledgers and sort bags full of receipts." She'd also meticulously avoided contact with Nathan Brodie, but Sherwood didn't need to know that. "Organization is definitely not one of Mr. Brodie's strong points."

A rich chuckle filtered through the line. "Maybe not, but the man has a definite talent for garnering loyalty," Bob told her. "Even though he quit two years ago, he's got enough support in the probation department to run for congress. The consensus is that he was the best P. O. on staff, absolutely devoted to the kids and his ranch is the greatest thing since sliced bread."

"In other words, you were stonewalled."

"That's about the size of it."

"Okay, Bob. Maybe I can find something out from my end."

"Well, good luck, kid."

"Thanks. Looks like I'll need it."

She dropped the telephone receiver onto its cradle and returned to the small ranch office where ledger books and bits of paper were scattered across the battered metal desktop. Another dead end. She felt like a rat in a maze.

Somehow, there had to be a pathway to the exit. Unfortunately, the map was still missing and she wondered if she should have told Bob Sherwood about the strange bank account she'd discovered.

Not yet, she decided. Not until she had a better grasp on what it meant.

Dragging the heavy ledger in front of her, Kristin flipped through the pages, double-checking the entries she'd noted yesterday. There was no mistake. Every month Brodie had received a check from the county for support of the three boys, and every month the entire amount had been transferred from the ranch's operating account to a separate fund. Kristin had tracked the money to a savings account and had found every penny received since the boys' arrival sitting there, unspent, gathering interest. And that wasn't all.

Besides the county money, smaller deposits in varying amounts had been made to the savings account each week.

"Where did the money come from?" Kristin mumbled aloud. "Why wasn't the county support money put in the ranch checking account to pay the bills?"

None of this was illegal as far as she knew, but it certainly was peculiar. The ranch itself appeared nearly broke, with revenues from cattle and hay sales considerably less than the cost of operations. Then out of nowhere, the money needed to cover the monthly deficit appeared and the ranch magically broke even. It appeared that Brodie had two mysterious sources of income.

Her pencil bounced a determined tap on the page. "Well, Mr. Brodie," she muttered. "You must have a rich fairy godmother tucked away somewhere."

Speculation, however, wasn't going to give her answers. She needed facts, and she'd spent enough hours scrutinizing the documents Brodie had supplied to realize that the facts she needed weren't there. He hadn't even given her the payroll records.

Her gaze shifted toward the small office window. From dinner conversation, Kristin knew that they were loading yearlings for shipment. She hadn't gone to the corral area since her first day at the ranch and had seen Brodie only at mealtimes. Since she still had trouble sleeping, many nights had been spent alone in her room, working on her book. She now kept the pages carefully locked in her briefcase. Whoever had been in her room that first night had pulled the manuscript out of the drawer and left it on the desk. Although nothing was ever missing, she'd had the feeling her mystery guest had returned several times.

She had to see Brodie. She either went to the corral now or she would have to wait until tonight and waste ten hours of the day.

She had little choice.

There were more records somewhere, records that contained answers instead of questions and Kristin was determined to get her hands on them.

She slammed the ledger closed and marched out of the house.

As she walked toward the rise, she saw a distant rider bent low in the saddle urging his mount flat-out up the slope toward the corral. She recognized Todd, noting the contrasting snakeskin strip wrapped around his hat. The boy rode with natural ease, his cheek nearly resting against the horse's black mane as he merged with the animal, more an extension of the beast itself than a separate entity.

In a few seconds, he crested the hill and disappeared and Kristin felt a qualm of regret. She hadn't spent much time with the boys, she realized, and her few attempts at conversation with them had been met with either suspicion or hostility. Silently, she resolved to rectify the situation.

Once she'd unlocked Brodie's skeleton closet, that is.

"Back it up now...more, a little more...stop!" Brodie swung his hands up and signaled the truck driver that the trailer of his huge rig was properly positioned against the cattle chute. He turned to Gus. "Have him drop the ramp. I'll make sure Merle's ready at the pen."

Gus divested himself of a mouthful of tobacco juice, then nodded and beckoned to Jess, who stood a few feet away watching the process. "Front and center, youngun," Gus called.

Jess complied, slowly and after a suitably rebellious pause.

Gus pointed to several sections of portable fence railing lying on the ground by the chute. "As soon as we get the ramp down, you start snappin' them rails up alongside it. Can't have them dogies fallin' on their tails whilst we're loading 'em."

"Yeah, okay." Jess wandered toward the pile of metal sections. He inspected them, then called to Gus, "Where's the clamps?"

"They're hooked on the dang post, boy. If they'd been a snake, they'd a'bit you."

"Got them," Jess replied, unperturbed, and began to drag one fence section over to the partially completed chute.

Brodie watched the teenager proudly. Jess had come a long way in the few short months he'd been at New Wave. At first, even casual suggestions had been provocation for a physical altercation; now, he accepted direct orders and instructions with no more than a careless shrug. Jess would always be a bit of a rebel, Brodie concluded, but he'd improved.

Gus had a soft spot for Jess, though Lord knows he wouldn't admit it. After twenty years, Brodie could read his foreman like the morning paper and had noted that Jess's work assignments always seemed to be situated where Gus could keep a paternal eye on him.

Brodie angled toward the holding pen where salable yearlings, cut from the herd during roundup, were bunched awaiting loading and shipment. The sound of Merle Deever's voice broke over the normal din of animal noises.

"Get off that fence, Ernie," Merle hollered.

Brodie swiveled and saw the boy perched on the top rail of the crowded pen. Grasping the splintered rail, Ernie was leaning over, reaching into the writhing mass of cattle with his free hand.

Apparently, the boy didn't hear Deever's warning because he made no attempt to climb off the fence. Brodie was on the opposite side of the pen and couldn't reach him, but Deever spurred his mount and plucked the startled teenager from his perch as easily as pulling a peach from a branch.

Merle reined the horse around the pen and deposited Ernie in a dusty heap at Brodie's feet.

"I dropped my hat," Ernie said, obviously surprised at the fuss. "It was sitting right on that cow's back." He tossed Merle a denouncing glare. "I almost had it, too, but it's probably trampled flat by now."

Merle grinned and reached down to ruffle Ernie's hair.

"Better it than you," Brodie told the disgruntled boy. "Merle's responsible for his men and you're on his shift. That means when he says 'jump,' you'd better already be in the air when you ask 'how high?'."

Ernie began to whine. "Aw gee, Brodie—"

"If you don't like the assignment," Brodie interrupted, "there's still a vacancy on Oaf's crew."

The whining stopped. None of the boys fancied spending the day up to their elbows in soapsuds and dirty dishes.

Ernie coughed. "Yeah, man...well, who needs a dumb hat, anyway?"

Brodie grinned. "That's the spirit."

As Deever and Ernie resumed their positions on the far side of the holding pen, Todd reined a red roan stallion up to the corral, sliding from the saddle almost before the horse had halted. He gave the reins a careless flip around the post, then dashed across the field to where Brodie stood.

"She's coming," Todd announced.

Brodie didn't have to ask who "she" was, and felt his muscles tense in response to the news. Reflexively, his gaze went to the top of the ridge.

She'd been avoiding him for days and frankly, he preferred it that way. Kristin bothered him, in more ways than one.

Brodie had known that eventually she would seek him out, especially since she'd been pouring through the ranch records. She was smart, that one. She would have a lot of questions and Brodie didn't particularly want to come up with the answers.

If only she'd stayed at the house for one more day, though, the cattle would be loaded and off to market. Then he could relax a bit and have a chance to think things through.

He saw her then, cresting the hill, pausing as she visually scanned the roundup field. Her gaze settled on Brodie and, after a moment's hesitation, she marched directly toward him.

No doubt about it. The rest of the day would be shot to cowcakes.

"You're working with Dwayne today, Todd." Brodie spoke absently, still watching Kristin's approach. "Go on and find him."

The boy scooted off and moments later, Kristin stood in front of Brodie, impaling him with the intensity of her silvery stare. Even in jeans and a loose, long-sleeved cotton shirt, she looked good. Too good.

"Good morning," she said.

Brodie issued a polite nod. "What can I do for you?"

Her eyes darted toward the holding pens, then briefly scanned the area immediately surrounding them. Brodie wondered if she was mentally plotting the location of every horse in the field.

"I've been analyzing your records and have a few questions." Brodie matched her gaze but didn't reply, so she continued. "I hoped you'd have some time to go over a few things."

"What things?"

"Well, bank accounts for one thing. I'm confused about the account at Mariposa Federal Savings." She paused, awaiting a response.

"Is that all?"

"No, as a matter of fact, it's not. The ranch seems to have another source of income that I can't track."

He smiled. "You suspect we're growing marijuana between rows of alfalfa?"

Kristin's eyes widened, then she returned his easy smile. "Of course not, but I *do* need to tie up the loose ends."

"Of course," Brodie agreed.

Kristin visibly relaxed at his affable attitude. She'd expected him to be secretive, maybe even hostile to her inquiries and was pleasantly surprised at his relaxed demeanor.

Inside, Brodie was far from relaxed. His mind churned rapidly, weighing and discarding options with breakneck speed. This was what he'd feared and he cursed himself for not having prepared for it. It wasn't illegal to use his personal money to cover the ranch's operating loss, but the savings account where the county support checks were deposited was possibly another matter.

Good intentions notwithstanding, Brodie knew he'd broken some rules and he may have even broken the law. He'd done it for the boys' future, but the slight infractions might be enough to lose everything. He could lose New Wave.

With a sinking feeling, Brodie decided that Kristin probably wouldn't let go until she found it all. He knew that her initial impression of the ranch had been less than favorable. In Brodie's opinion, it was the nature of bureaucrats to insist everything be done exactly by the book, regarding the slightest innovations as, at best, improper and, at worst, downright subversive.

Was Kristin like the rest of them? he wondered. Could he trust her or would she use the information to shut him down entirely?

Gus's raspy bellow echoed across the field and Brodie turned gratefully toward the interruption.

"Chute's ready," Gus hollered. "Time to load 'em up."

Brodie waved in acknowledgment then turned to Kristin and tried to disguise his relief. "Sorry, we'll have to go over this another time," he muttered. "Excuse me." Turning, he headed toward the large cattle truck at the far end of the roundup area.

Kristin saw that most of the holding pens, which had been filled to capacity during the branding operation, now stood empty and quiet. The two pens still in use were crammed with cattle and, as though the animals realized something monumental was about to occur, they began to clamor nervously, disgorging an outcry of panicked bellows.

Men on horses surrounded the pen and lined a kind of runway constructed of metal rail fencing that led to the open trailer of the cattle truck.

Kristin quickly ascertained that the cows in the pen were about to be herded into the truck via the rickety runway. She also decided that if one of the animals sneezed while it was in that chute, the whole darn thing would probably collapse.

She felt icy perspiration bead across her forehead and had the sudden image of herself wearing a sign announcing, Hooves Wiped Free. Kristin slowly backtracked, her eyes never leaving the activity around the cattle chute. Safely sheltered beneath the oak tree, she stopped to watch the rest of the loading process. It was frightening, yet it fascinated her.

A loud whoop resonated through the thick air and the metal chute swayed dangerously against the single-file surge of huge beasts. Bellowing loudly, they snorted down the narrow channel and up the ramp into the truck. Occasionally, one of the animals would balk, blocking the chute and mooing madly until a ranch hand prodded it with a long wooden stick apparently carried just for that purpose.

Each cowboy carried a walkie-talkie on his belt, holstered like a sidearm, and they used the radios to communicate through the din of stomping hooves.

Kristin watched for nearly an hour and after the first few minutes, found herself too engrossed in the sight to be nervous. When she'd seen the three teenagers actively engaged in the operation, she'd been instantly alert and concerned. But she'd soon realized, while examining the process, how closely the boys were actually guarded.

It wasn't particularly obvious to the casual observer, but Kristin noted that one ranch hand had apparently been assigned to each boy and was never more than a few feet from the youngster. Brodie seemed to be everywhere, moving from pen to ramp, checking on each cowboy and each teenager, then rotating to begin the procedure again.

Slouching beside the ramp, Jess scrawled on some kind of tablet as each animal stomped up the wooden platform and into the waiting truck. Gus hovered at the youngster's shoulder.

There was a shout, "It's a turnaround."

One of the cows shifted sideways on the ramp and stood bellowing in confusion, blocking the chute gate. The beast stumbled toward the edge of the ramp, some five feet above the ground.

To Kristin's dismay, Jess dropped the tablet and started to leap onto the ramp, but Gus grabbed the boy's belt, hauling him back. Gus's stubbled chin moved rapidly and Kristin was certain Jess was being categorically chewed out. With surprising agility, the older man swiftly swung onto the wooden platform, turned the cow and shoved the bawling animal into the truck.

Gus landed on his feet beside Jess, dusted himself, spit in the dirt and gave Jess a haughty, that's-how-you-do-it grin. To her surprise, Kristin saw the usually sullen teenager laugh and offer Gus a thumbs-up gesture of approval.

Brodie stood beside Todd, his arm tossed casually around the boy's small shoulders. He was a big man, dwarfing the boy, but he folded himself to Todd's level, pointing out something of apparent interest. Kristin could see the enthusiasm glowing on the youngster's excited face.

There was a camaraderie between them all, she noted, along with obvious affection. Strange. This behavior simply didn't fit Kristin's perception of the foul-mouthed ranch foreman and, after Brodie's uncomplimentary remarks about Todd's lack of morals . . . well, like everything else around here, it was all very unexpected.

She wondered about Ernie a moment before she saw him, hanging on the metal rails of the cattle chute. Then, as though he wanted a better vantage point, Ernie scrambled to the top of the swaying fence. Kristin noted wryly that the boy always seemed to be perched atop something.

There was a slight lull in activity. One pen was empty, but one was still full of cattle awaiting their turn and Merle Deever was fiddling with its gate.

The sound of Brodie's voice pulled Kristin's gaze back to the chute. "Ernie! Get down from there. Move it, boy!"

Startled, Ernie teetered forward and the fence swayed farther. The boy lost his balance, struggled briefly, then tumbled into the empty cattle chute.

Kristin went cold. Deever had opened the gate to the second holding pen and cattle were swarming through the connecting pen, hooves thundering toward the mouth of the runway where Ernie sat, dazed and dusty.

The first cow was muscling into the narrow opening when Brodie launched into the chute, positioning himself between Ernie and the steer. He grabbed the boy by the collar and belt, hoisting him up and over the rail to safety as the cow moved closer, closing in like a horned steamroller. The beast was less than five feet away when Brodie leaped the fence and catapulted, sprawling beside the stunned teenager.

Wind buffeted her face as Kristin dashed toward the chute, dropping to her knees between Ernie and Brodie as thundering hooves bellowed beyond the fence.

"Are you all right?" She meant both of them, of course, but found herself engulfed by Brodie's deep blue eyes as she directed the question.

His face was solemn. He nodded.

The gravity of the situation had finally hit Ernie. "Man, what a trip. Like, I saw that steer coming at me and I freaked, you know?"

Deever was looming above them, his face drawn and pale as he pulled Ernie to his feet, scrutinizing him anxiously. When he'd determined the boy wasn't hurt, his expression hardened. "You left your post," Deever reprimanded. "I should fire you for that."

Ernie's face crumpled. "No, man! Hey, I'm sorry, honest! I just wanted a closer look." He whirled toward Brodie, who now stood beside them. "Tell him, Brodie. Tell him I'm sorry."

Brodie's face was firm, but Kristin saw a flicker of compassion in his eyes. "You know the rules, Ernie," Brodie said. "Merle's your boss. If he fires you, you'll be reassigned."

Ernie's eyes widened, his voice a tiny whisper. "Oaf?"

"Yes."

The boy moaned, then whirled back to Deever. "I'm sorry. Please," he croaked.

"Well . . ." Merle appeared to be weakening.

Ernie pressed his advantage. "I'll practice roping for two whole hours every night," he promised.

Brodie turned away and Kristin noted he was fighting the smile cracking at the corners of his mouth.

Merle, however, kept his face admirably straight. Finally he told Ernie, "Get back to your post. I'll decide after dinner."

The relieved boy whirled and shot across the field like a bullet, probably, Kristin mused, trying to get away before Deever changed his mind. Merle winked at Brodie, then tipped his hat to Kristin and sauntered away.

When Brodie shifted toward Kristin, his expression had hardened. "I guess you've got another paragraph for that report of yours."

Avoiding his eyes, Kristin side-stepped, staring across the chute toward Todd, who was staring back with a sullen expression. Even Brodie couldn't deny the dangers, she thought, and was strangely saddened. Watching the loading operation, she'd begun to realize what precautions he took for the boys' safety. Obviously, precautions weren't enough.

"Yes," she answered slowly, "I guess I do."

She glanced peripherally toward Brodie and saw the desolation cross his face. It tore at her and she swallowed.

Get a grip on yourself. You can't change anything: you only report facts.

And the facts indicated that New Wave Ranch, operated by a mysterious man with a red-tagged past, was plagued by fiscal irregularities and presented a dangerous environment to the boys.

Trust facts, not instincts.

Her shoulders stiffened. "Now, Mr. Brodie, about those records—"

"We'll get around to it." He swiveled quickly away from her, angling back toward the loading truck.

"Get *around* to it?"

He was standing at the chute when she caught up, his back toward her as he motioned to his men, gesturing instructions.

"I can see that you're quite busy. Could we schedule some time this evening?"

He didn't even look toward her. "Maybe."

Kristin swallowed her mounting irritation. "I know that this investigation is a disruption. I've tried not to interfere with ranch operation, but every time I try to get an appointment with you when you aren't working, you put me off."

Brodie straightened and turned away, knotting his arms across the top rail of the five-foot-high cattle chute.

"Look, Brodie, if I don't get a little cooperation from you, I might as well climb into that rented car and head right back to L.A."

"We'll miss you."

Brodie's remark hit Kristin wrong. She stiffened. "Without more answers, my report will contain exactly what I've seen so far which, by the way, will not bode particularly well for your hopes of having twelve more strong backs to run your cattle ranch."

Brodie looked stunned. "Are you saying that these kids are being exploited?"

Kristin winced. She may have been provoked, but the implied threat of her statement was inappropriate. "Not exactly, but—"

"I should have known," Brodie said. "What else can you expect from a pencil-pushing power broker on a massive ego trip?"

"Now, just a darn minute—"

"Your idea of an abused kid is one who has to do his own dishes and buy his own Reeboks." Brodie spun to face her. "You made up your mind about the ranch before you even set one lily-white foot on the place."

"That's not true. I'm open-minded and objective on *all* my investigations. Even this one."

Kristin cringed. *Even this one?* Brodie had hit a nerve. *Had* she brought preconceived notions to New Wave?

She squeezed her eyes shut, rubbed her head and took a deep breath. "Look, we have to work together and it's to your advantage to cooperate." Good. Calm and reasonable.

Brodie's expression was dark. "I am cooperating."

"Not from my point of view," she said, then held up her palm as he started to interject. "It appears that the boys are being exposed to unnecessary danger."

"Oh, for crying out loud. The boys have been thoroughly trained and are supervised—"

"But *I* don't know that, because *no one will cooperate long enough to tell me.*"

Brodie jammed his hands in the pockets of his jeans. He was grim. "All right. Monday."

"What?"

"I said you've made your point and we'll get together on Monday."

"But this is only Saturday. That wastes two entire days."

"You've got two or three more weeks for your investigation. A couple of days won't matter one way or the other. Besides," he added, pausing to massage his forehead. "I'll be tied up until then, anyway."

Brodie looked up, saw Kristin's eyes darken with suspicion, and expelled a tired sigh. "Look. I said Monday and I meant it. The ranch will lose a bundle if these cows don't get out today, and with the barbecue tomorrow—"

"What barbecue?" This was a new wrinkle.

"End of roundup. Every year folks in the valley get together to celebrate with a giant barbecue. It's kind of a round-robin affair and, as luck would have it, this year is New Wave's turn to host it."

"You mean the entire population between here and Mariposa will be at the ranch tomorrow?"

Brodie smiled sadly. "Well, half anyway, but you can see the problem."

"Yes, well . . ." What could she do? It was Monday or nothing and, comments in anger to the contrary, she really didn't relish the idea of slinking back to her office with an incomplete report and a failed investigation. "Monday will be fine."

With a curt nod, Brodie turned back to his cows.

As she headed toward the rise, a movement caught Kristin's eye. She peered through the fence at one of the empty holding pens and saw Todd hunched in the corner.

Discovered, he straightened and gave Kristin a mutinous stare.

"Todd, what—"

"Are you going to send us back?" His eyes were narrowed, glinting like ice chips. The startling contrast of bitterness scarring the angelic young face took Kristin's breath away, leaving her stunned and mute.

Todd's mouth twisted into an ugly grimace. "You'd better not try," he warned. "You'll be awful sorry if you do."

Chapter Five

Fear. Bones bounced, jarred in their sockets as though shaken by a giant hand. Teeth crashed together with every pounding blow. Panic. A low, rumbling growl, like a thundering train vibrating land and air, raising icy fingers of flesh to encircle her spine with excruciating force. Terror. Falling against the earth, only to be overcome by snarling teeth and shattering pain.

Screaming, screaming, screaming. No one comes, no one cares.

Kristin's eyes flew open, glazed and vacant.

"Ssshhh, you're safe." Brodie stroked the frigid dampness from Kristin's brow as she thrashed against twisted sheets. Moaning, she struck sightlessly at him, hands flailing as though to protect herself. He captured the thrusting fists as her mouth warped in horror.

"Easy, Kris," Brodie crooned. "It's just a bad dream. You're all right, honey."

"Mama Lu," Kristin croaked, not awake, not aware. "Mama Lu, help me."

Gathering her trembling body in his arms, Brodie held her tightly, as though he could squeeze away her mental monsters. The wall between their bedrooms was no barrier to the sound of her terror and Brodie had listened, hearing her broken sobs as she fought unseen demons, ghosts of a sorrowful past.

Tonight those ghosts had possessed her fully and Brodie had gone to her as she'd screamed in abject terror again and again, until he comforted her with his touch and the sound of his voice.

Finally, she sagged against him, violent tremors reduced to an occasional shudder, her breath slow and even against his neck. He felt heat begin to seep from beneath the thin cotton nightgown as he stroked her back, massaging rigid muscles into pliability.

Murmuring sleepily, not yet fully cognizant of her surroundings, Kristin was aware of a heady male scent wafting the air, a clean, masculine smell. She breathed deeply, recognizing Brodie's special, earthy fragrance even in her sleep-drugged stupor. Hands were touching her, rough hands, Brodie's hands, spreading warmth over her skin. This was still a dream, Kristin's foggy brain told her, but it was a lovely one and she might as well enjoy it.

Forcing her leaden lids to open, she saw him and smiled. "Hello," she whispered huskily and Brodie's blood surged. She reached out to caress the hard muscles of his chest, tracing a mass of dark hair until it curled beneath the waistband of his briefs. Brodie moaned.

"Kristin..." Brodie choked back a groan as her fingers danced below his navel. He knew from the vapid glaze of her half-closed eyes that she was unaware of his torment. He couldn't take advantage of her condition, and his body rebelled at the realization. A bottle of sleeping pills was on the nightstand, the medication numbing her mind and leaving her woozy, unaware of what she was doing to him.

Fuzzily, she tried to focus. "You're a hallucination, aren't you?" Her voice was slurred and she smiled dreamily.

Clamping his jaw, Brodie tried to ignore the fiery need her soft touch had ignited. She was half drugged, he warned himself, and exhausted from the ordeal of her nightmare. He fought to control the throbbing hunger of his aroused flesh.

"Yes, Kris, I'm a dream. Close your eyes now, go back to sleep."

"Umm . . . you're a very nice dream," she said, drifting into a deep, sound slumber.

He continued to hold her as she slept, knowing he should release her and leave, yet unwilling to do so. Reluctantly heeding the dictates of his conscience, he lowered her to the damp sheets, tucking the bedclothes around her slim body. Eyelids twitching slightly, her brows squinched together and she whimpered at the loss of his reassuring warmth.

Brodie laid his palm across her forehead and felt her relax at the touch. Pale and soft, her skin was translucent in the silvery spray of the moon. Free of the defensive, cynical shield she carried in reality's harsh sunlight, her face now reflected the vulnerability of the child she once had been.

He slid a finger along her cheek, tracing the delicate curves. He choked at her beauty, too pure even to be marred by the whitened scars threading her ivory complexion.

What tore at her? Brodie wondered. What trust was betrayed, what monsters beckoned from her dreams?

The thick quilt rose and fell with easy rhythm and the sound of her tranquil breathing filtered through the darkened room. Forcing himself to stand, Brodie allowed a final glimpse of her face, now serene in peaceful slumber.

He had to leave her now, he told himself. He had to go before she woke again and found him standing over her bed, watching her, wanting her.

Kristin held her swollen head and wondered how she'd managed to swallow a Brillo pad in the middle of the night.

She must have, because her entire mouth now felt as though it were coated with steel wool and she was certain her head was filled with soapsuds.

Could one lousy sleeping pill result in this kind of a hangover? Moaning, Kristin vowed to dump the whole damn bottle and go back to hot milk. She'd told the doctor she didn't want the pills, but he'd insisted that they were mild and would allow her to get the rest she desperately needed. Last night, totally exhausted, she'd finally succumbed to the temptation. The cure, it seemed, was worse than the problem.

Wobbling to the door, Kristin cracked it and peeked into the hallway. Relieved to find it vacant, she teetered toward the bathroom and the nearest source of fresh, cold, splashable water.

When she returned to her room, her eyes were at least unglued but the aspirin she'd located had yet to soften the roaring ache in her brain. She felt as though she'd spent the entire night playing racquetball, using her skull as a paddle.

But she hadn't. After all these years, Kristin knew the symptoms. She'd had another nightmare, a massive one. Usually, she would wake up on the floor, tangled in covers and clammy with sweat. This morning had been strange, though. She was serenely sandwiched between sheets which were still neatly tucked beneath the mattress. Only stiffened muscles and a massive headache remained, mute remnants of her terror. If the medication hadn't eliminated the nightmare, it had at least dulled her memory of it.

Raising her arms above her head, Kristin stretched, painfully forcing each knotted muscle to unwind, then collapsed, bending at the waist like a rag doll until the tension ebbed and her bones moved freely. Straightening, she massaged her lower back.

"It's going to be a long day," she muttered, then rifled the closet to toss a pair of smoke-gray corduroy pants and a peach sweater on the bed. She moaned at the mirror but went to work with foundation and blush until she was satisfied that the reflection no longer appeared totally corpselike, just slightly zombified.

Noting she'd left her manuscript on the desk last night, Kristin hurriedly stowed it in her briefcase and shoved the locked case under the bed. She'd tried to work on the book last night, but ended up staring at useless pages which were blurred by images of Nathan Brodie.

Kristin was perplexed and frustrated. Brodie had gotten to her yesterday and she'd spent the rest of the afternoon mulling over yet another unpleasant episode in the New Wave saga.

How in the world could that man push all her buttons so easily?

Pencil-pushing power broker on a massive ego trip.

Not a particularly flattering description and, of course, totally inaccurate. Totally.

So why had it made her blood freeze to hear him say it? And why did she wake up with this peculiar image of Brodie holding her, stroking her head, murmuring softly?

Weird. The ranch was weird, her own reactions were weird and Nathan Brodie...well, he was just something else. Kristin hadn't exactly decided what.

Whatever he was, Kristin grudgingly admitted that everyone else on the ranch was obviously devoted to him. What was it Bob Sherwood had told her? "...a definite talent for garnering loyalty."

A talent Kristin didn't seem to possess. With one notable exception, Kristin's life since her parents were killed when she was seven had been a series of foster homes—some cold and impersonal, others manipulative and greedy—and one way or the other, none of the foster parents had seemed to care about Kristin's presence.

The Whitmans had been the worst, or perhaps it just seemed that way because the accident had happened while she was with them. She'd been assigned to them when she'd been ten years old and in two days the had put her to work in a neighbor's drug store. They'd collected her wages themselves, not trusting Kristin to bring the money to them.

Mr. Whitman only hit her once, when she had gotten the flu and asked to stay home, but Kristin had always been afraid of him, anyway. His wife was a mammoth woman with cheeks so fat her mouth was squashed until it resembled a pink Cheerio. The woman had rarely spoken to Kristin.

After the accident, Kristin remembered waking up in the hospital. After her release, she had been assigned to another foster home. The Whitmans, it seemed, had asked for another child. A healthier one.

Mama Lu was the exception. Kristin's eyes misted in memory of the only person since her parents had died who had really loved her. But Mama Lu was gone now, and Kristin was alone. Completely, frighteningly alone.

Well, she certainly couldn't continue to stand here in her nightgown dwelling on the past. Such thoughts always saddened Kristin and she abhorred moodiness, particularly in herself. It wasted time and energy, and to be depressed was to be inefficient.

Besides, the breakfast bell would soon be clamoring and Oaf had a tendency to sulk if anyone was late to the table.

Kristin smiled as she thought of the docile giant. She had learned that his real name was Olaf, but Gus's distinctive drawl had eliminated the *L* sound, and the nickname had stuck. Oaf was combination cook, housekeeper, paramedic and tutor. Exceptionally bright despite his plodding appearance, Oaf spent several hours each week assisting the boys with their more difficult homework assignments. Apparently, he excelled in theoretical mathematics and spoke four languages, English being the most recent addition to his repertoire.

Yes, Oaf was another New Wave enigma.

Yanking her drawer open, Kristin rooted through the contents for a fresh T-shirt. Stunned, her eyes widened as she saw the shirt move toward her under its own power.

Watching, nearly paralyzed, she saw the soft fabric undulate rhythmically, then realized that other items of clothing appeared to be gyrating, propelling themselves across the surface with a swaying, determined motion.

Hesitantly, she plucked at a corner of the fabric. Two glossy black eyes beaded back at her, glaring malevolently. A thready tongue whipped, flickering in Kristin's direction briefly before it disappeared beneath a heap of socks, followed by a shiny, black-and-white living rope.

Her breath gushed out in a single, hissing whoosh.

"Cute, boys," she muttered. "Very, very cute."

No expert, Kristin still recognized the harmless king snake and had a fairly good idea how it had suddenly appeared nestled in her drawer.

Fortunately, snakes themselves held no terror for Kristin. One of the boys in her last foster home had been an amateur herpetologist and she'd helped him care for his collection.

This particular snake had startled her but she wasn't afraid of it. However, she was incredibly grateful that horses were bigger than drawers.

For the moment, Kristin ignored her uninvited guest and slipped into her clothes. When the breakfast bell began to clang, Kristin finished running a brush through her hair. She reopened the dresser drawer, carefully peeling back layers of clothing until she found the snake, coiled and comfortable.

"Well, little fellow, I have a few folks I'd like you to meet. Of course, at least one of them will be an old friend," she added with a wry grimace.

She moved a finger in front of the snake's snout, capturing its attention. While it sniffed her hand with its tongue, she grasped the sleek body just behind its head and lifted the reptile from the drawer. It bucked and writhed at the movement, but by the time Kristin reached the bottom of the stairs, the snake had wound itself around her arm and seemed relatively placid.

Standard mealtime chatter sprayed into the hall, intensifying as she got closer to the kitchen. Just before she reached the doorway, she paused, changing her gait to a casual saunter.

"Good morning," she said, entering the bright room. "Beautiful day, isn't it?"

The snake squeezed her arm, whipping its tongue wildly.

Kristin smiled sweetly as the men's heads snapped in hilarious, slapstick double takes. Everyone seemed to freeze in place; mouths which were open stayed that way, forks locked in midair, hands stiffened midgesture.

"Oaf, perhaps you can find a fat mouse for my friend."

Her gaze swiftly swung to each of the boys, searching for some clue, some spark of recognition. Jess frowned briefly before his eyes veiled. Ernie lurched away from the table, plastering himself against the wall, wide eyes seeming to engulf his thin face.

Todd's eyes appeared to harden, a fleeting but frightening glimpse of fury. The expression flickered away. "Neat," he said, without enthusiasm, then forked a syrupy sausage into his mouth.

"Tarnation," exclaimed Gus, who had been uncharacteristically rigid for the past few minutes.

Brodie had been stunned, marbleized like a granite carving at the sight of Kristin nonchalantly carrying a snake into the kitchen as though it were an inanimate article of clothing.

Kristin sauntered casually to the back door, opened it and dropped the king snake into the dust. Then she smiled brightly and took her assigned place at the table.

Brodie could only blink in disbelief. Obviously, she's well-recovered from her harrowing night, he thought and wondered how much she remembered. He cleared his throat and kept his voice calm. "Ah…any particular reason you chose to favor us with a zoology lesson during breakfast?"

"Actually, I was trying to return it to its owner." Kristin looked innocently around the table and feigned surprise. "But no one seemed to claim it."

Brodie's eyes clamped into blue slits. "What are you talking about?"

"Pass the pancakes, please." Kristin heaped her plate and smiled her thanks to the cowboy handing her the syrup bottle. "I found it in the house, so naturally I assumed it was someone's pet."

"Snakes sneak into the barn, the house, everywhere," Gus pointed out. "That don't make the dang things part of the family."

Kristin nibbled a sausage. "That's true enough," she acknowledged. "But I found this one in my dresser drawer," she said smoothly, giving each of the teenagers a telling look before turning toward Brodie. "Snakes can't open drawers all by themselves, can they?"

Brodie moaned once, massaged his forehead briefly, then scowled, in turn, at every man and boy at the table.

"No," he grated, "they can't open drawers."

"Umm...I didn't think so."

Kristin continued to enjoy her breakfast as Brodie impatiently pushed his half-eaten meal away. He looked about ready to explode, a fact not unnoticed by Gus, who made a valiant attempt to defuse the situation.

"Let's get this shindig thing sorted out." Gus's suggestion was met with mumbled agreement. "Now, Merle, Dwayne and Ernie'll be taking the truck over to the Wilson place to pick up tables. Tug, you 'n Billy dig some pits up at the knoll, and you two lucky younguns get to shovel the stables."

"I'd be happy to help," Kristin offered, then blinked at Brodie's stunned look. "Since everyone will apparently be tied up today, I might as well contribute to the festivities. If I can, of course," she added, looking toward Gus.

"Well..." He scratched at his chin, his expression one of pure puzzlement, as if stumped by the thought. "Don't rightly know of anythin' what wouldn't get you plumb grimed up, missy."

"I *am* washable, Gus."

Brodie was seized by a convulsive fit of coughing.

"Well now, 'course you are," Gus said, placating her, "but it just don't seem fittin' for a pretty thing like you to be shoveling sh...er, stables."

"Oh. Well, stables really aren't my strong suit," she agreed, paling at the thought of sweeping under a horse. "But surely there's something..."

"Ja? Miss Kristin?" Oaf rarely spoke during meals, usually because he was engulfed in a flurry of activity loading and unloading the table. Heads swiveled toward him in surprise.

"Of course. I could help Oaf with the cooking! He'll probably be absolutely swamped."

"No!" Oaf looked stricken.

"I beg your pardon?"

"No, I cook, Miss Kristin, but I need things."

"Things?"

"Ja. Onions, tomatoes...things." He held up a list.

Kristin's brain light engaged. "Oh! *Things*. You want me to go into town for you?"

"Ja, please."

"It's settled then. Get your list ready, Oaf."

An hour later, Kristin bounced over the porch steps, pausing for a deep breath of the clean air. No salty tang, but she had to admit it was invigorating.

The truck was gone, so Merle, Dwayne and Ernie were apparently actively engaged in table pickup duty and Kristin saw two other ranch hands feverishly digging a large trench in the flattened meadow abutting the hill to the roundup area. Apparently, this barbecue was going to be a rip-roaring affair and half a cow would soon be rotating over coals glowing in that pit.

Rounding the corner of the house, Kristin headed toward the car that was parked beside the bunkhouse. She stopped, watching. Jess and Todd were standing nearby, kicking at the dirt and conversing quietly. Jess saw Kristin first and mouthed a warning that grabbed Todd's attention.

She offered them a smile and was surprised when she received dark stares in return, the boys' faces mirroring an expression that very much resembled extreme, unequivocal dislike. She watched them walk away from the car in the direction opposite the spot where she stood, feeling stunned and dismayed.

As she slid into the car and started the engine, Kristin realized that all the boys had become more hostile each day. Although she'd initially suspected Todd, any of them could have been responsible for the snake prank. Mentally, she amended that conclusion to exclude Ernie. He'd leaped from the breakfast table as though frightened half out of his wits by the reptile.

The car droned across the dirt road from the ranch, turning onto the narrow pavement that would wind through foothills and canyons to the main highway.

Rolling down the window, she allowed the cool breeze to finger her hair and relaxed as a collage of earth tones brightened by every possible hue of green smeared past the moving vehicle.

Soon the road hairpinned and the grade steepened. The terrain was mountainous with cliffs on one side of the road and deep gorges on the other. Downshifting, she slowed to execute the intricate maneuvers. The car jerked, startling her. Kristin's gaze swept the dashboard instruments and she cursed.

The thermostat's needle had swung into the red zone.

In moments, a hissing cloud of white steam burst from under the hood and she knew if she didn't shut off the ignition, the engine would fuse into a molten mass.

There were no shoulders along the narrow road, no place to pull off. It was straight down on her right, straight up on her left and room for precisely two small vehicles in between.

Ominous grinding noises filtered through the hissing steam as the engine lost power battling the steepening grade. She hit the brake pedal and the car vibrated to a halt. Kristin set the emergency brake lever and considered her situation.

The road curved in front and behind. Vehicles traveling in either direction would be on top of the stalled car before the driver could react.

Of course, that may not be a problem after all, because Kristin had been on this paved path for nearly twenty minutes and hadn't seen another car yet.

In either instance, one fact was indisputable: She was completely stranded.

The knoll was alive with activity.

Two truckloads of men appeared and charged toward the barbecue pit, spreading charcoal and mesquite, then setting up the rotisserie. Within two hours, coals glowing red as a hundred evil eyes watched the butchered carcass slowly roasting above them.

"There's enough tables over there, Dwayne. Set those over to the right, by the cottonwoods." Brodie pointed to clarify his meaning and with a grunt, Dwayne hoisted one end of the large wooden table. Billy, the youngest of Brodie's full-time hands, grabbed the other end and the two men trudged toward the trees.

"How come fixin' one darn supper can use up a whole day and cause all this misery, I'd like to know." Gus spat and stared gloomily.

"Seems you had yourself a pretty good time at last year's barbecue," Brodie said. "Good enough that it took three of us to fold you into the truck and get you home."

"Don't rightly remember," Gus said blandly.

Brodie chuckled. "I didn't think you would."

Oaf's voice lilted from the kitchen porch. "Mr. Goos, Mr. Goos," he called, having the same problem with Gus's name as Gus had with his. "I cannot paint the cow," Oaf said, obviously distressed.

Gus screwed his face. "Paint the cow?" he mumbled, then brightened with comprehension. "You mean the dang barbycue sauce?"

Oaf nodded. "Ja. I do not have the onion or the tomato..." He spread his huge hands dramatically. "I have nothing."

Something clicked in Brodie's brain. "Wait a minute," he said. "I thought Kristin went into town for those things."

"Ja, but the cow, it is ready."

"You mean she's not back yet." Brodie's eyes skimmed toward the bunkhouse area where she parked. No car. "When did she leave?"

Gus answered. "Shoot, I saw her drive off right after breakfast."

Oaf nodded. "Ja. She took my paper."

Brodie swore. "That was four hours ago. She could've been to town and back three times by now."

"Most likely got to gawkin' in some shop window," Gus offered helpfully. "You know how women are."

"Bull." Brodie was already swinging himself into the truck. He gave the ignition key a vicious twist and roared away.

Brodie maneuvered the narrow pavement winding along the mountain toward Mariposa. He was worried, his mind clamoring with images of Kristin's body sprawled in one of the steep canyons bordering the road. There were no guardrails, no pullout areas. A blowout could mean disaster.

Blast that woman, Brodie thought. He would be concerned for anyone who might be in trouble, but this gnawing fear went beyond that. She was under his skin, that lady, bringing out feelings that he hadn't experienced in a long time. The power of those emotions confused and frightened him. He felt out of control and control was Brodie's lifeline.

The grade steepened and as he rounded a sharp curve, Brodie suddenly screeched the truck to a halt. He stared at the sight before him, unable to believe his eyes. Flashing lights pulled at his subconscious, drawing from his unwilling mind the memory of other lights which once strobed across the L.A. night like slashing blades.

He could feel the sultry heat, the muggy night enveloping him as lights from a half dozen police cars blasted the darkness. Pulsing, illuminating the milling crowd, garish flashes of blue and red obscured the subtle green neon of Clancy's Liquors. The air was filled with the smell of death.

Icy sweat beaded his face and his hands trembled against a taloned grip on the steering wheel as he fought the memory.

These lights were amber, not red and blue, and they were attached to a large truck, not a police car. A tow truck. On the other side of the tow truck was Kristin's rental car.

Brodie pried his fingers from the wheel and shakily stepped from his truck. As an afterthought, he reached into the cab and flipped on the hazard lights, then surveyed the scene in front of him.

It looked abandoned. The car's hood was up, but Brodie saw no sign of either Kristin or the tow truck driver. He ducked behind the huge craned vehicle and spotted two pairs of feet extending from under the car's grill. Then he heard muffled voices.

"Kristin?"

The smaller pair of feet wiggled, scraping against the pavement as Kristin scooted from under the car. She was on the roadway, flat on her back, surprise etched across a grimy, grease-stained face.

Finally, she asked, "What are you doing here?"

"Looking for you."

Kristin stood and dusted herself. "Why?"

"Because," he replied tightly, "I thought you might need help." He eyed the lanky young man shimmying out from under the car.

Kristin cocked her head, her expression soft. "That was very kind of you. It didn't occur to me that my absence would be cause for concern. I should have called after I ordered the tow truck."

"Yes, you should have." Relief was turning to anger and Brodie was feeling more than a little foolish. After all, she was a grown woman and could obviously take care of herself. What would she think of him, roaring up here like some kind of jilted lover?

As though she could read his thoughts, Kristin placed her hand on his forearm and gave him a grateful smile.

"Thank you for coming," she said softly. "I really *did* need help."

Brodie stared down at the small hand warming his arm. "What happened?"

Kristin sighed. "The car overheated and stalled. I sat here for nearly an hour before someone came along and gave me a lift into town." She glared at the car. "I knew I should have rented a newer model."

"That wouldn't have helped much," said the tow truck driver.

Kristin and Brodie both turned toward the man, who was squatting in front of the car.

"What do you mean?" Brodie asked.

"Well, you see this here?" The driver pointed toward the grill and Brodie leaned down, squinting.

"What am I looking for?"

"See this nick in the chrome?"

Brodie nodded.

"The radiator's been torn right behind that nick." The driver straightened and brushed his hands together as though his statement should explain everything.

Brodie, still bent over the grill, looked up blankly. "So, what does that mean?"

Exasperated, the driver explained. "It means that the radiator wasn't punctured by some kind of road hazard. You know, a rock or a piece of metal. That would have caused the damage to be lower and the object wouldn't have come through the grill at this angle."

Standing, Brodie slitted a glance at him. "Do you know what *did* cause the damage?"

The man reached for a rag in the back pocket of his dungarees and shrugged. "Can't tell for sure," he said, then coolly met Brodie's narrowed gaze. "A knife, maybe, or something like it."

"A knife?" Kristin breathed, paling. "Are you saying someone deliberately sabotaged that car?"

The driver calmly swung his gaze toward Kristin. "That's not for me to say, lady."

Her own shock and disbelief was reflected by Brodie's astonished expression. Suddenly, Kristin was frightened. This wasn't simply a game anymore.

The stakes were too high.

Chapter Six

The scenic forest beauty passed unnoticed and unappreciated as Brodie guided the truck down the winding road back toward the ranch. He was quiet, somber, his features set grimly, as though sculpted in gray stone.

Kristin, too, was absorbed by silent contemplation. A slashed radiator went beyond the bounds of a youthful prank and Kristin was chilled to discover the extent of the boys' hostility. Why would they target her so ruthlessly? After all, she was there to protect them, to make certain they were treated properly and their individual rights were preserved.

The plain fact was that Kristin was on *their* side—couldn't they see that?

Then another fact weaved into her brain. If anyone had a motive to chase her away, it was Nathan Brodie.

She angled a covert glance at his rigid profile. Tight stress lines bracketed a thinned, cheerless mouth and his forehead puckered into hunched brows. But his eyes...Kristin glimpsed an intense sadness in those eyes, a hollow, almost hopeless sense of loss.

That Brodie could be responsible for this torment was difficult to believe. He'd seemed genuinely angry about the snake gag and it was Brodie, after all, who had searched for her when she didn't return to the ranch. Even now, he was quite obviously upset.

Still, Kristin's logical mind spurred into action. Brodie *could* simply be angry that the plan hadn't worked. Perhaps he'd expected to find a hysterical woman ready to grab her bags and run screaming back to L.A.

Kristin's instincts told her that Brodie wasn't—couldn't—be involved in the harassment, but instincts were unreliable. Facts were reliable. Facts could be trusted.

The smothering silence settled over them, filling the cab of the pickup like a humid cloudbank. It was suffocating and she fumbled to roll down the window, deeply inhaling as fresh air rushed at her face.

Seeking release from the tense atmosphere, Kristin mentally scrambled for the diversion of casual conversation. "Well, the morning wasn't a total loss," she said, glancing at the grocery sack nestled at her feet. "As soon as I fluttered a five-dollar bill in front of his nose, the tow truck driver was more than happy to stop at a store."

Brodie's response was a tightening jawline.

Kristin ignored his silence. "Since the car will be ready by tomorrow afternoon, do you think one of the men could drive me into town to pick it up?"

After a few seconds, Kristin saw his stiff, affirmative nod. So much for casual conversation. She folded her arms and stared at the window.

It was several minutes more before Brodie spoke, so softly she barely heard him. "Kristin, I'm sorry." His expression was desolate. "Whoever vandalized the car will pay for its repair. If they can't, I will."

She watched him carefully, ignoring the lump in her throat. Brodie's pain was a tangible, living thing and Kristin felt it cut through her own chest.

He appeared to be a man betrayed.

"Do you..." her voice faded and she swallowed, trying to clear her head as well as her throat. "Do you know who's responsible?"

"I think it's fairly obvious that the boys had a hand in it." He swung a sideways glance. "They were all in on the snake trick, you know."

"All of them?" She hadn't counted on that bit of news.

"Yes. Oh, Todd actually found the snake but the whole thing was Jess's idea and Ernie went along with it."

"How do you know all of this?"

"I asked them."

Kristin's mouth dropped. "You just *asked* them?"

Brodie glanced at her, then quickly turned back to the road. "Why does that surprise you?"

She mulled the question a bit. "It surprises me that they would just confess without... well, without some kind of..."

"Coercion?" Brodie finished grimly. "As in beating the truth out of them?"

Kristin flushed. "Of course not. I know you wouldn't beat them."

"Do you?" Brodie's eyes were hard. "It seems like there isn't much of anything you don't think I'm capable of doing to those kids."

"That's not true!"

Brodie made a sound of disgust and squeezed the steering wheel tightly. "Oh, no? You've already accused me of jeopardizing their safety, exploiting them and you've strongly hinted that you suspect me of embezzling county funds."

Unable to look at him, Kristin stared quietly out the window.

"Are you going to deny it?" Brodie demanded.

"No, I'm not going to deny it."

Brodie sighed. "The worst part is that I can't even blame you."

That startled her. "All the facts aren't in yet," she said.

"No, they're not," he acknowledged. "But one fact is that someone punched a nasty little hole in your radiator."

"And you're certain that one of the boys is responsible?"

"One of them, all of them—it doesn't really matter at this point."

Kristin was stung by the bitterness in his voice. "What do you mean 'It doesn't matter'? Of course it matters."

"Obviously, I've made some serious errors in judgment." His voice dropped to a whisper. "You could have been hurt, or worse, by that stunt. I never would have believed any of them capable of that." His mouth twisted. "Apparently, I was wrong."

Brodie jerked the steering wheel a bit harder than necessary. The truck veered onto the dirt road leading to the house and Kristin grabbed the dashboard in an effort to steady herself. "Maybe I've been wrong about a lot of things," he muttered.

"Like the New Wave idea?"

"Yes." Brodie swung the truck in front of the house and pulled to a shuddering stop, flipping off the ignition with a vicious, angry twist.

He wasn't invincible, she realized. The great Nathan Brodie was vulnerable to his own doubts and fears. Kristin suffered many uncertainties about the ranch, the boys—even Brodie himself. There was one fact, however, of which she was certain. Many of the problems she faced were rooted in her own erratic behavior.

"Brodie, you weren't wrong." Kristin barely recognized her own choked voice. "This entire mess is as much my fault as anyone's."

Deflecting Brodie's puzzled gaze, Kristin absently stared at the activity on the knoll. Some of the neighbors had already arrived and, although the main course wouldn't be ready for several hours, festivities were gearing into full swing.

Celebration, however, was the last thing Kristin was in the mood for. She, who'd always prided herself on objectivity, had arbitrarily jumped from one conclusion to another, creating her own theories, then searching out facts to support them.

Brodie had been right, she realized sadly. Oh, she hadn't consciously formed decisions about the ranch before she'd stepped foot on it, but she'd brought some strong, preconceived notions through New Wave's gate. Those notions may have colored her interpretation of the facts, or she may have been receptive only to information that substantiated her own subconscious views.

In any case, her behavior had been presumptuous, careless and totally unprofessional.

"I haven't spent much time with the boys," she said. "I've buried myself in records and when I *did* venture out, I've lost control, screaming like some kind of deranged fishwife." Unconsciously, she began to wind a silky strand of hair around her finger, biting her lip nervously. "The boys have seen it all, heard it all." She remembered Todd's furious face at the corral.

Are you going to send us back? You'll be awful sorry if you do.

"They've come to the conclusion that I'm here to close the ranch and send them all back to the city," she said softly. "Judging from my conduct, I can't say that I blame them." Kristin forced herself to meet Brodie's eyes. They were a startling, intense blue, and for a moment, Kristin's mind went blank under the power of his scrutiny. Then she regathered her thoughts and continued. "I will, of course, remove myself from the case. Arrangements will be made to assign another investigator as soon as—"

"No." Brodie's voice was clear, firm and adamant.

Stunned by his vehement response, Kristin explained. "I don't think you understand. I'm obliged to remove myself."

"I understand that it takes a strong person to look at herself so clearly," Brodie said. "I understand that everything you've done has been to protect these kids because you care about them. I also understand that you've had to overcome your own terror just to be here for them."

"That's part of the problem," she whispered. "I haven't overcome anything. Dealing with certain, ah, personal concerns has colored my judgment. I'm having some difficulty distinguishing genuine danger from normal routine. To me, it's all terrifying." Her voice broke and she turned the small sound into a nervous laugh. Admitting not only a humiliating personal weakness, but a professional one as well, was a formidable ordeal. "My ability to be impartial in this investigation has been seriously impaired."

Brodie saw her eyes shimmering, the too bright sparkle of unshed tears. Her lower lip trembled and he felt a tightness constrict his lungs as his breathing shallowed.

Yes, she was beautiful. A lot of women were beautiful and Brodie had certainly known his share of them. Kristin was special. She was strong yet soft, courageous but vulnerable. She cared, cared about the kids society had already tossed aside—and cared enough to see the frightened boys hidden beneath the armor of unacceptable, even cruel, behavior.

After the incident with her car, Brodie had felt defeat and disillusionment. He was unable to see beyond the foolish act and its potential for deadly repercussions. But Kristin *had* looked beyond the act itself and made him look beyond it, as well.

Besides, Brodie realized with a certainty that shook him to the very core, he wanted to be near her. He didn't *want* to let her go.

"Finish the investigation. You're staying." His tone indicated that he'd tolerate no further argument.

"I don't think you understand—I'm not certain I can be completely objective—"

"Objectivity is a crock," Brodie interrupted crisply. "Everyone carries old baggage, scars from the past. Most of us just aren't smart enough to know it or brave enough to admit it."

Swallowing once, then again, Kristin knotted her fingers, pressing her hands against her thighs to stop their trembling. "You realize that I would still have to continue my, er, research of your records?"

"I know," he whispered and Kristin watched, bewildered, as an expression of incredible sadness clouded his face.

The cow had been thoroughly and deliciously painted and the heady aroma of barbecue sauce mingled with pungent mesquite smoke, engulfing the knoll in a delightful blanket of fragrance.

Kristin plunged herself into the mood of the celebration, partly to dispel her own growing despondence and partly to prove to Brodie, and anyone else who was interested, that the morning's events held no lasting effect. Indeed, Kristin had been more deeply touched by her own inner revelations and the fact that, in spite of everything, Brodie still wanted her to complete the assignment.

Scanning the festive crowd, she finally spotted Brodie leaning against a cottonwood at the far side of the knoll, alone, looking grim and unhappy.

Kristin had not convinced Brodie to drop the radiator incident entirely, but he'd agreed to postpone any confrontation until after the barbecue. That gave her a few precious hours to spend with the boys and she was doing just that, forcing herself on them when necessary.

She and Ernie won the three-legged race, collapsing at the finish line into a tangled, laughing heap. Afterwards, they talked and Kristin discovered that sixteen-year-old Ernie was painfully shy when it came to discussing himself. The fifth of eight children, Ernie had soon decided that the most elusive prize of all was attention. To attain it, Ernie believed one must excel at something: be the best looking, the strongest, the smartest. Failing that, he could merely share the glory of others. If he just stood close enough, he could bask in their glow.

Kristin discovered another interesting fact about Ernie Fenton; the boy absolutely idolized Nathan Brodie.

Todd was more difficult. The youngster idolized no one. In fact, Kristin decided that he only tolerated people out of necessity and placed his loyalties with anyone who could provide him with what he wanted. At the moment, Todd wanted to remain right where he was—at New Wave, surrounded by the animals he loved. He was still angry and, Kristin suspected, disappointed that the king snake had failed in its mission to send her fleeing the ranch in terror.

Kristin had tried to coax Todd into being her partner for the egg toss, but the boy pronounced such antics as "dumb" and headed toward the stables for the third time that afternoon to check on Martha.

Now Kristin sought Jess. She found him standing with Gus in a small circle of men. Beer firmly entrenched in one gnarled hand, Gus was gesturing comically, apparently entertaining the group with some sort of lively tale. When a loud burst of laughter signaled the end of the story, Kristin sauntered casually toward them.

An uncomfortable silence heralded her arrival, but she plastered a determined smile on her face. "Hi. Sounds like everyone here is having a good time."

Shuffling awkwardly, the men replied by mumbling in agreement. Gus merely raised a bushy gray eyebrow.

She faced Jess. "I need a partner for the egg toss," she said cheerfully.

Jess's brown eyes narrowed, but he said nothing.

"How about it?" she persisted. "It's my favorite event."

He returned her smiling expression with a cold stare. "No."

Gus turned to him with disapproval. "No, *what*, young-un?"

Jess's eyes didn't waver. His voice was dry. "No, *ma'am*."

Kristin saw Gus's chin clamp. "Then how about taking a walk with me, Jess?" she said quickly. "I'd like to talk to you."

In the moment of silence that followed, Kristin was certain Jess would refuse, but Gus spoke to the rest of the men in the group. "You boys just come on with me and I'll show you the ornery horse what done it."

As the small horde of cowboys shifted away, following the bandy-legged foreman, Kristin heard Gus saying, "It's the gospel truth, I'm tellin' you. That old mare is so dang mean..."

Gus's voice trailed off as Kristin turned toward Jess. The boy's sullen glare indicated that her work was definitely cut out for her. Jess was not a particularly tall boy, but his shoulders were well developed and he was powerfully built. The red bandanna tied around his forehead held a thick mass of straight, black hair and gave him a menacing, almost savage appearance. He was the type one did *not* want to meet in a dark alley.

Forcing a bright snap into her voice, Kristin asked, "Well, Jess, are you enjoying the barbecue?"

His lips tightened. "Yeah, until you showed up."

Kristin smiled. "Don't beat around the bush," she said dryly, "just say what you mean."

Jess had apparently misplaced his sense of humor. If he ever possessed one, that is, which Kristin seriously doubted. The only time she'd ever seen this boy smile was with Gus.

Okay, she told herself, he wants it serious, he'll get it serious. Her smile died. "You resent me, don't you?"

"Yeah."

"Why?"

"You got no business here."

"Oh?" Kristin constructed her next question carefully. "Tell me, Jess, exactly what do you think *is* the purpose of my investigation?"

He shrugged. "To close the ranch."

"No," she said slowly. "Actually, it's to keep the ranch going."

Jess's expression clearly indicated he was unimpressed by her statement. "That's not what I hear."

"I'll admit that my conduct thus far has left a lot to be desired and I apologize for that. I have several responsibilities here—to verify adherence to county regulations, to audit county funding, that sort of thing." She tilted her head. "But my most important job is to make certain that you and the other boys are well treated and not abused in any way."

"Abused?" Jess scoffed rudely. "You mean, like beat up?" He uttered a concise oath.

"There are many forms of abuse." Kristin's voice was soft but her eyes were moored on Jess's and she'd deliberately ignored his foul language. "I'm here to make sure none of you suffer any of them."

"Lady, wasn't no one suffering anything until you showed up." Jess's face darkened ominously as he lowered his voice. "Go away, lady. No one wants you here. It'd be real smart for you to go back where you came from and leave us alone."

Kristin felt a sharp chill prickle her nape. Jess's eyes were deadly cold and his mouth was twisted cruelly. She sensed a palpable, unspoken threat.

Now what? she asked herself, almost desperately. She'd read all the juvenile psych books, but nothing had prepared her for this kind of hostility.

A shuffling sound caught Kristin's attention.

"I'd say that mouth of yours has been flappin' just about enough." Gus ambled casually past Kristin, stopping when he was less than two feet in front of Jess. Only the hard set of his roughened jaw and a dangerous glint to his pale eyes gave warning of the older man's anger. "Apologize to the lady," Gus said, his voice deceptively quiet.

Jess's lips lifted in a sneer. "What lady?"

In a flash, Gus held a handful of the black jersey of the boy's T-shirt and with a single, convulsive jerk, Jess found himself hoisted to his toes.

Shocked, Jess stared down at the wiry old man whose fist was pressing into his throat. "Geez, Gus." Jess's voice was understandably choked. "You taking her side?"

"Ain't no sides here, boy. There's right and there's wrong, and you're dead wrong." Gus twisted the fistful of shirt. "Apologize to the lady."

Face reddened by embarrassment and the steady pressure against his Adam's apple, Jess finally gasped, "Sorry."

Instantly, Gus released him. "Do it right now, youngun, so she believes you."

Kristin was stunned to see the normally arrogant adolescent contritely stare at the ground, shifting nervously from one foot to the other. "I apologize for my behavior, Ms. Price," he whispered. "I shouldn't have been rude to you."

When the boy slanted a glance at Gus, the old man nodded sagely and Kristin was shocked to see the gleam of unshed tears in Jess's eyes as he slumped away in dejection.

Kristin licked her lips. "Ah . . . thank you, Gus," she began, but the weathered cowpoke stopped her by raising a crooked hand.

"No need, missy," he told her quietly. "Never could tolerate disrespect to a lady."

Kristin felt a piercing pang of sorrow. She knew that Jess was Gus's favorite and he obviously doted on the boy. Yet Gus had come to Kristin's defense and disciplined Jess firmly. Kristin realized the entire episode had hurt Gus as much as it had hurt Jess.

"You didn't have to step in," Kristin said. "You could have figured it was my own darn fault and let me handle the problem myself."

"Could have," Gus acknowledged. "But you got a job to do and ain't none of us makin' it any easier." He paused, emitting a brown stream of tobacco juice. Gus squinted toward the meadow where an exuberant throng was cheering the finalists in the egg tossing competition. Then he looked across the knoll where the broad-shouldered youth sat alone on the grass, hugging his knees to his chest.

Gus's eyes softened briefly before squaring his thin shoulders. "Right is right," he mumbled, then tipped his hat to Kristin and disappeared into the crowd.

The late afternoon sun had lowered, a giant orange ball perched on the hills, allowing itself a final glimpse before turning the valley over to the shadows of night.

Laughter and banal chatter hummed over the knoll and Oaf passionately sliced the last bit of charred beef. Guests were still enjoying the succulent meal and those who'd been first in line were now on a return trip for seconds.

Seeking solitude after her confrontation with Jess, Kristin sat at a table away from the bustle, observing without participating, indulging her quiet mood.

Brodie's voice startled her. "Oaf will be upset if you don't sample his masterpiece." He held two plates piled high with steaming slices of rare meat, creamy potato salad and hot, fresh biscuits. Brodie set one plate on the table in front of Kristin. "Beer or soft drink?" he asked.

"Pardon me? Oh, a soft drink would be fine."

Angling through the crowd, Brodie plucked two colorful cans of cola from a bed of ice cubes, then returned, swinging his leg over the bench and seating himself beside her. Popping both can tabs, he handed one to Kristin and took a huge swallow from the other.

"You could have had a beer if you preferred it," Kristin told him. "It seems that most of your men do." Nearly every cowboy on the knoll had a fist wrapped around a beer can, almost as though it were an extended appendage.

Skimming a glance at his men, Brodie acknowledged, "They seem to." He set the can on the table. "Alcohol just doesn't agree with me." For a moment his face was shadowed by a guarded, distant expression. It had been just a flash, like an unpleasant thought and Kristin felt she might have imagined it when he quickly smiled, nudging her plate. "Oaf will sulk," he reminded her.

Kristin eyed the huge portions on her plate without enthusiasm but managed a genuine smile as she thanked Brodie for his thoughtful gesture.

"You don't seem to be enjoying yourself," he commented before sampling a large forkful of potato salad.

Kristin shrugged. "I guess I'm just not a party animal."

She nibbled at a biscuit and they ate in silence for a few minutes. Dark shadows rested beneath her eyes. She looked tired and tense, still not sleeping well, Brodie noted.

"This hasn't been a particularly good day for you," Brodie said. "As a matter of fact, this whole week has been pretty tough. I'm sorry."

"I'll survive, I always do." She glanced toward him. "I have the distinct impression that you'd just as soon write off the past six days as well."

Brodie grinned and Kristin caught a glimpse of the boyish charm that had captivated her that first day on the ranch. "It's had some advantages," he said.

"Name one."

His eyes softened. "I met you."

Under the intensity of his gaze, with the soft, sweet intimacy of his husky voice still ringing in her ears, Kristin felt herself flush.

Her voice was a tad shaky and it irritated her, but she forced a light, joking tone. "Somehow, I'm surprised you find our meeting advantageous in any way at all."

Brodie ignored the teasing inflection. His expression was solemn, as was his voice. "No, you're not surprised," he whispered.

His eyes darkened and Kristin found her own gaze riveted to his mouth. Strange, she hadn't noticed before how full his lips were, how sensuous. She dragged her eyes away, fixing a stare on an anonymous branch stretching from the trunk of a distant tree.

She feels it, too, Brodie realized, *the electricity that seems to crack the air between them.*

He wanted to touch her, to reach out and stroke her soft cheek, to rest his fingertips against the pulsing hollow of her throat. God, how he wanted to, but he didn't have the courage. Brodie sensed that if he reached out at that moment, she would skitter away. He had to back off, go slowly.

Forcing himself to redirect his attention, Brodie began to mechanically attack his cooling meal. He tasted nothing, but felt Kristin relax beside him. When she picked up her fork and began to poke at her plate, Brodie made another attempt at conversation.

"How long have you been with the county?" he asked casually.

Kristin speared a potato chunk. "Since college, about five years."

"Have you been an investigator all that time?"

"No," she said. "I started at the bottom, like everyone else, but I sure learned how to file during the first couple of years."

The sun was now submerged behind the foothills, flinging its last vestige of color across sky and clouds in a glorious farewell. They watched the spectacle in silence.

Lifting her left hand, Brodie stroked her bare fingers. "No husband?"

Kristin glanced at him in surprise. Quickly, she looked away, contemplating whether or not she should allow their conversation to progress into such a personal area, then deciding that sharing some of her own past might encourage Brodie to do the same. There was, after all, a great deal of Nathan Brodie's past yet to discover.

"I was divorced about four years ago." Kristin's eyes clouded. She really didn't want to discuss the subject and shifted the conversation. "What about you, Brodie? Have you ever been married?"

Smiling, Brodie shook his head. He still stroked the captive hand and Kristin made no move to withdraw it. "The women in my life came second to my work," Brodie said quietly. "And they knew it. Eventually, they all got tired of being stood up every time one of my kids had a crisis."

"Never even came close?" She made a disbelieving sound. Men like Brodie didn't come along every day. So what if his work came first. So did hers.

"Yes, I guess I did get pretty close to the big step once, in my rebellious youth." He could think about it now, but the experience had taken a fierce emotional toll at the time. "She was tall and lithe, supple as a stream willow, with these huge brown eyes. She was also a Sioux princess." His voice flattened on the last phrase.

Kristin felt an irrational pang. "It sounds as though you were truly smitten. What happened?"

"I came back to L.A. She stayed to teach on the reservation." He offered a nonchalant shrug, but his eyes couldn't quite veil the pain evoked by the memory. "We both felt a devout calling, so to speak. She made her choice, I made mine."

"You sound as though you haven't forgiven her for staying."

He laughed dryly. "You're probably right. I was angry. I figured that if she really loved me, she'd have come with me."

Kristin absorbed that. "Perhaps she felt that if you really loved her, you wouldn't have left."

Brodie seemed strangely disconcerted by the notion, as though it had actually never occurred to him. Kristin was overcome by a sudden, intense need to erase the sadness from his eyes. She didn't want him to think about anything painful, particularly a supple, brown-eyed princess. Forcing her tone into a light, conversational banter, she asked, "Did you grow up on a ranch like this, Brodie?"

"Yes and no." He easily flattened the empty cola can. "Actually, I grew up in Boyle Heights, East L.A. My mother worked days in a hospital laundry and nights cleaning offices in one of the downtown high rises."

"Sounds rough. Where was your father?"

"In the living room, usually. Drunk."

"I'm sorry," she said, really meaning it. "I had an alcoholic foster father for a while. I remember the social worker coming for a routine check—there were four foster children living there at the time—and he staggered out of the bedroom in his underwear, clutching a beer can. He belched twice, then passed out flat on the floor."

"Sounds like a real champ." Brodie dropped the squashed can on the table. "At least he did it in front of someone who could get you out of there."

"Actually, the social worker stepped over him and muttered something about coming back when everyone was feeling better." She shrugged and sipped at her tepid drink. "I was there six more months."

That made Brodie angry. Unreasonably so, perhaps, since it had happened so many years ago. Yet, he could picture the small, frightened little girl she must have been and wished fervently to run into this foul excuse for a man someday. Preferably, in a dark, quiet alley. "It makes me sick to think of you living like that," he said. "What happened to your parents?"

"They were killed in an automobile accident when I was seven."

"I'm sorry," he said, and Kristin had never heard those two words expressed with more feeling or sincerity. "It must have been rough on you."

"It's rough on a lot of kids. Orphans who are alone, confused, frightened, tossed like so many vegetables into a big government stewpot where they're stirred and dished up for the first paying customer."

"And you want to change all that?"

She nodded stubbornly. "If I can."

Brodie cast a thoughtful gaze across the murky line of shadowed hills. "Were all of your foster homes like that?"

"No. There was one." She tenderly fingered the pearl at her throat.

"Tell me about it," Brodie urged, fascinated by her rapt expression.

"Mama Lu was a wonderful, warm-hearted woman with so much love to give. She made each of us feel so... so special. I loved her so much. We all loved her, but to me, well, she became the mother I could barely remember."

Reaching out, Brodie touched her throat, sliding his finger down the gold chain. Kristin realized she was rubbing the gleaming pearl and recognized the unspoken question in Brodie's gesture. "Yes, it was from Mama Lu," she acknowledged. "A gift for my fifteenth birthday. It has sentimental value, I guess, because it was the first birthday present I'd received since my parents died and because it was Mama Lu who gave it to me."

"You miss her."

"Oh, yes. Too much."

"Where is she now?"

She'd known he would ask, but that knowledge didn't stop the lump from forming in the base of her throat. "She died a few months after my birthday. I found out later that she'd been ill for months, but she never told us."

"It still hurts," Brodie said softly. "Grief stays with us always. It just moves over a bit so we can deal with the rest of life."

The man never ceased to surprise her. "That's beautiful. You must have had a great deal of sadness in your own life to describe it with such understanding. But then, I guess everyone has to experience grief at some time."

"Only those who are capable of love, because we can only truly grieve for the loss of that love. It's frightening, that power. Sometimes people withhold love because they're terrified of losing it, so afraid of the pain that will follow." Brodie saw he'd hit a nerve. He'd known he would. "The brave ones give love, anyway."

She stiffened. "And cowards avoid it?"

He smiled, understanding. "Not cowards. They're more like walking wounded who have reached the threshold of their pain tolerance. They are . . . healing."

Something in his voice squeezed at her heart. "Are you healing, Brodie?"

"Yes, I suppose I am. Perhaps that's what New Wave is really about."

Silently, she waited, knowing he wanted to share more, hoping he was ready to do so.

Brodie cast a thoughtful gaze across the murky line of shadowed hills. The air seemed suddenly muggy, smelling of ozone and exhaust fumes, as it had two years ago. Pulsing flashes of red and blue, the crumpled form sprawled across the sidewalk, a soul-wrenching cry of despair that shattered the night and twisted his guts.

"There was a boy," Brodie said quietly. "His name was Martin Alvarez, a bright, happy kid who wanted to escape the barrio, to make something of himself."

"You were his probation officer?"

"Yes, he was one of my boys. I'd been working with him for over a year." Brodie stared across the blackened valley at the moon rising between silhouetted pines. "Martin had dropped out of *Los Diablos*—that was the neighborhood gang—and he was determined to do something worthwhile with his life."

For several minutes, Brodie stared silently into the night. The red embers of the barbecue pit had cooled to smoldering ash. "What happened to Martin, Brodie?"

"*Los Diablos* didn't take kindly to his defection. They stuck a gun in his hand, a gun in his back and forced him to hold up a liquor store." Green neon. Clancy's Liquor. Blood on the sidewalk. "The police killed Martin."

"But if he was forced to participate . . ."

"The cops didn't know that. All they saw was Martin holding a gun." The somber voice of Lt. Donald Dexter flashed through Brodie's mind. *Damn shame,* Dexter had said. *He was a good kid. Damn shame.*

Then, in the dark recesses of his memory, Brodie saw the scene that still haunted him. He spoke without realizing, describing the horror that flickered like a filmstrip through his brain.

A piercing scream had shattered that night.

The portly woman had pushed through the crowd to stand with her arms flung toward the lifeless body of her son. She'd dropped to her knees, gathering the bleeding boy to her breast, rocking him with the rhythm of her anguished wails.

Maria Alvarez had looked at Brodie, her eyes shimmering with bewildered agony, her handsome face contorted by grief.

"Madre de Dios," she had cried, as she had when her oldest son had lain dying from poison he'd injected into his own scarred veins.

"Why?" she had begged, as she had when her second son was shot to death on his own front porch, victim of a rival gang's vendetta.

And Brodie saw her still, holding the body of her youngest and final child, swept away by the bloody, raging current of the barrios.

How could the woman cope with such grief, such unbearable loss? Helpless, he had watched, wanting desperately to offer comfort, yet knowing he was powerless to relieve her suffering.

"I resigned, kissed the probation department goodbye and waved a not-so-fond farewell to L.A.'s ghetto." Brodie's voice was a dull monotone. The raw emotions of that horrible night had poured out of him like a cleansing salve. "New Wave was born that night. The ranch took its first breath of life as Martin Alvarez took his last."

A single tear slipped across her cheek. Brodie wiped it away with his fingertip, touched that she would be so moved by the tragedy of a boy she'd never known.

Kristin's eyes were luminous, shimmering silver like the reflection of a full moon on a mountain lake. Brodie traced the contour of her jaw, the rough pads of his fingertips whispering across her skin, delighting in the silky feel of her. His fingers lingered briefly on the thin, white line at her brow, then followed it to her temple.

Kristin sucked in her breath as Brodie gently traced the ragged line. He was going to ask how it happened and she couldn't even think about it, let alone speak of it. Her eyes widened and she tried to turn her head.

Brodie recognized her gesture of avoidance and cupped her chin with his thumb and forefinger, turning her face toward him. He slid his free hand to the small of her back.

"You're beautiful," he murmured. "Beautiful outside, beautiful inside."

Kristin's heart was hammering a frantic rhythm against her ribs. He was going to kiss her and she desperately wanted him to.

This was madness. She couldn't get involved with this man. She had to be objective, she had to be professional.

But regardless of her mental distress, Kristin found her hands splayed on his hard chest, moving against its rippling strength, fingers testing the springy texture of hair hidden beneath his thin cotton shirt.

Brodie lowered his head as he pulled her closer, their lips inches apart when he hesitated, hovering uncertainly until, with a whimper of urgency, Kristin slipped her hands around his neck and drew him to her.

Lips met, molded, withdrew, then met again.

It was a caressing kiss, gentle and healing, yet profound, almost reverent. In his softness, she tasted strength. Like Irish coffee—sweet, rich cream concealing a hot, potent liquor. Intoxicating, dangerous and exquisitely delicious.

Warmth enveloped her, an earthy, musky heat rising from deep inside, radiating outward until her skin glowed with its energy. His lips brushed her throat, slowly, unhurried as they tasted and savored. So delicate, like the touch of a whisper, the caress of a lullaby.

She felt safe, protected, cherished.

No groping hands and lusting bodies. That, she could have fended off, deflected. But she had no defense against tenderness, no protection from the surge of emotion choking off rational thought.

The hollowness deep inside was filling, the void she'd carried next to her heart was pulsing with fulfillment, yet crying with need. She wanted to take, but ached to give, was overwhelmed by a sense of deep contentment, yet throbbed with unmet desire.

Brodie swallowed her soft moan as his tongue slipped into the soft recess of her mouth, exploring her sweetness gently at first, then thrusting with command, deeper and stronger until they clung together as though famished for the taste, for the feel of each other.

Kristin felt feverish, as though her skin would burst into flame, then suddenly shivering as icy chills racked her body. A molten knot in her abdomen suddenly exploded, pouring liquid flame into her loins.

She wanted him.

She wanted him with such desperation, she would never have believed it possible. Yet, here she was, clawing at his back, hauling herself onto him as though she could actually merge into his body, as though they could share the same skin.

And tomorrow you may discover he's a fraud.

Kristin's head was spinning, but she heard the tiny voice in her mind and listened. Tomorrow she would continue her investigation and soon she'd have the answers she sought, answers Nathan Brodie had done everything in his power to keep from her.

Brodie felt her stiffen in his arms and groaned in protest. He couldn't turn her loose. His mind was on fire, his blood was in flames. If she pulled away, she would take something vital from the pit of his soul, and he'd simply explode.

But Kristin did pull away, trembling and confused. With every ounce of control he could muster, Brodie forced his knotted fingers to release their steel grip.

"Kris," he rasped. "Kris, I—"

"No." She touched his lips with her fingers to silence him. "No," she repeated in what sounded like a moan.

Then she stood with quiet dignity and disappeared into the darkness.

In the safety of her room, Kristin swung the door shut, leaning against it until her heart slowed and her breath no longer caught in her throat.

What had happened to her?

She knew better than this. It was the most dastardly of deeds, becoming romantically involved with the subject of an investigation.

It was particularly foolish when said subject seemed to have a dozen little secrets dangling around like loose threads. Kristin knew those threads would have to be either mercilessly slashed or woven back into the fabric, and she simply couldn't allow herself to be diverted by the primal instincts of her own renegade body.

Calming herself with some effort, Kristin finally managed to change into her nightgown and began brushing her hair with an almost cruel vengeance. Something strange, out of place, caught her eye in the dresser mirror and she turned.

A piece of crisp, white paper had been fed into her typewriter, paper she knew hadn't been there a few hours earlier. Walking to the desk, she saw a message on the sheet. It sent a freezing shudder down her spine and raised the hairs on her neck.

GET OUT WHILE YOU CAN.

Chapter Seven

Kristin awakened with a start. She listened for a moment, then swung her legs across the mattress and sat on the edge of the bed.

Muffled voices filtered through the thin wall that separated her room from Brodie's. The sounds moved to the hall and Kristin recognized Todd's high-pitched squeak. The boy seemed agitated and Brodie answered in deep, soothing tones.

She slipped on her robe when a hurried thud of boots vibrated wooden floors, echoing down the hallway toward the stairs. By the time Kristin reached the front door, the house was dark and silent.

Stepping out onto the front porch, she saw that the stables were lit and recognized the silhouetted forms moving past the open door of the long, rectangular building. Todd emerged from the stable and ran toward her as if the devil himself were on his heels. He hit the porch at a full gallop, whizzing past Kristin as though she didn't exist.

He was hollering, "Oaf! Call Dr. Amatti. Brodie says we need him *now!*"

Message delivered, Todd whirled and sped back toward the stable. Kristin managed to snag his arm, slowing, but not stopping, the determined youngster. She hung on, half running to keep up.

"What is it, Todd? Martha?"

Todd looked positively stricken. "She's sick," he cried. "Brodie says something's wrong with the foal."

"Oh, no." Kristin knew Todd would be absolutely devastated if anything happened to either Martha or her foal. "What can I do to help?"

Tears streaked Todd's face. "When the vet comes, tell him to come to the stable," he sobbed, then tore his arm from Kristin's grasp and dashed away.

Within moments, Oaf ducked through the front door and lurched from the porch with a single massive step. When he reached Kristin, he stopped, wringing his hands, shiny scalp reflecting moonlight, big face furrowed with concern.

"You go on, Oaf," Kristin told him. "They need you. I'll wait for the doctor."

Satisfied, Oaf grunted toward the stable.

Kristin paced, oblivious to her casual attire as the nylon nightgown's hem dusted the ground, swinging freely beneath the folds of her short robe. Absently, she wrapped the terry cloth more securely, although she hadn't consciously noticed the night's damp chill. Her eyes kept darting toward the open stable door, catching glimpses of movement. Instinct told her that the situation must be serious. Brodie wasn't the type to panic.

It seemed an eternity, but had only been thirty minutes or so when Dr. Amatti's ancient Jeep finally jerked into the driveway. Kristin rushed to meet him.

"One of the mares having problems?" he asked, heaving his stout frame from the confines of the vehicle.

"It's Martha," Kristin blurted, as though to personalize the situation. "This way."

She led the veterinarian toward the stable area, seemingly unaware that each step brought her closer to the New Wave's entire congregation of horseflesh.

"Is this her first foal?" Dr. Amatti asked.

"Er, I don't really know."

"How long has she been in labor?"

"I . . . uh . . ."

They had reached the stable and Kristin saw the gathering of men standing just beyond the door.

"Never mind," the vet said, pushing past her and heading directly toward Brodie.

Kristin hesitated, then took a few more steps to stand in the open doorway, her heart hammering loudly as she forced herself to look inside. The scent of animals mingled with hay and human sweat. Compared to the crisp night air, the stable was humid and uncomfortably warm.

The foaling stall was nearly as large as Kristin's bedroom and was enclosed by a four-foot, open rail fence, through which she could observe the activity. Gus, Oaf and Brodie were all inside the stall and Dr. Amatti joined them. Todd stood outside the fence and Kristin assumed he'd been instructed to do so. The look on Todd's young face convinced her that nothing less than a direct order from Brodie would have kept him from Martha at that moment.

Kristin could hear the nervous snorts and pawing of the other horses housed in the stable. From her vantage point, she could see that beyond the foaling pen, smaller stalls lined both sides of the building. A large black head stretched from one of them, peering from the far end of the stable, as though engrossed with the activity. Kristin idly wondered if the handsome stallion could be the father of Martha's foal.

That's ridiculous, she told herself. Animals have no sense of parenthood. To them, the entire process is merely a normal biological function. Still, the animal had seemed, well, concerned.

As one of the men shifted position, Kristin saw a dappled gray rump. She moved to the other side of the doorway for a better look. The mare was lying on her side, snuffling loudly, huge brown eyes wide and wild. Her barrel was distended, bloated grotesquely by the unborn foal. Suddenly, the mare issued an almost human screech and began kicking furiously before her legs stiffened, quivering.

Kristin's blood froze. Brodie and Gus were both kneeling beside the animal, dodging the deadly, flailing hooves.

The mare's frenzied cries ceased as suddenly as they'd begun and to Kristin's shock, the animal swiveled its head and seemed to stare directly toward the open door. Kristin looked into large liquid eyes and felt an eerie sense that the mare was communicating, sharing her pain with an understanding female.

Then Martha's head dropped to the straw and she nickered softly.

Dr. Amatti was examining the animal. "Breech," he pronounced ominously, then began applying generous portions of a jellylike substance to the entrance of the birth canal. At the same moment, Martha emitted a low, echoing moan.

Todd jerked to life. "What are you doing to Martha?" he squeaked, leaping to the fence and hanging there like a cat on a screen door. "Leave her alone!"

"Just helping her out," the doctor replied. "This is a sterile lubricant to make the foal's trip a bit easier."

Although the portly veterinarian's voice was calm, Kristin noted tense lines of concern creasing his forehead. Even she knew that "breech" meant the foal was presenting itself feet first, rather than head first. A breech birth in humans was usually more difficult, but somehow she had never really considered that animals could have the same problems, suffer the same pain.

Martha's agitated whinny echoed louder, her legs stiffened rigidly and Kristin saw Todd's face contort as he watched, helpless.

Somehow, Kristin found herself inside the stable, standing next to the stall fence with her arms around the terrified boy.

"It'll be fine," she soothed, "just fine."

Whirling, Todd buried his face in her shoulder and sobbed, allowing Kristin to comfort him as his own mother never had. She stroked Todd's prickly thatch of hair, brushing tears from the freckled cheeks and murmuring encouragement.

The labor process seemed to go on forever and Kristin marveled at the courage of the mare, wondering if she herself would be as brave under similar circumstances. Todd's arms tightened around Kristin's waist with each of Martha's contractions, as though he were feeling every pain in his own small body.

Finally, the vet told Brodie, "It's coming, but we're going to have to help her. She's nearly worn out."

What happened next shocked Kristin to her very core. With Gus still at Martha's shoulders continuing to stroke her head and offer comfort, Brodie positioned himself next to Dr. Amatti. The vet had reached inside the mare, carefully cupping the foal's hoof as he withdrew one spindly leg, then repeating the process for the other leg.

"What's wrong with its hooves?" Todd was staring with obvious revulsion. "They're deformed."

"That's just nature's way of protecting the mare," Dr. Amatti answered, somewhat distracted. "The rubbery covering on the hooves peels off as soon as the foal's up and about." As he spoke, the vet continued manipulating the foal, moving it slowly back and forth with a seesawing motion.

Martha emitted a weak, bubbling sound and Amatti's brows crashed together. "That's it, then," he muttered grimly, then quickly tied a length of rope to the tiny wet legs. He and Brodie both pulled on the rope with all their strength.

Kristin had never been more horrified in her life.

Finally, it was over. Looking tired and worn, Dr. Amatti stood and muttered a curse before meeting Brodie's bleak stare.

"I'm sorry, Nathan," he said. "It had just been in the birth canal too long."

Brodie massaged the back of his neck. "I know, George. There was nothing else to be done."

Martha lifted her head, wobbling with the strain of effort, and nuzzled the tiny limp body. She butted weakly at the foal with her head, then looked straight at Kristin with an agonized expression of almost human grief before falling back, exhausted into the straw.

Todd emitted a wrenching shriek, then screamed, "No! No! No!" He jerked away from Kristin and ran sobbing into the soft gray dawn.

"Todd!" Kristin took a step, as though to follow the boy, then stopped, meeting Brodie's weary eyes. They shared a look that communicated the full measure of their own sorrow over the tragedy and mutual understanding of Todd's enormous anguish, his need to be alone for a while.

Gus sat rigid, holding the mare, his expression grim. Oaf's big head hung and he looked as though he might break into tears at any moment.

Rustling through his leather case, Dr. Amatti extracted a huge hypodermic needle and several flasks. He filled the syringe, injecting the contents into Martha's flank, then reaching for another vial.

"I've given her a tranquilizer and something that will help the uterus contract." He sucked the contents of the second flask into the syringe. "This is Banimine, for the pain. Since the medication affects a nursing mare's milk, I usually don't prescribe it, but under the circumstances . . ." His voice trailed off as he looked at the weary animal.

Finally, he'd done all he could. George Amatti snapped his bag shut, then clasped a warm hand on Brodie's shoulder, offering a consoling smile. "The mare will be fine," he said. "Bleeding's under control and there's no sign of shock. She'll be on her feet in a few hours."

"Appreciate your help, George," Brodie told him.

"Anytime, Nathan. Just wish it'd turned out different." The men walked from the stable. "Nearly morning," George said, to no one in particular. "Don't look forward to this day, I can tell you. My assistant's been on vacation for a week and some kind of pneumonia has been rampaging through Farley Greene's sheep." The vet scratched his sparsely-covered scalp. "Sure hope I can figure out what's ailing them before it wipes out the entire flock."

Dr. Amatti stepped into his Jeep, extending his arm for a handshake with Brodie, surprised to find his hand being firmly grasped instead by all ten of Kristin's slender fingers.

"Doctor," she said. "Could I have just a few more minutes of your time?"

Kristin found Todd an hour later, slouched behind the hay barn, flinging pebbles into the dust. His face was composed, his expression bland, the extent of his pain betrayed only by the reddened eyes over which he had no control.

As he sensed Kristin's presence, his pudgy shoulders stiffened and he ducked his head slightly, as though scrutinizing the small patch of earth between his outstretched legs. His face was shadowed by the white, snakeskin-garnished hat he always wore, but misery and grief saturated the air.

Quietly, she dropped beside him, leaning against the rough wooden planks of the barn wall. She picked up a pebble, skimming it across the dust, as he had done earlier. Todd palmed a small rock, weighing it momentarily, then flicking it expertly, making it dance across the ground in a series of choreographed hops.

"Very nice," Kristin said. "Can you show me how to do that?"

"It's dumb," Todd replied, then proceeded to shred a twig into pulp.

"I don't think it's dumb at all." To make her point, Kristin flipped another pebble. It rolled sickly and she sighed. "I wish I could do it as well as you, but each of us has different talents, I guess."

The look Todd gave her clearly indicated that he didn't consider pebble-flicking to be particularly high on the list of admirable traits with which a person could be blessed.

Kristin, however, was leading toward a more important point. "Take animals, for instance. You seem to have a real talent for working with them." She watched Todd carefully as she spoke. His round face remained impassive and Kristin continued. "I don't relate to animals very well. In fact, I'm...well, I'm rather afraid of them." She hoped that, by sharing personal feelings, Todd would be encouraged to recognize and discuss some of his own painful emotions.

Todd dropped the last of the mangled twig into the dirt. "That's dumb," he finally announced.

"Yes, it probably is," Kristin agreed. "But why do you think so? I mean, take horses, for example. They're big and heavy, they kick and—"

Todd was indignant. "Horses are neat. They only kick people who are mean to them." He glared at Kristin. "If someone was trying to hurt you, wouldn't you try to hurt them back?"

"I guess it would depend on how that person was trying to hurt me."

"Like, what if someone was going to hit you? Maybe with a belt, or something?" Todd was looking at the ground again, his voice becoming softer, more childlike. "Wouldn't you kick to stop him from hurting you? If you were a horse, that is."

"I don't know, Todd. How would you try to stop him from hurting you?" Kristin knew Todd was discussing himself. No matter how abstract, the boy was finally sharing invaluable snatches of his inner fears, his past terrors.

The boy shifted uncomfortably, then shrugged. "If I was a little kid, I guess I'd just cry and run away."

From his alcoholic father, Kristin imagined. Her file records indicated a history of abuse, Todd finally being removed from his father's care after a particularly brutal attack. Apparently, the boy had eventually defended himself by threatening his father with a knife. Instead of treating Todd as a victim, the courts had, in their infinite wisdom, decided the boy was a threat to society, prone to violent outbursts. Of course, being beaten with everything from fists to clubs would tend to make one a bit testy.

The files also indicated that Todd would never discuss the incident with any of his counselors, stating only that his father was "dumb," the incident was "dumb," and the counselors were "dumb."

Kristin hardly dared hope the boy would open up now, but she delicately prodded anyway. "That would be difficult for a little boy. After he grows up, how would he protect himself from . . . people who wanted to hurt him?"

His mouth set grimly. "He'd hurt them back." Todd squinted at the sun, just visible above the jagged horizon. "Got to go to school," he pronounced without enthusiasm, then stood rigidly, his actions proclaiming their discussion over.

Kristin didn't press the issue. There would be other opportunities, she hoped, to further promote such discussions. Now, however, she had a specific reason for having sought him out. She'd forgotten that spring break was over and the boys would be going back to school, so there was no time left for just casual conversation.

Scrambling to her feet, she walked beside Todd toward the main house.

"Todd, I've a favor to ask."

He didn't reply, but slid her a sly, curious glance.

"Dr. Amatti needs some help at the clinic and he'd like to hire you."

The boy's eyes rounded, then quickly narrowed. "He killed Martha's foal."

They stopped walking and Kristin contemplated Todd's response. She saw the slight tremor of his lip and noted his eyes were reddening again. "I know how hurt you are," Kristin said quietly. "Do you really believe Dr. Amatti is responsible?"

He met her direct gaze, and for a moment Kristin feared that, in his grief, he would simply have to blame someone for the mare's tragedy. But the small chin finally wobbled.

"Guess not," he whispered.

"I think the doctor tried very, very hard to help Martha. A veterinarian helps so many animals, it must hurt a lot that he can't help them all."

Todd managed a mumbled "yeah" and Kristin was suddenly hopeful her plan would work.

"Think of what you could learn by working with him." Her voice echoed persuasion, encouragement and the merest touch of desperation. She was certain Todd needed this diversion, and working with many different animals just might bring him out of his shell. "It would only be on weekends, to start, and you'd have to keep up with your schoolwork. Brodie says it's okay. In fact, he told Dr. Amatti that you'd be the best helper he would ever have.''

Todd's face twisted with uncertainty and Kristin brought out her big guns, firing the final round. "Dr. Amatti would be paying you, of course. He says he just doesn't know how he's going to manage that new litter of puppies if he doesn't get some help soon.''

Todd's eyes rounded. "Puppies?''

Kristin nodded.

"Well, I guess I could do it. I mean, like, if he really needs me and everything.''

"Oh, he does.''

"Okay.'' The boy was brightening fast. "When can I start?''

"Brodie will take you over to the clinic tonight and the doctor will answer all your questions,'' she replied, delighted by the turn of events. "Meanwhile, school comes first.''

Looking like he'd just sucked a lemon, Todd made a noise to indicate his opinion of Kristin's last statement, but he was all smiles as he bounded toward the bunkhouse.

Suddenly, Kristin was as tired as she was relieved that Todd had accepted the idea of working at the animal clinic. Her mind couldn't seem to erase the sight of Martha poignantly nudging her stillborn foal. It had touched her deeply.

"You handled that well.''

The deep male voice startled Kristin and she jumped, shifting quickly to see Brodie leaning casually against the porch railing, booted feet crossed at the ankles, thumbs hooked carelessly into the back pockets of his jeans.

Brodie had been watching, listening from a discreet distance. Not really eavesdropping, he told himself, but Gus had mentioned Kristin's problem with Jess and considering the harassment she'd suffered already, well, Brodie simply didn't want to take any chances.

But she'd been wonderful. Brodie had been stunned to see Kristin in the stable overcoming her own fear in order to comfort Todd. You just naturally had to admire that kind of gumption. She'd gotten Todd to open up in a way Brodie never could and her idea of having the boy work with George at the clinic might be a stroke of pure genius. Brodie was a bit cha-grined not to have thought of it himself, but he certainly wasn't going to let Kristin know that.

She had a way about her, a way of wriggling into a man's heart before he even realized she'd thrown her hook out. She made him feel strange, kind of exposed.

Last night at the barbecue, he'd been completely lost in the smoky depth of those eyes and told her things about himself that he'd never shared with anyone else.

Watching her now, Brodie thought she seemed so small and fragile, yet her chin stuck out in that funny, determined way. He remembered the feel of her mouth under his, her sensual little gasps of surprise and pleasure, and his heart leaped. The lady got to him.

He forced a smile. "I wasn't at all sure Todd would go along with this crazy scheme of yours," Brodie said. "Obviously, your powers of persuasion extend to males of all ages. First you manage to sweet-talk George and now you have Todd eating out of your hand."

"It's not a crazy scheme, it's perfectly logical. And unfortunately, my batting average with 'males of all ages' is considerably less than major league."

Brodie stood beside her now, so close she could see each whisker of morning stubble shadowing his jaw, and tiny fatigue lines creased beneath his eyes. It had been a long night.

"You're major league, all right," Brodie said, his voice soft. "It seems to me you're conquering us all, one by one."

His nearness and the quiet admiration in his voice thrilled her, and Kristin remembered the feel of his warm breath on her cheek as Brodie's soft lips and rough hands had awakened every erotic nerve in her body. Her own response had shocked, per-haps even frightened her. Instead of handling the situation with quiet aplomb, she had become flustered, flittering away like a reluctant virgin. But if she hadn't . . .

She turned away, ashamed and embarrassed. Kristin hadn't meant to fall into his arms and it certainly would never happen again. It was simply an isolated incident, induced by too much moonlight and Oaf's secret barbecue sauce.

Right now, all she wanted to do was to break the tension of this moment and direct the conversation back to the boys. But it wasn't easy with Brodie standing so close she could taste him.

She forced a nervous laugh, shifting aside to allow a safety net of air between them. "I don't think I've exactly conquered Jess."

"I heard about that. Jess was out of line and he knows it. He'll come around."

"Umm, maybe." Maybe Jess would come around, thought Kristin, or maybe he was busy thinking up more ideas to get her off the ranch and out of his hair. Briefly, she considered telling Brodie about the note she'd found in her typewriter, then discarded the option. The radiator episode had yet to be satisfactorily resolved and Brodie was already dangerously disillusioned by the harassment.

Instantly, Kristin realized she was jumping—no leaping—to conclusions again. She'd decided that Jess had been responsible for the note simply because of his hostility toward her, and she'd concluded that Brodie'd had nothing to do with it simply because she didn't want to believe that he had.

The startling revelation stiffened her resolve as well as her shoulders. She turned to Brodie.

"This is Monday. I believe we have an appointment."

For the third time in the past thirty minutes, Kristin rearranged her handwritten notes and tried to mentally rehearse the questions she would ask. She leaned back in Brodie's rickety office chair, wincing as the springs emitted a grating squeal. Glancing at the wall clock, as she had every five minutes, Kristin realized Brodie would appear at any moment. When she'd reminded him of their appointment, he'd asked for a couple of hours to take care of something, promising to meet her in the ranch office by 10:00 a.m.

It was now five minutes past the appointed hour and Kristin fidgeted nervously. This was it. This was the day she would finally get some answers. Suddenly, she realized she was no longer anxious to get them. She was frightened.

Since the office was situated off the entry hall of the main house, Kristin could easily hear the front door opening, followed by muffled male voices. Then Brodie loomed in the office doorway and the room seemed to shrink with his presence. Tense, obviously wary, he tossed his hat on a dented file cabinet and hesitated before taking the armless, wooden chair across from the desk.

"Please, sit here." Kristin stood instantly, motioning to the battered swivel chair. "I didn't really mean to commandeer your desk."

"No problem," Brodie replied, motioning for her to sit down. He appeared enormously unhappy and Kristin swallowed a pang of guilt by reminding herself that he'd insisted she finish the investigation knowing that this would be part of it. But he looked so tired, so defeated, yet so incredibly handsome....

Kristin yanked her mind back to the business at hand. Seating herself, she shuffled through the clutter of papers strewn in front of her. "Let's see now...ah, here they are." She studied her notes briefly, then cleared her throat. "As I mentioned earlier, I have some questions..."

She hesitated, not certain where to start. Brodie slumped impatiently, plucking a stray paper clip from the desktop and twisting it into a mangled wire knot. Kristin decided to broach the subject with finesse and diplomacy. She took a deep breath, smiled sweetly and blurted, "Why have the county support checks been deposited in a separate account?" Ouch. So much for finesse.

Brodie shifted. "What difference does it make?"

Kristin blinked. "I beg your pardon?"

Standing so quickly the wooden chair rocked, Brodie began to pace the small room. "Is it illegal to have more than one account?"

"Why, no..."

"Then what's the big deal?"

Kristin ducked her head, pretending to stare intently at her notes. Something definitely was amiss here and Brodie was being obviously evasive. Again. She anchored her gaze on his narrowed eyes.

"I have no intentions of arguing the point with you. If you have any questions regarding my authority to ask these questions, I suggest you get on the phone right now and call some of those highly placed contacts of yours." Her voice cooled. "Otherwise, I'd appreciate a little cooperation and some answers."

Mouth flat, eyes dulled, Brodie emitted a long sigh and raked his fingers through his hair. He hadn't really expected that she would be vulnerable to intimidation. Kristin, he'd discovered, was not easily bullied. It had been worth a try, though.

Since he couldn't think of anything better, he told her the truth. "It's a trust fund."

"A what?"

"A trust fund." Brodie dropped heavily back into the chair. "For the boys."

Disbelief clouded her eyes, a flat, gray mist of a cold winter day. "Are you telling me that all of the county money you receive is put into a trust fund for the boys? Why?"

"College. These kids won't have a shot in hell of getting enough money together for college and without an education, they'll never escape the barrios." He faced her with calm dignity, yet a plea for understanding echoed from his eyes. "You can verify the terms of the trust with Sol Freeburg at the bank. He's the executor."

Shocked, Kristin could only fidget with a slightly chewed pencil until she regained control of her voice. "Just what are the, ah, terms?"

With a careless shrug, Brodie absently plucked a second paper clip from the clutter and began to twist it. "Tuition paid, one hundred percent, directly to the college of their choice. If they don't go, the funds held for them revert to the pool and are reallocated to the rest of the boys. It's supposed to be an incentive."

"Yes, well..." Kristin cleared her throat. "I don't understand why you were so secretive about the entire matter."

"You're right, I should have told you," he said, standing quickly. He stretched his long legs once and grabbed the doorknob. "Is that it, now?"

Kristin's spine straightened. "No," she said firmly. "That is *not* it."

Brodie sank back into the chair, glowering. At the moment, his sullen stare reminded Kristin of Jess and she stifled a smile. "There are other deposits. Weekly, in fact." She faced him with her most professional expression. "Where do they come from?"

"Payroll. A percentage of their wages are set aside in the trust."

"Wages?" She mulled that over. "I didn't realize you paid them wages."

"Same rate as any novice ranch hand." He cocked his head and eyed her solemnly. "I suppose that's going to look pretty bad in the report."

Kristin lifted her head in surprise. "What?"

"The fact that I . . . appropriate a portion of their wages."

"No, I don't think so." She leaned forward. "Brodie, the funds you've been putting away for the boys have been allocated by the county for things like food and clothes. Who's paying for that? The ranch itself is in the red, or would be if it weren't for the mysterious deposits every month in the exact amount of the deficit." She sighed. "Why don't you just give me the whole story?"

Realizing he was backed in a corner, Brodie took a deep breath, uttered something rather concise and walked around the desk. Unlocking the top drawer, he dropped a small red ledger in front of her.

"I think that should answer your questions," he told her.

Kristin absorbed Brodie's determined expression, then inspected the small book in front of her. With a final, cautious glance toward Brodie, she lifted the cover and began to read.

The book contained a detailed monetary breakdown of the trust amount currently established for each boy. It also contained a narrative of the overall function of the ranch written in a first person viewpoint. Kristin realized that this was more than a ledger; it was a diary—Brodie's diary.

The major goal of New Wave, Brodie wrote, was to give the kids something they could carry with them for a lifetime. Their experience at New Wave was a start, a push in the right direction, but Brodie was convinced that education was the key to their final escape from poverty and violence.

The ranch would eventually become self-supporting, Brodie wrote, which allowed all the county money, along with savings from the boys' wages, to be set aside to ensure their future.

With a soft thump, the cover settled into place and slim fingernails drummed across the red leather surface. Kristin was stunned and confused, and made no attempt to hide it. "Why were you afraid for me to know that you've put some of the boys' wages in the trust?"

Brodie speared his hair with his fingers. The thick curls were already well-ruffled by the nervous gesture. "These boys have families who are desperate for money just to live on, or to drink on. I can't help them all, so—"

"So, you put the money away for the boys and kept it secret so the families wouldn't claim it." A glimmer of comprehension. "And the mysterious monthly income that balances New Wave's books is your money, isn't it?"

"Yes, for as long as it holds out." He rubbed at his forehead. "That's why we absolutely have to make this ranch operational and efficient. I'm not exactly wealthy."

Watching him, realizing the extent of his dedication to a cause he believed in with all his heart, Kristin felt a surge of admiration. He may not be wealthy in the material sense, but in all the ways that really count, he could be considered a very rich man.

A trust fund. For the boys' education, no less.

Remembering her early visions of a major exposé of the ranch's embezzlement and fraud, Kristin was feeling incredibly foolish. She'd already drafted her notes into a rough outline based on that original hypothesis, pages that detailed speculation as fact, judgment as evidence. Her theories had been way off base. She'd failed to abide by her own unbreakable rule: trust facts, not instincts.

She shuddered.

"Kristin?"

With a start, she realized he'd been speaking to her. "I'm sorry. What did you say?"

"Is there anything else you want to know?"

"Oh. No, thank you." She stood and followed Brodie to the door.

He opened it, stepped into the hallway and turned, his expression serious, voice somber. "I . . . well, I just wanted to tell you that I understand your position. I know that my methods have been unorthodox..." He squeezed his eyes closed and emitted a weary sigh. "The whole thing might even be illegal."

"Illegal?" Kristin's eyes widened. She hadn't even thought of that.

Brodie nodded tiredly. He might as well play out the entire hand. "I ran the idea past a friend of mine in L.A.—an attorney. He told me that since the boys were minors and since, under the terms of the trust, if they don't go to college their actual earned wages could be used to benefit someone else, well, there just wasn't any real precedent."

"I see." Kristin's heart squeezed. Actually, without careful research of the specific laws involved, even she wasn't certain whether Brodie's appropriation of the boys' wages, purity of motives notwithstanding, was legal or not. She didn't even know if he was required to pay them at all for chores around the ranch.

She managed a thin smile. "I plan to do a little discreet research on the subject. Maybe we'll both learn something."

Brodie's eyes flickered in comprehension. Discreet, she had said. To him, that meant she wasn't going to blow any whistles until she found out whether or not a problem even existed.

"Thank you," he said quietly, then he strode out the front door.

Kristin returned to the desk and stared down at the small red book. Part of her mind said that no matter what the letter of the law on this point, it was the spirit of the law that counted, and no one could fault Brodie's good intentions.

Still, Kristin couldn't allow herself to swing across the imaginary ethics line by accepting everything she was told as gospel and interpreting law to suit her own preference. No, Kristin realized that, having recognized her error, the tendency would be to overcompensate, become gullible to deception, and she couldn't allow that, either.

Mr. Freeburg would be contacted to verify the terms of the trust. She would also pull the ranch's payroll records and validate any deductions from the boys' checks with the trust deposits.

Sighing, Kristin realized it was time for another call to Bob Sherwood. That should start the ball rolling on some "hypothetical legal questions." Even if Bob ascertained the real reason for her question, he could be trusted not to divulge the information.

Stiffened by silent resolve, Kristin vowed to proceed with the analysis in a completely logical, totally objective manner.

But she would keep those distorted manuscript notes, if only to serve as a reminder that her judgment could be as fallible as her instincts.

Chapter Eight

The morning air snapped like a bite of crisp apple. Kristin pulled the lightweight jacket tighter and buried her chilled fingers in her armpits. The day was a fresh, tangible reminder that springtime in the Sierras, unlike the bland, temperate climate of Los Angeles, was a distinct season with a personality of its own.

Though barely past seven o'clock, the main house and peripheral buildings were bustling with activity. Breakfast was over and the boys were in the bunkhouse readying themselves, albeit a bit reluctantly, for school.

The stable area was quiet, though, as the hands had already selected the horses required for the day's work. The large double doors of the building stood open, and Kristin could see that Martha still occupied the foaling suite. Brodie had mentioned during breakfast that the mare was well enough to be allowed some time in the exercise arena today. It had been little more than twenty-four hours since her tragic stillborn delivery.

To Kristin, it seemed much longer.

Merle had driven her into Mariposa yesterday to pick up her beleaguered car and she'd verified the trust with Sol Freeburg at the bank. Today Kristin planned to validate the deposits with payroll records, but actually had no doubts that the figures would balance satisfactorily.

Todd had returned from his "job interview" with Dr. Amatti beaming and ecstatic, simultaneously extolling the virtues of veterinarians and fat puppies.

Everything was coming together wonderfully. In fact, it was beginning to look as though she would be able to complete her assignment considerably ahead of schedule.

Why, then, Kristin wondered, did she feel so restless? Why this gnawing sense of uneasiness, of impending loss? Kristin kicked at a flat gray rock. She didn't want to acknowledge it, but she was beginning to realize what her problem was and she didn't like it.

Nathan Brodie was her problem.

The man invaded her thoughts. In the middle of her work she would remember the feel of his lips, his touch.

She tried to logically sort through these unexpected and un-welcome emotions. She was, after all, in a strange place surrounded by all manner of secret terrors. The very nature of her assignment garnered a great deal of resentment, so she was disliked and distrusted by nearly everyone on the ranch. It was natural for her to be drawn to someone who made her feel safe, protected. Someone like Brodie.

The harassment had taken its toll as well. Kristin had decided to keep the most recent incident, the threatening anonymous note and its contents, to herself. After dinner last night, Brodie had gathered the boys in his office to discuss the vandalism of her car. Kristin winced, remembering his grim expression—a hard mask, like the crust of a volcano with the fire of his fury boiling beneath the surface.

A cold breeze lifted her hair, stinging her cheeks and she absently prodded the stone with her toe. Brodie had supported her, Kristin realized, through all the unpleasantness. Oh, they'd had their differences, to be sure, but somehow she always felt he would well, look out for her.

It was perfectly logical that she would deal with the mental stress of the past week by conjuring images of the one person she believed would ensure her safety. The fact that her visions were so...ah, personal, was simply a matter of...that is, it was perfectly normal to...

Nuts. With a final kick at the hapless rock, she glanced up and noted with some surprise that she'd wandered within a few feet of the stable door. Martha was standing at the stall fence, watching Kristin with apparent interest. The mare gave a snort of invitation, bobbing her big gray head as though to offer reassurance. The large brown eyes still held a tinge of sadness, Kristin decided, and smiled at her own newly discovered penchant for endowing human emotions to inhuman creatures.

But Kristin found herself inside the stable. The building was quiet now, its occupants hard at work. Only Martha remained, and the mare appeared as lonely and in need of company as Kristin herself.

"How are you feeling today?"

The sound startled Kristin, and she laughed to realize the voice was her own. She was actually talking to a horse!

"Who'll ever know?" she asked Martha, her voice becoming bolder. The mare snuffled and whinnied in conspiratorial agreement. This was no ordinary animal. Kristin was convinced that a real person lived behind those huge eyes and only the cruelest quirk of fate had condemned Martha to spend her life cocooned in a horse suit.

The mare stretched her powerful neck, reaching across the railing and Kristin froze, the familiar chill of terror rolling down her spine. She'd moved too close. The beast could actually reach her.

Kristin's eyes darted wildly. She commanded her feet to move, but they remained firmly entrenched, as though her sneakers had been nailed to the floorboards.

Then Kristin felt the mare's warm, hay-sweet breath on her cheek, followed by a feathery touch as the animal softly nuzzled Kristin's neck. Such a gentle touch, so sweet, almost loving.

The mare withdrew, watching, eyes questioning.

As though controlled by some remote force, Kristin saw her own hand extending until fingertips brushed the velvety gray muzzle, withdrawing, then stroking again with more confidence.

Martha nickered with pleasure.

"I know," Kristin whispered, caressing the mare's sleek neck. "We all need love, don't we?"

They stood together, woman and mare, comforting each other, communicating in a very special, very female way, their friendship blossoming with petals opened slowly under the warming rays of mutual trust.

"She . . . she might like these."

Startled, Kristin whirled, heart hammering, unnerved by the unexpected intrusion. Martha, however, snorted a delighted welcome.

Brodie stood in the open doorway, filling it with his presence. Even in the crisp morning air, he'd rolled the sleeves of his plaid shirt to his elbows and a down vest was his only concession to the chill. He stretched a balled fist toward Kristin, then opened his fingers slowly, displaying two small white cubes dwarfed by his large palm. She stared at them stupidly.

"Sugar," he explained. "Martha loves it." He wriggled his hand in encouragement. "Take them."

Kristin wasn't ready for this. "You mean, *feed* them to her?"

Trying to keep his face impassive, Brodie fought the insistent smile twitching at his mouth and nodded silently.

"Uh, I'm sure Martha would rather have them from you," Kristin said.

"Nonsense." With his free hand, Brodie snagged Kristin's wrist, holding it steady while he dropped the sweet squares into her palm. She stared at the cubes in abject horror.

Brodie watched her thoughtfully. Maybe he was pushing her a bit too fast. When he'd come to the stable and had seen Kristin crooning to the mare, his heart seemed to leap into his throat. He knew she was overcoming whatever horrors haunted her, knew she could learn to love animals, love the ranch. She had so much love inside her, Brodie thought, and she didn't even realize it.

Martha snuffled impatiently, eyeing the sugar.

Kristin began to tremble. Teeth. Martha had teeth and she would have to use them on the sugar cubes, cubes that nestled on Kristin's unprotected skin. Her mind whirled wildly, seeking escape, yet she was somehow unwilling to let Brodie know how terrified she was at the thought of feeding a horse.

To change the subject, she blurted out, "How did your meeting with the boys go?"

Brodie's lips flattened. "Jess confessed."

Her mouth went dry. She'd expected that but somehow, hearing her fears confirmed jolted her. "I see," she murmured.

Absently reaching out to stroke Martha's sleek neck, Brodie's brows furrowed and the grooves etched in his cheeks deepened. "I don't believe him."

Kristin looked at him in astonishment. "Why not?"

"Something doesn't sit right." He jammed his hands into the pocket of his vest. "First, they all denied it and Jess looked genuinely surprised. When I told them if I didn't get to the bottom of it, I'd send them all back to L.A., Jess shrugged and said he'd done it."

Automatically, her hand tightened around the grainy squares. Brodie looked so sad, so incredibly bleak that Kristin had an overwhelming urge to touch his face and offer comfort. She fought the desire and cleared her throat nervously. "Well, at least he didn't let the others suffer for his actions."

Brodie seemed distracted. "Umm. Except Todd pipes up and says Jess was with him from breakfast until you drove off."

An image jogged Kristin's memory. "Well, they *were* standing by the car together," she affirmed.

His mouth twisted and pursed thoughtfully. "Ernie accused me of blaming the three of them for everything bad that happens. He said everyone at the breakfast table that morning knew you were going into town and anyone on the ranch could have done it." He paused before adding, "Even you."

"Me?" Kristin's jaw dropped. "Why would I sabotage myself?"

"You wouldn't." He bit off the words, then lifted his hat, sighing as he dragged his fingers through his hair. "Ernie's just grasping at straws."

Kristin was beginning to see Brodie's predicament. "So Jess, who never lies, confessed, and Todd, who frequently ignores the truth, said Jess couldn't have done it. Where does that leave you?" Kristin was concerned about Brodie. She knew he was feeling frustrated and angry, possibly even betrayed.

He shrugged stiffly. "It leaves me with a decision." And that, his tone inferred, was the end of the discussion. Blinking, Brodie looked down at Kristin and managed a tight smile. "Now, what about Martha's sugar?"

Eyes widening, Kristin opened her palm and stared helplessly at the now sticky cubes, her face twisted with apprehension.

Her distress was not unnoticed.

"You're right," Brodie said finally. "She'd probably be disappointed if I don't feed her myself."

Looking up at Brodie's strong face, Kristin saw the compassion in his eyes. Martha didn't give a fig who gave her the sugar and they both knew it. He was offering a graceful way out and she desperately wanted to take it. And yet . . .

Hesitating, Kristin swung a glance at Martha. The mare cocked her big head, eyes patient, as though she understood Kristin's fear and liked her anyway.

Slowly, Kristin extended her palm with a fitful, jerky motion. She stopped breathing, squeezed her eyes shut and wondered how fast she would be able to type with one hand.

A light, tickling sensation grazed her palm. Kristin opened one eye. Her hand was empty and Martha was chewing contentedly.

"Congratulations," Brodie said, obviously proud of her accomplishment.

Kristin grinned, warmed to the core by his approval. "Nothing to it," she said casually, then burst into delighted laughter.

Brodie laughed with her, then, unable to stifle his need to touch her, reached out to stroke her face. He brushed the pale, silken strands from her cheek and saw the laughter die on her lips as he slid his fingertip to her mouth, testing its softness, tracing its fullness. Her eyes darkened, turning from silver to the smoky color of desire that incited his senses, aroused his flesh.

"You're special, Kris," he whispered, gathering her hand in his calloused palm. "So very, very special."

"Brodie, I..." Her voice broke with a gasp as he brought her hand to his lips, then lightly nipped the sensitive pad of flesh beneath her thumb.

As though starved for the feel of her, he caressed her throat, traced the ridge of collarbone exposed by the neck of her shirt, then skimmed to the base of the open V, hooking over the button between her breasts as his lips fluttered over hers.

He teased her, softly caressing, then withdrawing to touch the corner of her mouth and to brush across her eyelids.

Kristin tingled with anticipation and already her body was signaling its need. She wanted to be captured by his strength, as she had been captured the last time he had held her in his arms. She wanted to feel his lips tormenting her with urgency and passion, as they had tormented her then. She wanted to feel his skin against hers, fevered and damp as he moved with her, inside her, loving her, as he had loved her in her dreams.

But Brodie continued a slow, tantalizing assault on her senses, his finger still nestled against her cleavage, demanding nothing more than to snuggle in her warmth. His lips skimmed hers, then paused, barely touching her as he outlined her mouth with his tongue. Moist and warm, it contoured the fullness of her lower lip, then feathered over each curve, lightly stroking the inner softness, but never quite claiming it until her own tongue met him at the threshold, welcoming, an invitation to share and savor.

His gentle quest became hotter, more demanding and finally, a scorching, thrusting possession that left Kristin gasping and nearly senseless. Of their own accord, her arms wound around his neck, drawing her to him as her fingers tangled in the thick hair curling over his collar.

Hands that had been content merely to rest against her skin now roamed urgently over her body, as though memorizing each contour, molding themselves to every curve. The roughened skin of his palm caught on her thin cotton shirt, then slid across her ribs and softly, intimately cupped her swollen breast.

He tore his mouth from hers. "Kris," he rasped. "You do things to me, lady. In another minute, we're going to give Martha quite a show."

As they stared at each other, gasping and fevered, Brodie continued to massage her breast and Kristin kept her fingers firmly knotted in his hair.

"The feelings between us," Brodie murmured against her ear. "They're right, Kris. I've waited a long time for you, I've waited all my life."

There was no mistaking the depth of feeling in Brodie's voice, the sincerity. This was not a man searching for a convenient roll in the hay. He was looking for someone, Kristin realized, someone to share his life. She wasn't that person and yet she allowed him to think she was by responding to his touch with unbridled passion, a passion she hadn't even realized was a part of her.

Hands trembling, she unlaced her fingers, sliding them across his hard chest, pushing him gently away.

He grasped her shoulders. "Don't turn away, Kris. Look at me."

"No," she said quietly. "I'm not the person you think I am. This is wrong, Brodie. I'm sorry."

"It's not wrong and you know it's not. You're afraid, honey, and..." His expression softened, his rugged features melting around the midnight intensity of his eyes. "I don't mind admitting I'm a bit nervous myself. I've never wanted a woman the way I want you, Kris." Brodie straightened, clamping his jaw into a determined line. "Accept what's happening between us."

"Nothing is happening." Kristin was carefully enunciating each syllable, revealing her own inner turmoil. "I've been a bit lonely, that's all. I miss my apartment, I miss the ocean, I miss my friends..." She whirled toward Brodie, her eyes wide, veiled with pain yet begging him to confirm what she was saying. "Don't you understand, I haven't been myself lately. It's not your fault and please believe that I never meant to lead you on, to let you believe that we might...that we would eventually..."

"We *will*, eventually," he said, with a flash of that boyish allure.

Frustrated, Kristin turned away. That cocky confidence was infuriating. And exciting. Squaring to face him, she lifted her chin defiantly. "No, we won't."

To her chagrin, he laughed. It was a deep, rich sound that rumbled through the building and reverberated through her entire body. She stiffened. "You find me amusing?"

"No." Tiny laugh lines crinkled his eyes. "I find you delightful." He slid a fingertip around her rigid jaw. "And I find you desirable."

He was close—too close. "I have no intention of sharing your bed."

"Umm." He rested the fingertip against a pulse point below her ear. "I don't recall having invited you to my bed," he said huskily. "But you will invite me to yours. Soon, I think."

Her skin flamed. "When hell freezes."

She was furious, more with herself than with him. He could control her with a touch, a soft whispering caress and he knew it. He was confident in his ability to arouse, to excite. Even now, she trembled.

With a maddening, lazy grin, Brodie continued his erotic assault on her senses. "When hell freezes, Kris?" He brushed his lips across her ear and whispered, "Honey, it's getting mighty cold already."

Suddenly Kristin realized what Brodie already knew. He'd held her motionless with the merest touch of a single finger. She wasn't trapped. She could have stepped away at any time, ended the moment, stopped the sweet torture.

She could have, but she didn't. At that moment, their eyes met. Snow was falling on the gates of Hades.

Or would have if a dull rasping noise, like something scratching on the outside of the stable wall, hadn't captured their attention. Reluctantly dropping his hand, Brodie walked toward the open door, but the rapid-fire crunch of shoes meeting ground in a fast sprint was a clear indication that whoever had been outside was not willing to hang around.

Who was it? Kristin wondered nervously. How much had he seen and heard? Lord knows, he certainly could have gotten an eyeful, and she blushed in remembrance.

Brodie had gone outside, then returned, now standing in the open doorway, silhouetted against the glare of morning sunlight.

"You're wrong about yourself, Kris, and you're wrong about me—but you've been wrong before. Eventually, you'll work things out and come around." He raked at his hair, then tugged his hat back over the thick curls. "Until then, keep your snow shoes handy."

Turning, Brodie took two strides, then halted, looking over his shoulder. Sunlight streamed over him now, illuminating the teasing glint in his eyes, his mischievous grin. "I think we're in for a late spring frost."

Before she could respond, he'd banked to his left and disappeared, leaving Kristin to stand stunned and gaping like a giant grouper.

Martha sniffed sympathetically. After all, two-legged or four-legged, the male of any species could be arrogant, stubborn and downright frustrating.

Females understood these things.

"Are you sure, Gus?"

"Yep." Gus scratched at his chin and scanned the distant hills with shrewd, narrowed eyes. "Just like last winter."

Brodie sighed, then leaned against one of the wooden posts supporting strands of stretched barbed wire. He took off his hat and gazed intently at the horizon. "How many this time?"

Gus spat noisily. "Two. Killed one calf, hurt the other so bad, we had to shoot it."

"Damn," Brodie muttered, then slapped his hat against his knee and repeated the oath more vehemently. "It's spring. What are wolves doing down here in the middle of spring?"

"Don't rightly know, unless that big fire last year has something to do with it."

Brodie mulled that over. That could be one reason, he decided. The fire last September had burned over fifty thousand acres of prime timber on the western slope of the mountain. Those animals that had survived had moved to lower elevations in search of food and were followed by their natural predators.

Driven by starvation, a small pack of wolves had attacked New Wave's herd last winter but, with the help of the Forest Service, Brodie's men had managed to capture and relocate about four of them.

Winter in the Sierras was a bleak, desolate season. Food was scarce in the best of times and Brodie could understand the animals' desperation. In the spring, however, small rodents and other animals were coming out of hibernation, along with an abundant collection of newborn fawns. All were listed on the wolves' menu. There would be no reason for them to be down in the foothills, unless, as Gus had said, the effects of the fire were still being felt throughout the forest.

"Could you tell how large the pack was?"

"Weren't no pack," Gus replied. "Just one stray, near as we can figure. Probably a rogue male, might even be hurt. Not likely to take down a full-growed steer, but them calves'd suit it just fine."

That was true enough, Brodie thought, grateful that only one animal was involved. A full pack of wolves was something else. They were clever, fearless, intelligent, and there was no animal on earth that a hungry pack couldn't make into a meal.

Pulling on his hat, Brodie said, "That's it, then. Have Merle and Tug pull out the traps. We'll get an early start in the morning."

Lazily scratching his armpit, Gus squinted up at Brodie. "Best not tell the lady about them traps. She'd probably be accusin' us all of abusin' them poor critters and sic the sheriff on us."

Eyes narrowing, Brodie's lips tightened. "Those traps are rubber-jawed and toothless. I think you're underestimating

Kristin's intelligence and if you'd all stop using her as the butt of your smart jokes, you might notice what a fine woman she is.'' Brodie turned stiffly and marched toward his horse.

Raising a bushy eyebrow, Gus noted Brodie's angry stride. The old man's leathery skin creased, his eyes crinkling in amusement. "Mite touchy," he observed, then casually sauntered toward his own mount.

Kristin stood on the bunkhouse porch and peered through the open door. The boys had returned from school over an hour ago and Todd was busy with his chores in the stable. She'd seen Jess leaving the bunkhouse a few minutes earlier and was hoping to catch Ernie alone.

"Hello," she called through the door. "Anybody in there?"

There was no response, still Kristin hesitated to violate their privacy by entering without an invitation. "Ernie? Are you in there?"

A shuffling noise greeted her inquiry. Within a few minutes, Ernie appeared in the doorway looking nervous and surprised. The mop of tightly wound curls was even more disheveled than usual, as though he'd combed it with his fingers, then left it to fend for itself.

"Uh . . . hi," he said awkwardly. "No one's here but me."

Kristin offered a bright smile. "That suits me fine, Ernie. It just so happens that you're the one I wanted to see."

Ernie's eyes widened, engulfing his thin face. He swallowed, his Adam's apple bobbing anxiously. "I didn't do nothing wrong. Honest."

"Of course you didn't," Kristin said, startled by his defensive response. "I just wanted to spend a little time with you."

"Oh. Yeah."

"Why would you think I'd believe you'd done something wrong?"

The boy shrugged. "The snake and all. I didn't have nothing to do with that," he said quickly. "Todd and Jess did it. I didn't."

"But you knew about it." It was not a question and Ernie shuffled nervously without replying.

Kristin continued. "What about the car, Ernie? Did you know about it, too?"

"I don't know nothing about the car," he said vehemently. "Jess did it. He doesn't like you."

Kristin lifted her eyebrows in surprise. Obviously, loyalty was not one of Ernie's strong suits, Kristin thought dryly, then switched to another tack. "Why doesn't Jess like me, Ernie? Do you know?"

He stammered for a moment, then coughed. "Because you're trying to close the ranch and send us away."

"But I told Jess that wasn't true."

Ernie's expression hardened before his gaze slipped to the ground. "Maybe he doesn't believe you. You said the ranch 'provided the opportunity for un-unscrupulous activities and abuse of county funds.'"

Even Ernie's mangled pronunciation couldn't conceal the intent of that statement. Kristin winced. "I said a lot of things I shouldn't have said, Ernie. I apologized to Jess and I'm apologizing to you." Kristin managed a weak smile. "Even adults make mistakes and are capable of poor behavior. Can't we be friends?"

The boy's resolve seemed to be weakening. "Yeah, I guess so."

Wanting to change the subject, Kristin glanced past him. "You know, I've never seen a real bunkhouse before. How about a quick tour?"

"No!" he said too quickly. "I mean, I don't know if the other guys would like it."

Surprised, Kristin watched him thoughtfully. His Adam's apple vibrated rapidly and he looked for all the world as though he wished nothing more than to disappear through the floorboards. When she spoke, Kristin's voice was tinged with weary skepticism. "If you're concerned about giving me permission, I'd be happy to ask Brodie to show me through your living quarters." She watched Ernie's eyes twitch, then added softly, "It's all part of my job, Ernie."

"Yeah, well, I guess it'd be okay." Ernie shuffled his skinny legs, fidgeting uneasily before stepping aside to let Kristin enter.

The large room was light and airy. Two overstuffed sofas were arranged in one corner, almost engulfing the end table between them. A tall driftwood lamp sat on the table, along with an assortment of magazines and hardcover books.

Several other chairs were positioned around the area. Some were simple wooden seats, others were thickly upholstered and comfortable looking. None of the furnishings matched and all were situated to face a large television set. A table and some chairs were pushed against the farthest wall and Kristin deduced from the clutter of papers and books that the boys probably did most of their homework there.

"This is just like a living room." Although not a particularly clean one, Kristin noted. It smelled of leather and dust and unlaundered socks. "I expected, well, a row of cots lined up, kind of like a barracks. Where do you sleep?"

Ernie pointed toward a very long hallway lined with doorways. "Down there. We each have our own room."

Kristin was surprised. "You do?"

"Yeah." Ernie was relaxing a bit. "We have a bed, dresser, everything, just like home. *Better* than home."

Smiling, she said, "With seven brothers and sisters, I don't imagine you had the luxury of your very own room."

"Nah. There were four of us in one bedroom. I had to sleep in the same bed with my little brother and, man, that was a bummer." Ernie's face was solemn. "He was a real geek. Snored, you know? And he jumped around all night long."

Nodding, Kristin assured Ernie that she fully understood his appreciation of the ranch's private sleeping accommodations.

She'd wandered to the table and was absently glancing at the papers strewn across its surface. "Were you in the middle of your schoolwork?"

"Yeah. I dunno, it just takes me a long time. Jess and Todd are through already." He picked up a piece of paper and Kristin noticed it was covered with smudges, as though the eraser had been given a considerable workout. "They're smart, real smart," Ernie intoned. "Especially Jess. I'm kind of dumb, but Brodie says that's okay."

Kristin glanced up from the papers. "I don't think you're dumb, Ernie, and I can't believe Brodie does, either."

"Well, maybe not stupid-dumb," he conceded. "Just schoolwork-dumb, but Brodie says each of us has a different ah . . . po-ten-tial?" He looked anxiously at Kristin for confirmation of the word, continuing when she nodded. "Anyway, Brodie says all we can do is our best and that's all he expects. I got a D in math, but Brodie said it was okay because I tried real hard and it was the best I could do." Ernie's voice lowered, his eyes skittering as though he feared being overheard. "Jess got a C last time and Brodie was real mad, put him on restriction and everything."

"Why did he do that?"

"Because he said Jess was goofing off and I wasn't." The boy's skinny chest seemed to puff with pride.

"I see." Kristin smothered a smile and continued to scan the scattered papers. Something, partially covered by a sheet of math homework, caught her eye and she pulled at the paper, freeing it. It was a pencil sketch of a horse, beautifully rendered, crisply detailed and realistic.

Turning the drawing toward the window for a better look, she murmured, "This is wonderful. Who drew it?"

Ernie lowered his eyes, scratching at the carpet with the toe of his sneaker. "I did. It's no big deal."

"I disagree. You're very talented, Ernie, and this piece is absolutely wonderful." Kristin was amazed. "Do you have any more?"

"Some." He grinned sheepishly. "Want to see 'em?"

"Oh, yes, I do."

Ernie disappeared down the immense hallway, emerging moments later with a large manila folder from which he extracted a dozen drawings of similar quality. As Kristin admired each one, Ernie beamed.

After she'd examined each sketch carefully, she asked, "Did you ever take art classes in school?"

"Art classes cost money. You've got to buy special paints, all different kinds of pencils and drawing paper. My folks couldn't afford that junk."

"But you're earning your own money now," Kristin pointed out. "Has Brodie seen these?"

"Nah. He wouldn't be interested in this stuff."

"Oh, yes he would, Ernie, he'd be terribly interested." She wrapped her fingers around his bony wrist. "May I show these to him?"

The boy hesitated, his eyes veiled.

"Brodie would be so pleased with this work, Ernie."

"Well..."

"Please?"

A small, shy smile played at his lips. "I guess it's okay."

Triumphant, Kristin carefully replaced the sketches in the envelope and tucked them under her arm. Her excited grin froze as a thumping sound emanated from one of the rooms down the hall. Ernie's eyes widened and his face paled. A rasping noise, like something dragging across the wooden floorboards, grated through the room and Ernie bolted, reaching the front door in two strides. Whipping the door open, he stared at Kristin as though imploring her to leave. "I—I got to finish my homework now..."

Kristin made no move toward the door. "What's that noise?" she demanded, planting her heels and fixing Ernie with a no-nonsense stare.

"W-what noise?" he mumbled, wincing as another thump rolled down the hall.

Irritated, Kristin marched toward the hallway.

Ernie sprinted after her. "No...Ms. Price, I wouldn't do that..." He skidded to a stop beside Kristin, who stood in front of a closed door at the far end of the hall. She raised an eyebrow in question. Ernie shuffled and mumbled. "This is Todd's room and he don't allow no one in here." His eyes seemed to plead with her. "He'll skin me alive."

"Who is in there, Ernie?"

"Nobody. Honest." Ernie moaned as the soft squeak of springs echoed behind the door.

Twisting the knob, Kristin pushed the door open. The room was small and dim, daylight blocked behind a narrow window shuttered with tightly knit venetian blinds. Squinting into the gray pall, she saw the obscure outline of a lean dresser and a thin bed. There seemed to be a large lump in the middle of the room, and Kristin stepped inside for a better view. Suddenly, the lump unfolded and expanded, swelling until it was almost as high as her chin.

Nearly paralyzed, Kristin felt her skin slither as a low rumble filled the room. Ernie's drawings fluttered to the floor. A flash of white teeth was followed by a heart-stopping growl. The animal was standing on the bed, his eyes reflecting the brightness of the hallway, refracting the light into two glowing red orbs.

She was frozen with terror. Snarls filled the room, louder, thundering like the roar of a freight train in the night. White flashes, fangs bared like jagged lightning, seemed to lunge at her.

Teeth. A lot of them. In her face.

Chapter Nine

Brodie found her by the cottonwoods on the far side of the knoll. She was crumpled at the base of a tree, rolled into a rigid ball with her arms wrapped tightly around her head. Her small body was racked with great, gulping sobs.

His heart coiled, reacting to her pain.

Silently, he swore that Todd would rue the day he'd decided to sneak an injured dog into the bunkhouse. Brodie had been in the office when he'd heard Kristin scream and by the time he'd reached the front porch of the house, she had been dashing blindly across the meadow.

Watching her now, curled like a frightened child, Brodie realized he would give anything to help her, do anything to ease her mental torment.

Feeling helpless and frustrated, Brodie finally went to her, dropping to his knees to gather her shuddering body against his chest and rocked her, crooning and soothing until he felt her knotted muscles soften and relax.

"You're all right, Kris, honey," he murmured against her ear. "You're safe now."

Finally, her sobs reduced to shaky hiccups, she moved against him, raising her head to peer up, dazed, bewildered, frightened. Rubbing wet eyes with the back of her small hands, Kristin blinked at him, as though she knew him to be merely a mirage and was patiently waiting for him to disappear.

"Brodie?" she croaked.

"Yes, Kris, I'm here."

"I—It came after me," she said, stammering and hiccuping. "I'm so sorry...I couldn't seem to control myself."

"There's nothing to be sorry about. You weren't expecting a huge animal to leap at you like that." He felt her slump against his chest and tightened his arms around her. A lump wedged in his throat at her gesture of trust and acceptance. "It's okay, honey. You're safe."

Brodie continued to hold her, stroking her head, until she was somewhat controlled. When she sat up and pushed the hair from her face, he reluctantly loosened his grip.

Her voice was dull, monotone. "I feel like a fool."

Stroking her cheek, Brodie offered a smile of encouragement. "If I'd been in your place, I'd have been a bit startled myself. You've got no reason to feel foolish, Kris."

"I...ah, I mean, it was real, then?" Kristin had been terrified by the thought that her nightmares might have taken hold of her mind and caused her to hallucinate the entire episode. She could be going mad, stark raving mad.

Eyes hardening, Brodie's jaw twitched. "It was real. A dog at the clinic had been hit by a car and had a broken leg. The dog was not particularly fond of most people but apparently took to Todd."

A glimmer of comprehension hit Kristin. "So Todd brought the dog back to the bunkhouse."

"Yes, a decision he'll live to regret."

Closing her eyes, she allowed her head to rest against Brodie's hard shoulder. She felt the warmth of his body seep through her skin, heating muscles still in spasm from her violent reaction to terror. Kristin felt safe now, cherished, and although she knew this tender comfort couldn't last, she savored it. How long had it been, she asked herself, since anyone had held her like this, demanding nothing, receiving nothing, giving only kindness and love? Love. Strange, that after all these years of loneliness, a man she'd known less than two weeks could make her feel accepted, valued and yes, loved.

Nathan Brodie was a very special man, Kristin realized. He had an almost magical power, the ability to filter through a false facade and touch a person's heart. Images of him comforting the boys, much as he comforted her now, filled her mind. That's why he's so perfect for them, she decided, and so perfect for me.

The thought pierced her mind unbidden, stunning her upright. *So perfect for me.* Good grief, what was wrong with her? The man was merely offering solace and she was mentally deifying him, visualizing Brodie as her lifetime soulmate.

Flames of embarrassment fanned her face as she tried to pull away. "Don't blame Todd, Brodie. Or the dog, for that matter. It's my fault. Ernie told me not to go into the room, but I just had to play detective and plow right ahead."

Brodie allowed her the distance she sought, yet confined her withdrawal to the circle of his arms. "The dog shouldn't have been there. Todd knew better."

Something decisive in Brodie's voice issued a warning and Kristin responded quickly. "Please, don't take the dog away from him. He's opening up now, allowing himself to feel again. To lose that animal so quickly after the loss of Martha's foal could set him back weeks."

Brodie's voice gentled, his fingers continued to stroke and soothe. "What about you, Kris? Can you handle it, knowing that animal might be just around the corner?"

"Todd shouldn't have to suffer just because I don't care for...certain animals. Now that I know where it is, I can avoid it. Besides, I won't be here that much longer."

A pang spiked through him at the thought of her leaving, but he pushed it away. It was her pain that mattered now, not his. "You know, Kris," he whispered, "your fear goes a bit beyond simply not caring for animals. Your terror is almost phobic." She stiffened and tried to pull back, but he held her. "You can't go on like this. Whatever has happened to cause your nightmares can be dealt with, but you need help."

Twisting away, she mumbled brusquely, "No one can help. It's my problem."

Not allowing her to retreat, Brodie gently cupped her chin in his hand, turning her head until she faced him. "At least share it with me, Kris. Sometimes just talking about it helps."

"No. I don't want to talk about it." Each syllable rolled from her tongue like a concise, round marble. "I don't want to think about it."

With a brisk jerk, she stood and swiftly walked to the edge of the knoll, knotting her hands as she gulped great lungsful of the fragrant spring air.

"Kris..."

"No. Please, Brodie, just... just leave me alone right now. I appreciate your concern, but I need to be alone."

Tracing her steps, Brodie stood behind her, so close the clean, light scent of her circled him like a soft cloud. He gazed over her head at the distant silhouette of sunlit hills. "Being alone right now is the last thing you need."

Kristin forced a light laugh. "I think I should know what I need."

"You should," he agreed tersely, "but obviously you don't."

Winding her arms around herself, Kristin shielded herself physically from the soft breeze and psychologically from Brodie's prying questions. Why wouldn't he leave her alone? Why was he hounding her this way?

"What are your nightmares about, Kristin? The time you fell off the horse?"

He saw her stiffen. So that was it. Remembering her terror the first day on the ranch, he'd suspected that her fear of animals was somehow tied in with her nightmares.

"Yes," said Kristin. "It's about the time I fell off my horse." If she could simply convince him that was all there was to it, maybe he would go away. She feigned a weak smile. "Silly isn't it? But, I'm scared spitless of the beasts and there you are." She whirled, issued a weak shrug, then started toward the house. "Thanks again for your concern. I really appreciate it."

Firmly but gently, Brodie snagged her arm, pulling her to a halt. "Tell me about it. What really happened?"

The flimsy smile flattened. "I've already told you. I was riding to work and I fell off. No big deal." That was partially true. Kristin really couldn't remember why she fell off the horse, she only saw vague images.

Brodie was obviously skeptical. "I doubt that." His fingers brushed the scar on her temple. "How did this happen, Kris?"

Shaking, she pulled away. "Stop it. I want to leave now."

Insistent hands grasped at her shoulders, holding her firm. She felt the panic bubble into her throat and thrashed against it as she fought his imprisoning grip. The images were gathered in her mind, like a filmstrip, a horror movie she couldn't watch yet couldn't block from view. He was causing it, creating it with his words.

"Stop!" Small fists balled and pounded on his chest, as ineffective as moths fluttering against concrete. He was making her see it . . . the teeth, the teeth.

"God, no," she moaned, her head falling to his collarbone. "No, no, no."

"No. Tell me, Kristin. Let me help you."

"Help me? *Help me?* Are you some kind of psychiatrist?"

She was trembling visibly, her face smeared by dried tears even as her eyes shimmered with fresh moisture. Brodie could see tiny droplets perched on her lower lashes as her lips flexed.

"Maybe you're a plastic surgeon," she babbled, twisting in his grasp, pushing her hair back to fully reveal the jagged white lines. "Maybe you think you can patch me up and make me pretty again."

Tears splashed across her cheeks and Brodie grazed her skin with his knuckles to push them aside. "You're beautiful, Kristin," he said softly, but she didn't hear him. Her entire body was vibrating, her eyes wide with glazed terror as she fixed her horrified gaze on something only she could see.

Perhaps he'd gone too far, pushed too hard again. He mentally cursed himself, her torment tearing at him.

Then she spoke, a husky whisper, suddenly calm. "It doesn't matter if I'm pretty or not, don't you see? I'm weak. I'm like a sniveling mouse, afraid of everything on four legs. *I can't control it.*" Her gaze swung around, smoky gray locking with midnight blue, and he was chilled by the futility in her eyes and the desperate tremor of her voice. "I thought I could—but I can't." Her next words were nearly inaudible. "I'm too weak."

"You're not weak, honey. You're the strongest, bravest woman I know." Brodie gathered her in his arms, closing his eyes as he held her quivering body tightly against him. "You were on the horse, riding to work. You were ten years old. Think, Kristin, think. Why did you fall off the horse?"

"I don't know! I—I don't remember."

"Yes, you do," he soothed. "Just relax and let your mind show you."

She fought it, fought the images crowding her mind. Then Brodie's soft voice, his reassuring touch, slackened her rigid muscles. It would be all right, she realized. Brodie was here, and it would be all right to remember. He would help her, he would keep the demons away.

Slowly, she allowed the vision to clear and solidify in her mind. "I-It was frightened," she finally whispered. "The horse was frightened."

"Of what?"

She buried her face in his chest and he couldn't understand her muffled response.

"What was it? What frightened the horse?"

"Something huge and black. I-It was snarling, growling." She looked up, almost surprised that she could remember so clearly. "I think it bit him."

"Bit the horse?"

Kristin nodded vehemently. "Yes, yes, that's it. I remember now, it attacked and the horse reared up...I tried to hold on, but there was no saddle..."

"What attacked the horse, Kristin? What was it?"

"Some kind of dog...I don't know. It was so big, so vicious."

Brodie led her to the dappled shade of a cottonwood, then sat beside her on the soft earth. "Tell me the rest of it."

Calmer now, Kristin began to share the secret that had been locked in her mind for eighteen years. When the horse had thrown her, she'd landed on her back, winded and gasping. The dog turned its attention from the horse to Kristin, its sharp teeth tearing at her face and shredding her arms as she tried in vain to protect herself. She remembered screaming for help, but none came and the animal continued to maul her.

Then the horse was suddenly there again, its hooves raised high in the air before they slammed into Kristin, breaking three ribs and crushing her shoulder. It'd taken a total of two hundred stitches to put her back together and she'd needed two separate surgeries on her shoulder.

Brodie listened, wiping her tears, holding her, allowing the grief and pain to roll out.

"When I woke up in the hospital, the doctor told me that they hadn't been able to find the dog that attacked me, so they gave me the entire series of anti-rabies injections." She managed a wet smile and accepted the handkerchief he offered. "I don't like shots now, either. Anyway, I was in the hospital for a couple of months and then was assigned to a different foster home." She sniffed, wiping at her nose, laughing softly. "Lord, I'm a mess, and I've nearly drowned you."

Brodie smiled and tightened his grip, pulling her head to his chest. "You look good to me, honey. You always look good to me."

She snickered and dabbed her eyes. "My very first hero."

"Not your first hero, though I wish I had been."

"Sure you are. I ought to know how many heroes I've had."

Smiling softly, Brodie said, "I think you overlooked one."

Kristin was puzzled. "Who?"

"The horse."

"What?"

"After the dog turned on you, most animals would have run like the devil. Their first instinct would have been to get as far away as possible, fast. Granted, the horse's aim left a bit to be desired, but I suspect he was trying to protect you."

Swallowing hard, Kristin attempted to digest this hypothesis. "Are you telling me that the horse was trying to trample the dog?"

Brodie shrugged. "The way you told it, it sure sounds that way."

"Well." Kristin twisted her arms against her chest, her lips pursed thoughtfully. Suddenly, her eyes welled with fresh tears.

Brodie was instantly concerned. "What's wrong, Kris?"

When she looked up at him, her eyes were misted with sadness. "They told me the horse was badly injured in the attack. They had to...put him to sleep." Her voice began to break. "What if I've spent all these years hating that poor animal and it really gave its own life to save me?" She grabbed at his arm anxiously. "Can horses think like that, Brodie? I mean, are they intelligent enough to...make that kind of a decision?"

"I don't know for sure, honey," Brodie said softly. "No one does, really."

But Kristin remembering Martha's grief the night her foal had died, recognized understanding and patience in the mare's eyes as she had fearfully approached the stables this morning.

And Kristin wept.

Wadded balls of paper filled the wastebasket and decorated the surrounding carpet. Disgusted, Kristin turned off the typewriter. Obviously, she wasn't accomplishing anything except a guarantee of employment for the entire paper industry.

Standing, she wrapped the robe more tightly around her body and paced, circling the small guest room twice before halting in front of the window.

Moonlight swept across the valley, outlining a jagged silhouette of distant hills, spraying treetops with gleaming silver. Hoisting the sill, she allowed the night chill to surge through the room. Kristin breathed deeply, taking in the flavors of the earth, fragrant pine and succulent hay, the sweetness of a nearly wild land. She tried to recall the ocean's salty tang, but the memory was fuzzy now, overwhelmed by new scents, new sounds. The rumbling crash of surf was buried beneath the symphony of a thousand crickets' songs, the comforting drone of traffic was forgotten, replaced by nightbirds warbling their love.

The home which had been her anchor, a place of security and peace, seemed now to be merely a faint memory. And that confused her.

Her soul had been opened this afternoon and she'd faced a horror that had been as much a part of her life as breathing, taming it to a vision of the past, where it belonged. And that awed her.

A man had held her with such compassion, such pure, unselfish love, that her heart felt his presence, even now. And that frightened her.

Brodie. It was two o'clock in the morning and here she stood, pacing the small room, her mind filled with thoughts of Nathan Brodie. She couldn't work, she couldn't sleep. Kristin almost wished she hadn't thrown her medication out. She would have felt lousy tomorrow morning, but at least she wouldn't be standing here tonight, aching to feel his arms around her.

This was ridiculous, she told herself firmly. Psychologically, it was only natural to feel a sense of gratitude, even a deep affection, for someone who had shown such kindness and caring. Perhaps she was again suffering from the dreaded disease infatuation. Yes, that was it. The only other time she'd found herself infatuated with a man, she'd married him. It was not the first disaster in her life, but it was certainly one of the biggest.

Infatuation. Once recognized, it could be handled. A childish emotion, of course, but one Kristin was certain she could deal with.

Yet this aching heat uncurling in the pit of her each time she visualized his face, remembered the touch of his hands—this was different. Her skin seemed to steam against the cold air, her stomach felt tight, yet she was empty inside, like a hollow jug.

A muffled sound filtered through the wall, footsteps in Brodie's room. Kristin froze, ears straining, relishing any sound he made as though hearing it was like seeing him, being with him. Closing her eyes, she tried to picture what he looked like now. Did he wear pajamas, or did he sleep nude? The image caused a delicious shudder. Was his bare chest glistening in the moonlight?

Another noise, a soft click followed by a faint squeak. A door opening? Was he, too, plagued by sleeplessness? Perhaps he was going to the kitchen for something. Kristin felt an immediate urge for a glass of milk. Would that be too obvious?

Of course it would.

A light knock on her bedroom door seemed to reverberate through the room like the rolling thunder of a pounding drum and Kristin jerked spasmodically, adrenalin squirting through her veins. Whirling, she clutched her robe to her throat and stared silently at the door, her heart thudding against her ribs.

The knob turned slowly and her gaze was riveted on its movement.

Then he filled the doorway, half shadowed, half golden, all man, skin shining across hard planes and curved muscles. Soft lamplight danced around his chest, skimming the tips of dark, curling hairs which contoured his body like an inverted pyramid, then disappeared into denim. His jeans had been hastily donned and Kristin saw the top snap was undone, allowing the cloth to gap open slightly.

His voice was tight, coiled as tautly as his bunched biceps. "Are you all right?"

She remained rigid, but managed to drag her gaze up to meet his. "Yes."

Brodie's eyes seemed to burn into her skin. "I heard you moving. You seemed . . . restless."

"I—I couldn't sleep." A stiff smile pulled at her lips. "You couldn't, either?"

"No." Stepping into the room, he closed the door behind him, then leaned against it, watching her. His gaze swept over her like a hot wind, yet she shivered against it, unable to look away. "I hear there's a blizzard in purgatory." His voice was soft, husky and very male. "Come to me, Kristin."

She wanted to. God, how she wanted to. "I can't," she whispered, then stepped closer anyway, as though in a trance. It was dreamlike, unreal, yet it was real. Air that had cooled her body moments earlier now fanned her with fingers of heat, and she felt a slick sheen film her skin.

His eyes seemed to glow like sapphires reflecting flame, faceted jewels that spoke silently to her mind, repeating the gentle command. *Come to me, Kristin.*

And she did.

So close, the scent of him surrounded her, dazed her. He smelled of earth and clouds, of sweet grass and musky passion. He could have reached out and touched her now, but he didn't. Instead, his eyes worshiped her, reflecting and sharing the treasure of her beauty.

And Kristin saw her own beauty reflecting from the indigo depths. For the first time in her life, she felt exquisite.

She was desirable, beautiful, sensuous. Brodie saw her smoky eyes darken with passion, her soft lips part, an unconscious invitation to taste paradise. Brodie balled his fists and held them rigidly at his sides to keep from grabbing her at that moment. If he touched her now, he would take her right there on the carpet. Control. He fought for control. It had to be Kristin's decision, he would take only what she offered, give what she needed.

He wanted her, God only knew how much. But more important, Brodie knew that he loved her. It had been so long since he had loved. Wanted, yes. Needed, yes. But never loved, never known the gut-tearing pain of having someone become so much a part of your body and mind, that her loss would amputate part of his very soul.

Kristin still clutched the bodice of her robe. Slowly, she released the bunched cloth and, trembling, extended one slim hand toward him, hesitantly touching the springy mat on his chest. She traced the muscular curves with her soft fingertips, then followed the dark ribbon until it disappeared. She paused at the zipper tab, feeling the cool metal as it was warmed by the heat of her skin.

A shudder racked Brodie's body, her silky touch tearing him with exquisite agony, filling him with astonishing desire. He closed his eyes tightly and brought his hands into fists, his flesh throbbing dangerously as he neared the summit of his restraint. He groaned, a low rumble of desperate need.

The zipper slipped slowly downward, followed by the soft slither of cloth as denim pooled at his feet. A tiny gasp escaped her as Kristin absorbed his beauty, the powerful strength of his desire.

His breath was as jagged as her own. "Take off your robe for me," he said huskily. "I want to see you."

Suddenly shy, Kristin lowered her eyelids demurely as she fumbled with the knotted sash of the robe. The cloth fell open, exposing a narrow strip of ivory skin from throat to thigh. With a graceful shrug, the terry cloth tumbled to the floor and she gave herself to his hungry gaze.

"You're beautiful," he whispered. She was like a silken statue, sleek and shining, yet gently curved. Small breasts peaked upward, round and firm, softly tipped with a coral blush. She was silver and moonlight. He was awed, as though in the presence of a goddess. "I want to touch you," he murmured.

Hesitating, Kristin raised her eyes to him and her heart melted. He wasn't going to grab at her, she realized. He was waiting for her permission, waiting for her to set the pace of their lovemaking. Kristin had never experienced this kind of consideration, this tenderness.

Reaching out, she took one of his fists, cradling it in her hand while she coaxed his stiff fingers to unwind. Laying his open palm on her breast, she felt her nipple harden at his touch. Her head toppled limply back as she moaned at the delicious sensation. She heard his sharp intake of breath, followed by a low groan as he brushed his flattened palm over her breast, then teased the rigid peak, grazing it with his knuckles.

"I want to love you, Kris." His voice was quiet, almost reverent as he slid his fingers lightly across her skin, circling her breasts, then exploring the curve of waist and hip. "I want to touch you everywhere, taste every inch of you."

She gasped when he tangled his fingers in her delicate feminine curls, yet went no farther. Sliding his hand to the small of

her back, he held her firmly as she writhed beneath his questing search.

He brought his lips to her hair and buried his face in the
silken strands. "Touch me," he urged gently. "Feel my desire
for you, feel how I need you." Responding, she eased her hand
slowly down his chest, then hesitated, teasing until he felt he
might explode from the pain. Suddenly, she was there, fluttering fingertips against his inflamed flesh, testing the strength of
his passion, curling around his warmth until, with a wrenching gasp, he grabbed her wrist. "Oh, God, Kris," he moaned.
"See what you do to me."

She tasted his neck, nipping sweetly, and delighted in the
quiver of his flesh under her mouth. "It's what I want to do to
you," she whispered, her voice low, throaty, filled with passion. "I want to drive you mad with desire, because you've already driven me mad. Make love to me, Brodie, and let me
make love to you."

The sensations were dizzying as he swooped her into his
arms, then laid her gently on the soft mattress, as though she
were made of fine china. He stretched beside her and she turned
to him, hungry for the feel of his body on hers, the taste of him.
Seeking the warmth of his lips, she brought her mouth across
his throat, her tongue flicking the rough texture, until, unable
to withstand the torture, he captured her with a searing kiss.

Lips touched, scorching. Tongues probed, questing, thrusting and withdrawing in a burning, aching love dance. Tiny cries
of pleasure and moans of delight were swallowed, consumed by
the driving hunger. Thought suspended, the world belonged to
touch, to taste, to scents of passion.

Brodie's whispered words promised ecstasy, then his lips and
his hands fulfilled the promise. Kristin was soaring, whirling in
a sea of desire unlike anything she'd ever experienced.

And still he teased her, bringing his mouth to her breast,
flicking his tongue across the sensitive nipple until she cried out
for release. He brushed the inside of her thighs, with the
roughened pads of his fingertips, tracing the silken triangle, yet
never quite touching the secret part of her that begged for his
caress.

As though he read her thoughts, Brodie brushed her ear with his lips. "Show me, honey. Show me what you need."

He had to know, her mind screamed. He had to know that her body was throbbing, empty, begging for him to complete her, release her from the clawing pain.

She felt him shudder against her and knew his need was as great as hers, yet he still held back. For her, she realized.

He rested his hand low on her abdomen, and she covered it with her own, then urged it lower, gasping as he slid his fingers down to touch her moist warmth. Brodie moaned into her mouth, claiming it with his tongue as his fingers possessed her body.

"Love me," she whispered against his lips. "Please, please love me."

The weight of him pressed on her, hot, slick, smooth as polished stone beneath her fingers. She opened herself, emitting a whimper of pleasure as the heat of his arousal nestled at her threshold. She arched against him, but he held back, giving her only a trace of what she so desperately wanted, then withdrawing. She cried out at the loss, raising herself to recapture his strength.

With a groan of surrender, Brodie thrust deeply, sheathing himself in her softness. Then Kristin's world whirled purple, violet mist revolving around her, encircling her with a sweet torment that swept through her so intensely that she felt her very soul had been fused.

White lights exploded, glittering diamonds flashing through her brain as her body contracted, then seemed to burst into a thousand electric sparks.

It was mystical, it was real. It was spiritual, it was flesh-and-blood. And it was the end of Kristin's carefully constructed wall. Her emotional barricade had just been hurdled.

Chapter Ten

Where's the guilt?

Hairbrush poised in midair, Kristin studied her reflection in the dresser mirror. The woman smiling back had new sparkle to her eyes, a glow to her skin, some intangible inner illumination and yet, she showed no trace of remorse. Logically she should feel all those things, Kristin decided. Guilt, remorse, even shame.

Since her failed marriage, Kristin had scrupulously avoided intimate relationships, preferring instead to end friendships that appeared to be heading toward a romantic conclusion. More significant was the knowledge that she had broken her own strict professional code of ethics.

So why in the world did she feel like hanging out the window and singing a rousing chorus of "Oh, What A Beautiful Morning"?

The fact was that she'd further complicated an already complex case by becoming emotionally involved with Brodie.

Highly improper, to be sure, but her instincts insisted that she'd never done anything so right, so utterly and absolutely proper, in her entire life. In Brodie's arms, Kristin had felt a deep, profound sense of belonging, of coming home.

Brodie. Her lips curved at his mental image. Powerful yet gentle, caring and loving, giving of himself to help the kids society wanted to throw away. Her heart leaped at the thought of him, her brain whirled at the sight of him, she was intensely, completely and totally... emotionally involved.

Emotionally involved.

A frown marred her serenity as she considered the dry, colorless words. The words were factual enough, but they didn't even begin to describe the feelings that boiled deep inside her, the sweet ache squeezing her insides. Exactly what *was* she feeling?

Kristin dropped the hairbrush on the dresser and turned her attention to tidying the rumpled bed. She didn't want to analyze her feelings this morning, she simply wanted to enjoy them. Fluffing the pillows, she gave in to the urge and buried her face in the downy softness, inhaling Brodie's earthy scent. Memories washed over her, flooding her mind with sweet sensations and her body reacted with renewed yearning.

She wished he was still with her.

But he wasn't. He'd been gone when she had awakened, and Kristin hadn't been surprised when she had seen how late she'd slept. After all, Brodie had work to do, she reminded herself firmly, and, if she was quite through swooning around like some kind of starry-eyed adolescent, so did she.

Still, Kristin found herself humming as she bounced down the stairs toward the kitchen.

"Ah, Missy Kristin, you rest well?" Oaf was up to his blocky elbows in soapsuds. As Kristin slid onto the polished oak bench, he wiped his wet arms on his apron and announced, "You are needing breakfast."

"No, thank you, Oaf." Kristin wasn't the least bit hungry. In fact, she felt as sated and content as if she'd just downed a six-course feast. "Coffee would be just fine."

Unconvinced, Oaf frowned. "You must eat. You are skinny."

Kristin smiled. Obviously one couldn't worry about tact while still in the throes of mastering a new language. "I'm fine, Oaf. Really. Coffee is all I need this morning."

Forehead puckering with doubt, Oaf nonetheless fetched a large coffee mug and filled it, clucking his disapproval. She sipped the hot liquid carefully. It was rich and strong, just the way she liked it. "Wonderful, Oaf. I've never tasted coffee as good as yours."

Oaf beamed. "Ja." He jammed his hands back into the dishwater, which sloshed over the edge of a sink barely large enough to contain his bulky fists. "Ja, coffee is good."

"How long have you been here, Oaf?"

"Here?" His fat lips pursed, then he brightened. "Oh, *here*. Two years. Mr. Brodie brought Oaf first," he added proudly.

"You've been here at New Wave since the beginning, then?"

Nodding enthusiastically, Oaf said, "Ja. Oaf came first."

Kristin considered that. "Do you mean Brodie hired you before he hired Gus and the other ranch hands?"

Grin broadening to display a row of incredibly tiny teeth, Oaf's round head bobbed with pleasure. "Ja. First."

Amused by the big man's delight, Kristin said, "Well, everyone has to eat. Personally, I think your job is just about the most important one on the ranch."

"Important?" He thought a moment, as though translating the word, then lit up. "Ja! Important," he said triumphantly. "*Most* important." He slammed a fist into the sink for emphasis. A tidal wave of foamy, gray water crested and shattered, sheeting walls and windows and flooding the tiled floor.

Tiny blue eyes blinked as Oaf inspected the result of his enthusiasm. A cluster of soapy bubbles slid from smooth cheek to round chin and Kristin choked in an attempt to stifle her laughter.

Somewhat subdued, Oaf wiped listlessly at his apron, soggy ruffles limply dripping into the growing puddle at his feet. His timid smile was endearing and he issued a sheepish shrug. "To cook is important," he said sedately.

Kristin's lips were pressed into a tight, quivering line and she held them together with her teeth. Not trusting her voice, she managed only an agreeable nod.

Satisfied, Oaf returned to his duties and Kristin concentrated on her coffee mug until she'd regained control.

She cleared her throat, testing it. "Ah, where do you come from, Oaf? I mean, what country were you born in?"

"I am Danish," he said proudly. "My papa made pastry, the finest in all of Copenhagen."

"So that's where you got your talent." He stared at her blankly and Kristin hastened to explain. "Cooking. Did you learn to cook from your father?"

Oaf looked genuinely surprised. "No."

"Oh. Well, then where did you learn to cook so well?"

"McDoo-nalds." He grinned. "I cook the Big Mac."

The answer caught her midswallow and she was seized by a coughing spasm. Wiping at her watery eyes, she regarded the exuberant, childlike hulk who stood before her, obviously exceptionally pleased with himself.

"Well, ah, you certainly have expanded your repertoire over the years," she mumbled.

"Ja," Oaf agreed happily, then swung his attention to the back door as it creaked open. Following his gaze, Kristin saw Todd peeking tentatively into the kitchen.

"Come in, Todd." She patted the bench beside her. "Have you got time before school?"

"Uh…yeah, but…just a minute." Todd ducked out of sight behind the door and Kristin heard muffled voices. In a moment, Todd was standing across the table from her, shuffling uncomfortably. "I just wanted to, you know, 'pologize." He stared intently at his scuffed sneakers.

"Apologize for what, Todd?"

"You know, the dog and all. I'm real sorry he scared you." Todd looked up and his round eyes seemed to plead with her. "He's really a good dog, honest. He's hurt, that's all, you know?"

"I know. Brodie told me." She took a deep breath. "I guess I kind of owe you an apology, too." Perplexed, Todd's nose wrinkled and Kristin hurried on. "I'm certain you realize that you should have gotten Brodie's permission before you brought the dog here, but I really shouldn't have gone into your room. I guess you could say we're even."

Todd brightened. "Yeah, well it's cool. I mean, like you could've let Brodie send Butch back to the clinic and all."

"Butch? Ah, yes, Butch."

"Yeah, well, Butch doesn't like people much." He grinned proudly. "He likes me, though. Doc Amatti said I was the very best person to take care of him until his leg gets better."

"That's what I heard."

"Anyway, Butch...well, he's sorry, too. I talked to him about it, you know?" Todd's face was solemn. "He's right outside."

Kristin stiffened and tried to keep her voice calm. "Is he?"

"Yeah, and I thought...like if you met each other, then maybe neither one of you'd be so scared."

"I see. Yes, well, I wouldn't want to, umm, upset Butch again, Todd." With shaky hands, she raised the mug to her lips, swallowing the cold coffee without tasting it. "Perhaps another time."

"He's on a leash," Todd insisted.

Standing quickly, Kristin backed away from the table. "You know Brodie said the dog wouldn't be allowed in the house, Todd. I—I wouldn't want either one of us to get into trouble again."

Her heart pounded on her ribs as though attempting escape and she couldn't seem to get enough air. Todd's disappointment gnawed at her, but Kristin couldn't help it. She couldn't, simply *couldn't* be in the same room with that ferocious beast.

"Yeah, okay." He pushed at the floor with the toe of his shoe, then slumped toward the back door.

"Todd?" The boy stopped, looking up expectantly. "Perhaps if you and, ah, Butch stayed outside..." She paused to wet her lips. "That is, if I stood on the back porch, then you could, uh, introduce us."

"Yeah! That'd be awesome!" Todd vaulted through the door.

Legs trembling, Kristin followed like a convicted felon on her way to the gallows. If only the boy hadn't seemed so desperate for her to make friends with his dog, if only he hadn't seemed so desolate when she'd refused . . . if only she wasn't such a damned fool, Kristin decided, she wouldn't be in this lousy predicament.

Peering cautiously out the back door, Kristin saw that Todd had kept his word. He was standing in the yard a good twenty feet from the back porch. Even so, Kristin was grateful the porch was elevated. She kept her hand firmly on the door-knob, determined to leap back into the kitchen and bolt the door at the first sign of trouble.

The dog, however, was not with Todd. "Is this far enough?" the boy called. Kristin nodded and Todd jammed two fingers in his mouth and emitted a piercing shriek. From her vantage point, Kristin saw Ernie step from behind the house into the yard, tugging on the long rope. Then *it* appeared on the end of that rope—huge, frightening, dragging one of its front paws. She tightened her hand on the knob as icy sweat gathered on her upper lip.

Ernie led the animal across the yard, handing the end of the rope to Todd. The dog was indeed very large, but seated doc-ilely beside the youngster, it didn't appear as big as Kristin remembered. Nor was it solid black, sporting instead a sleek, rather mottled gray-brown coat. The dog's front leg was wrapped in white from paw to shoulder and Kristin realized that the scraping noise she'd heard coming from Todd's room must have been the sound of the dog dragging that heavy cast across the wooden floor.

"This here's Butch," Todd announced, then promptly kneeled, tossed his arm carelessly around the dog's neck and carried on an animated, if one-sided, conversation with the animal. Kristin couldn't hear what the boy was saying, but he pointed in her direction occasionally and the dog dutifully fol-lowed Todd's gesture, focusing beady brown eyes directly on her. It looked hungry.

Finally, the dog gave Todd a single, sloppy lick and the boy stood, beaming. "He understands now, and he won't bother you no more."

"Uh, thank you." Kristin watched Todd happily lead the limping animal back to the bunkhouse and concluded that she'd finally lost her mind entirely. Yes, indeed. Kristin's mental trolley had finally slipped off its little track and she was quite obviously deranged. There was simply no other explanation for participating in this little charade and, Todd's assurances notwithstanding, Kristin had no intention of *ever* going near that animal again. Even twenty feet had been too close.

By the time she returned to the kitchen, Oaf was busily slathering bread slices with mayonnaise and the steam rising from her mug signaled that it had been refilled with fresh, hot coffee.

She sipped the coffee gratefully, then shifted her attention to Oaf. "Isn't eight in the morning a bit early to start lunch?" she inquired.

"Brodie says you will leave soon, so must make lunch early." Oaf's nose wrinkled. "You like the ham with the cheese?"

"I beg your pardon?"

"The ham," he repeated, wiggling a thin, pink slice in her direction. "You like the ham with the cheese, or no with the cheese?"

"Oh. Well, with cheese, but . . ."

"Ah, good. Is better with the cheese."

"Yes, but I still don't understand. What exactly did Brodie say?"

Oaf looked puzzled, then brightened. "Brodie say with the cheese, too."

Sighing, Kristin rubbed at her head. "I meant, why did Brodie say I'd be leaving soon."

Shrugging, Oaf wiped his big hands across the apron and reached for a leafy head of lettuce. "Brodie says to make for a picnic and that you leave soon, so I put food in this—" he tapped a large wicker basket on the counter "—so you can carry." Oaf grinned. "Is okay?"

A picnic? Quickly performing a sandwich count, Kristin realized that Oaf had prepared a meal for two. She and Brodie would be going alone. Alone. A small, secretive smile played upon her lips. "Yes, it's okay," she purred. "It is most definitely okay."

The sky was blue, threaded with high, thin clouds and as the truck bounced over the rutted dirt road, Kristin realized she was happier than she'd ever believed possible. Brodie steered around a particularly deep pothole, surreptitiously watching Kristin out of the corner of his eye. She'd been studying the strong lines of his profile and grinned when she caught his sly glance.

With a deep breath and a muttered oath, Brodie crushed the brake pedal, jarring the truck to a halt, then turned off the engine.

"Come here, woman," he growled, hauling her across the wide bench seat until she was snugly cradled beneath his arm. "That's more like it," he murmured against her lips. "I want you close to me."

Her lips parted provocatively as she trailed a fingertip lightly across his face and whispered, "How close?"

Capturing her in a searching kiss, Brodie answered her question, wrapping her in his arms and fusing her body to his. She responded instantly, arching against his hard chest, tangling her fingers in his hair. Her questing hands dislodged his hat but Kristin ignored it, needing only to hold him closer.

The fires within were erupting, bursting into searing need as they twisted in the tight confines of the cab until the steering wheel responded to the pressure of Brodie's elbow with a shrill horn blast.

Startled, Brodie released her with a muffled curse.

Kristin pushed at her hair and blinked out at the deserted road, confused and a bit disoriented. "What happened?"

Brodie's hands shook slightly as he tugged his hat back into position. "This truck wasn't exactly designed for passionate encounters," he muttered, then gave Kristin a rather embarrassed smile. "I thought I'd outgrown back-seat wrestling matches, but I can't seem to keep my hands off you."

Kristin leaned toward him until her lips brushed his ear and she felt his frame quiver at the touch. "This is the front seat, but you're right, we're both much too adult for this kind of thing," she whispered, softly nipping his earlobe. "You'll simply have to learn how to control your crude carnal urges."

Shuddering under the sweet assault of her mouth, Brodie grated, "If you keep doing that, you're going to find out just how crude my carnal urges are."

Feigning shock, Kristin said, "Oh, my. Is that a threat?"

A wicked smile curved his mouth as he assessed her lazily. "You keep nibbling my ear, honey, and you'll know soon enough." With a flick of his wrist, the truck engine roared to life. "You might just like it."

Kristin settled back in the seat, snuggling against Brodie's broad shoulder as he swung the truck onto the road. "I might at that," she murmured, and saw him smile.

Completely relaxed, Kristin allowed herself to enjoy Brodie's warm strength. It felt natural to lean against him. "Brodie?"

"Hmm."

"Have you seen any of Ernie's drawings?"

"Drawings? What kind of drawings?"

"If you'd ever seen them, you wouldn't have to ask." She shifted and sat up. "He showed me some of his work. Pencil sketches, mostly, animals, a few portraits." The truck bounced over a rock and Kristin grabbed at the dashboard to steady herself.

"Sorry," Brodie mumbled, straightening the wheel. "I didn't know Ernie had any hobbies."

"I think it's more than a hobby." Her voice was serious. "He's good, Brodie, exceptionally good."

"Really?" His interest had been piqued. "I'd like to see these pictures."

"Drawings," Kristin corrected. "Or sketches or renderings. Pictures come from a camera, art comes from the soul."

"A thousand pardons," he muttered, but slid her a respectful glance. "How is it he showed these, ah, drawings to you?"

"I stumbled across one he was working on and cajoled him into letting me see some others." Her expression was thoughtful. "You know, he's never had a single lesson. Without professional instruction, his potential could be severely limited."

"Why do I feel like I'm being herded into a one-cow chute?" Brodie complained, but his smile was tolerant. "Spit it out, Kris. What's on your mind?"

Scooching sideways on the seat, she faced him. "I'd love to see him enrolled in the high school art program. He could pay for the supplies he needs out of his wages." She paused. "I mean, the portion he receives, of course."

"A tactful retreat," Brodie mumbled, then quietly considered her request. "I don't see any problem with a few art classes."

"Great." She was pleased with Brodie's acquiescence, but had one more bridge to cross. "About the trust fund..." She hesitated, seeing his wary expression.

"What about it?" Cautiously, Brodie waited for the other shoe to drop.

"Nothing, really, it's just that, well, the money has been set aside for the boys' education, right?"

"Right." What was she up to?

"There's all kinds of education, isn't there? I mean, besides a regular university there are trade schools and specialty colleges... you know what I mean," she finished, with a helpless gesture.

So that's it. Biting back a smile, Brodie said, "I think so. You'd like Ernie to use his scholarship for some kind of special art school."

"As an option, if he really has the talent to make a career out of it."

"I don't know..."

"It would be a wonderful incentive," she coaxed.

Brodie's mouth pursed as he pretended to contemplate her request. He had no intention of denying it. In fact, he thought it was a fine idea and was pleased that she cared enough about Ernie to have put so much thought into his future.

The sight of Kristin's anxious face convinced Brodie that he'd feigned indecision long enough and he ended her torment. "You're right. It would be an incentive for Ernie to know the option was available." Kristin's face lit with immense relief. "Why don't you tell him tonight?"

"Absolutely not." She looked genuinely shocked. "You should tell him."

"Why? The idea of an art scholarship option is yours. You should take credit for it."

"Without you, Nathan Brodie, Ernie would have no options at all." So said, Kristin snuggled back into the curve of his arm.

About three miles before they reached the highway, Brodie turned onto a road that seemed to ribbon up into the mountains flanking the ranch. Kristin felt the word "road" seemed a bit pretentious for the two skinny grooves they were following.

"I gather this little path doesn't see a lot of activity," she commented.

"It's primarily a riding trail." Jerking the wheel sharply, he avoided a large rock blocking the path. "Usually, we ride horseback up to Campton Creek, but I thought you'd prefer the truck."

"Oh, yes." Not much doubt about that.

"We'll have a bit farther to walk, but I figured you could tough it out."

"Umm, I think I can manage."

"Good. I can't carry both you and the lunch. Of course," he hastened to add, "if I had to make a choice, I'd certainly take you."

Kristin's eyebrow arched. "What a sport."

"I thought you'd be pleased to know that."

"Delighted," she said dryly. "I can't remember when I've been so highly complimented."

The path had all but disappeared into a line of slightly flattened weeds when Brodie pulled to a stop. "End of the road," he announced. "We walk."

Reaching behind the seat, Brodie pulled out a hunting rifle and shouldered it, sliding his arm through the canvas sling. Kristin stared at the weapon and Brodie noticed her discomfort. "Ever fire one of these?" he asked, lifting the picnic basket from the truckbed.

"No." Her reply was curt. "I've never found it necessary to arm myself for a picnic."

"This is just to discourage uninvited guests."

Her eyes widened. "I've always used ant spray."

Brodie laughed. "I'll admit Mariposa ants don't take no for an answer, but I haven't had to shoot one yet. This is in case we get any four-footed party crashers."

The images that comment evoked did little to quell Kristin's clammy palms.

"Don't worry. I doubt if we'll need it, but a rifle is the American Express Card of the wilderness. We don't leave home without it."

She smiled sickly and Brodie gestured toward the tiny footpath into the forest. He lifted her hand, kissed it, and led her into the wilderness.

Although the hike took nearly a half hour, Kristin took one look at Campton Creek and proclaimed it the most beautiful place in the world. From the rise above them, a crystalline cascade splashed over a nest of granite boulders, pooling into the clear waters of the creek below. At the base of the waterfall, a small green meadow was carved into the forest of mossy oak and poplar.

"Oh, I can see why you love it. It's breathtaking," she said, kicking off her shoes and wriggling her toes in the lush meadow grass.

Brodie spread a large, colorful quilt on the thick turf then stretched out, tilting his hat over his face and tucking his arms behind his head.

Kristin watched in disbelief. "What are you doing?"

"Resting," he drawled.

"*Resting?* This is a picnic, not a slumber party." Playfully, she kicked at the soles of his boots. "How could you possibly take a nap in the midst of all this natural beauty?"

"I had a rather strenuous night," he pointed out, his voice somewhat muffled by the hat. "And *I* didn't sleep in until half the morning was gone."

Kristin snatched the offending hat. "Strenuous, was it?"

"Hey! Give me my hat."

Kristin waltzed across the soft grass. "Perhaps, Nathan Brodie, you're getting too old for such athletic endeavors." She plopped the hat on her head and it promptly settled to the middle of her eyes. "Over the hill at thirty-five? Tsk, tsk. I'm *so* disappointed."

She danced to the edge of the creek and dunked her big toe in the icy water. "Good grief, that water's cold."

"If you get that hat wet, woman, you'll find yourself up to your cute little armpits in that cold water," he warned.

Undaunted, Kristin snatched the hat from her head, pretending to examine it carefully. "My, my. We're just full of threats today, aren't we?" She grinned brightly. "You know, this would make a swell Frisbee."

"Don't even think about it."

"Catch!" The suede Stetson sailed for only a few seconds before looping sickly and plummeting into a thick, sprawling blackberry bush at the edge of the forest. "Ooops."

Muttering colorful descriptions of exactly what he'd like to do with her for that stunt, Brodie fought the thorny bush for possession of his prized hat. After he'd retrieved it, he moaned loudly and clutched at his hand.

Alarmed, Kristin sobered instantly. "What's wrong?"

Brodie dropped to his knees, still moaning as though he were in horrible pain. "Oh no," Kristin whispered, sprinting and skidding beside him. Her eyes were wide with fear as she threw her arms around his shoulders. "Where are you hurt?" she demanded.

With a movement more rapid than the flick of a bee's wing, Brodie grabbed Kristin's waist and they tumbled to the ground in a tangled, sprawling heap. He laughed at her stunned expression, then scooped her up in his arms and carried her toward the waterfall.

"It's not a question of where I'm hurt, my sassy little wench, but rather a question of where *you're* going to hurt when I'm done with you."

Kristin looked from the shimmering curtain of frigid water to the amused, but determined, set of Brodie's jaw, and blanched. "You wouldn't."

His eyebrow lifted. "No?"

She wound her arms around his neck in a death grip. "If I go, you go."

Lips pursed thoughtfully, Brodie seemed to cogitate the consequences before giving her an evil grin. "It'll be worth it," he said, then plunged into the icy shower as Kristin squealed in his ear.

Brodie's breath caught with a tight hiss as the frigid water swirled around his hips and pounded chilled needles into his scalp. The soft breasts writhing against him shot a blast of hot electricity through him, mingling with cold to envelope him in a blanket of steam. He felt Kristin's hands tangle in his hair, the tiny serration of her teeth nip playfully at his neck. An inner warmth spread downward, oozing through his blood, turning chill to hunger.

Kristin felt his shudder as she traced the sensitive rim of his ear with her tongue. He buried his lips in the curve of her neck and she felt his breath, hot and sweet, caressing her throat.

He groaned. "Honey, you're frying me."

"But I've just learned how to cook." She tugged at his earlobe. "I need more practice."

"Any more practice and we'll both be poached and fricasseed." Lowering her more deeply into the icy stream, he allowed the rising water to emphasize his point. "Or drowned."

"Right," she gasped, sputtering and tightening her grip on his neck as a rumbling chuckle rolled across his chest.

Sloughing out of the stream, Brodie carried her to the small meadow effortlessly, as though she weighed no more than a whisper. He laid her gently on the quilt, tracing the line of her jaw and throat with the pad of his fingertip as his eyes darkened into blue-rimmed, fathomless orbs, speaking his desire more eloquently than any sweet utterance.

She felt his passion, saw raw hunger in his eyes and her body responded, rippling at his touch, turning toward his warmth. She tangled with the wet cloth of his shirt, tugging until she heard the soft click of snaps and the fabric fell open, allowing her access to the hard, furred muscles beneath. She scratched lightly across his nipples and smiled as his heart raced under her hands.

For a few brief, glorious moments, she would allow herself to feel. Tomorrow would come soon enough. Today—now— was all she had, all anybody had, really. Kristin released herself to the sensations of heat uncurling in her core, pushing her mind away, seeking the sweet oblivion of a passion she'd never experienced before Brodie, never needed to experience.

With a swift movement, they rolled together, leaving the quilted fabric for the natural blanket of the meadow. Supple grass blades tickled her naked back as Brodie swept her wet cotton blouse away with an easy stroke of his hand. Shrugging his own shirt off, he buried his lips in the pulsing hollow at the base of her throat, tracing the softness with his tongue, then moving lower, drinking fat drops of creek water from her skin, replacing it with his own, intimate wetness.

Her breasts hardened under the sweet assault of his mouth, and a sound curled from her lips, a soft moan that could have been his name. When his cheek brushed against her belly, rough against soft, sandpaper on satin, she gasped, her legs flexing in unconscious welcome.

"I love how you respond to me." His voice was husky with passion, his breath hot against her sensitized skin. "When I touch you here—" his tongue slipped into her navel and he felt her body contract as she whimpered helplessly "—you turn to fire under my hands. I want to bury myself in you, make love with you until the world explodes, until the nightmares are gone and your mind and your body are filled only with me."

"Yes." Her head rocked and she moaned as his fingers grazed a burning, feather-light trail along her inner thighs. "Yes," she repeated, whispering, ignoring the quiet warning in her mind, the soft, insistent voice urging her to think of tomorrow, remember yesterday. Those she'd loved had left her, those she'd trusted had betrayed her and yet, even as her mind acknowledged the inevitable truth, she opened herself to accept him knowing that, in future days she would relive the pain of the past.

A shadow blocked the sun's spray of hot light as Brodie moved over her, a silhouette of potent power eclipsing the sky's brightness. She reached for him, welcoming, wanting.

He filled her slowly, powerfully and she arched to meet him, fusing with his searing heat, melting under the force of her own liquid passion. Rocking with a primal rhythm as old as time yet uniquely their own, they rose together as two ethereal souls merging for eternity.

Suspended, she seemed to levitate, drifting in a universe of sensations almost painful in their exquisite torment. Then she cried out as he shuddered, her eyes snapping open in the midst of their mutual climax to savor his face at this moment, and seeing his features lit as though the earth now glowed with celestial fire, casting their images back to the heavens, their shadows on the sun.

Slowly, the white-hot light of passion faded into sweet contentment. They lay together, bodies in full-length embrace, entwined like fibers in a tightly woven rope. Kristin emitted a soft whimper of protest as Brodie stirred.

Smoothing his hand over her back, he caressed her spine with the ball of his thumb. In the unforgiving sunlight, Brodie saw the thin white scars crossing her forearms. The accident had been more extensive, caused more damage than he had realized. He felt a surge of protectiveness, of anger that she'd been forced to endure so much. With exquisite tenderness he caressed her nape. Nothing would hurt her like that again, he decided. He simply wouldn't allow it.

"I'm going to see if our clothes are dry." He nipped lightly at her shoulder. "I wouldn't want you to get sunburned somewhere, umm, sensitive."

A groggy mumble filtered from the crook of his shoulder where Kristin's head was comfortably nestled. Smiling, Brodie cupped her chin and lifted her lips for a deep, sweet kiss, then he eased from her sleepy embrace, lowering her head gently to the ground. She stretched languidly, starting at the swishing plop of her clothes as they landed in a heap next to her head. With a grunt, she pushed them impatiently away. She felt entirely too warm, too free, to be bothered with the confining restrictions of cloth.

A low chuckle echoed over the rush of the waterfall. "That's fine with me, honey. I like the view just the way it is." Blinking, she squinted up at Brodie's smug grin. "And I'll just love rubbing the sunburn lotion over every little peak—" his eyes swept from her breasts downward "—and valley."

"Tyrant." Kristin grabbed at the wadded garments and dressed, lost in thought. No one had made her feel like this before and she couldn't recognize her own behavior. She'd made love with Brodie, wild, magnificent love, in a green meadow beside a bubbling waterfall and then wanted to spend the rest of the afternoon lounging naked in the grass.

She was happy. Too happy. Happiness foretold loss. A lonely childhood and the disillusionment of divorce had taught that lesson. Kristin's mood sobered. Her job here would soon be completed. She would go back to the city to pursue her dreams and Brodie would go on pursuing his.

Kristin realized that she'd let herself care too much for Brodie. She felt suddenly vulnerable and frightened.

Brodie settled on the quilt beside her. His expression was serious. "You're special, Kris. The only thing all the women I've known ever wanted from me were sweet words, a roll between the sheets and a gold ring through my nose. Not one of them cared about my work or those kids, and not one of them was worth the polish on one of your pink fingernails."

"Brodie, I . . ."

"Ssshhh." Gently, he caressed her lips with his fingers, wiping away her whispered protest. "You understand me, Kris, and you understand these boys. We're alike, you and I. Our lives are devoted to these kids, to making their lives better, offering alternatives to their poverty. They need you. *I* need you." His voice dropped to a hoarse whisper. "Stay with me, Kris. Don't go back to L.A."

Stunned, Kristin sat stiffly, as though she'd been cast in concrete. "I—I can't . . . my work—"

Brodie interrupted. "Your work is here, don't you see? Think of what we could accomplish together, what we could build for these kids."

"New Wave is *your* dream, Brodie, not mine."

"It could be yours, Kris."

Kristin's stomach twisted. The ranch was her nightmare. It forced her to confront every emotion, every weakness that had lain dormant since her childhood. Those feelings rushed at her now, joined by a sweet ache that warned of future pain. She was losing control of her emotions, Kristin realized. Brodie had become too special, her feelings for him ran too deep. It was dangerous. It was frightening.

Now Brodie was asking her to abandon everything she'd worked for over a lifetime—her career, her independence, her home—for a few more moments in the sun. Eventually, those moments would end, they always did. In one way or another, Kristin had always been abandoned by the people she'd loved.

"No," she said. "I have to go back."

"I see." Hard eyes glinted from beneath hooded lids. "Sweet words and a roll between the sheets. Everything but the gold ring."

She blanched. "You don't believe that."

His expression turned bleak. "No, I don't." Silently, he cursed himself for rushing her, frightening her away. He should have waited, given her more time to be involved with the boys, learn to care for them as he did. Time. He needed more time to convince her that the New Wave could be her dream, too, if she would let it. "I guess we'll just have to make the most of the time we have left."

Brodie folded the quilt and gathered the forgotten picnic basket. Reaching out, he laced his fingers with hers and silently, Kristin followed him down the footpath toward the truck. It was a long, quiet drive back to the ranch. Brodie's hurt and confusion at her refusal to stay was a tangible, throbbing wound pulsing through the small truck cab.

When they arrived at the main house, Oaf greeted Kristin at the door with a message to call her office immediately. As soon as she was able to excuse herself and duck into the relative privacy of Brodie's office, she dialed the familiar number. Bob Sherwood's voice came on the line.

"Hey, kid. How's it going?"

"Fine, Bob. I should be finished in a few days."

"Great." His voice lowered slightly. "Are you sitting down?"

Kristin became instantly alert. "Did you find something?"

He chuckled richly. "Let's just say that Nathan Brodie isn't the only one with contacts in high places. You see, I've got a little, er, acquaintance in the Court Records Department, and—"

"Get to the point." The hairs on her nape were standing straight up and her voice had uncharacteristic bite.

"Uh . . . sure. You all right, Kris?"

"I'm fine," she said through clamped teeth. "What did you find out?"

"I could hardly believe it myself, but there it was, and the file was sealed by the Honorable Judge Markham himself."

"Bob!" Kristin's patience was stretched thin and threatening to snap, but she made an effort to control her voice. "Why was the file sealed, Bob?"

Sherwood took a deep breath, exhaling into the receiver. "Honey, Nathan Brodie was convicted of assault and battery two years ago. He nearly killed a man with his bare hands."

Chapter Eleven

The telephone receiver slid from Kristin's cold palm to its cradle with an echoing clatter. She stared blankly at the instrument. If Brodie had done such a thing, there had to be a reason, something Sherwood hadn't unearthed. Bob had offered no real details of the incident. Something was definitely amiss.

Nathan Brodie was kind and gentle, a man who had devoted his life to caring for society's rejected youth. He had comforted her with softness and sensitivity, had made love to her with exquisite tenderness and fierce passion.

Perhaps Sherwood's information was wrong. After all, Brodie had been subjected to a thorough background check. He never could have gained guardianship of the boys if he'd been convicted of a felony.

"You don't give up, do you?" Brodie's voice grated through the silence like fingernails on a blackboard. He knew she hadn't seen him appear in the office doorway, where he'd stood, listening. She winced at his acrid tone, and her desolate expression knifed him. He softened. "Find what you were looking for?"

His answer was a slow shake of her head as she raised her eyes, displaying disillusionment, her bewilderment. With a sound that could have been a groan, or a muffled curse, Brodie stepped into the room and swung the door shut behind him. He leaned against the door frame, closing his eyes to blot out her shattered expression. He absently kneaded the throbbing knots forming at the base of his skull.

Kristin's voice was no more than a whisper. "Is it a mistake?"

When he opened his eyes, meeting hers with unwavering intensity, Kristin's breath hissed out. She had her answer. "Why didn't you tell me?"

Brodie sounded tired. "You didn't need to know, honey. It's not something I'm particularly proud of."

"Didn't need to know?" Her eyes flashed. *"Didn't need to know?"* Her back stiffened on each clearly enunciated word. "You want me to put a stamp of approval on a dozen more vulnerable kids, you ask me to give up my career and stay here with you to work with those kids, and you tell me I didn't need to know that you nearly killed a man with your bare hands?" Kristin was standing now, palms flat on the desk, her entire body quivering with each word, voice husky with leashed emotion. "My God, Brodie. How could you *not* tell me?"

"Because I didn't want to lose you," he said simply.

Deep grooves bracketed his tight lips and stress lines creased beneath his eyes. Kristin felt a hot mass rise from her chest to lodge painfully in her throat. It hurt to breathe. It hurt to see him so defeated, so exposed. She wanted to throw her arms around him and say it didn't matter, to kiss away his pain, his desolation.

She wanted to, but she wouldn't. Facts, not instincts.

Lowering herself shakily back into the creaky swivel chair, she stared sightlessly at the scarred desktop. "Tell me. Please."

In the silence that followed, she heard only his breathing and the pounding of her own heart.

"All right." Weariness etched his tone. "It was the night Martin Alvarez was killed."

She raised her eyes then, watching him, remembering his agony when he'd shared that experience with her at the barbecue. "That was also the night you resigned from the Probation Department, wasn't it?"

Nodding bleakly, he looked beyond her, fixing his glazed stare on some invisible point in time, remembering what he didn't want to remember. "I cleaned out my desk and walked out. The night was hot. I smelled blood in the air and felt sick, but I couldn't go back to my apartment." He paused, his lips twisted. "Martin had been there that afternoon. He'd been excited about the scholarship he'd just won..." Blinking, Brodie turned his attention toward Kristin as though he'd just recalled she was there. "Did I tell you how bright Martin was?"

Kristin nodded.

"He was a crackerjack in school, smart as they come. He wanted to be a doctor." A sad smile. "A brain surgeon, no less. Martin didn't fool around. He always wanted to be the best and he was." The smile faded. "I couldn't face going home, so I decided to get good and drunk first. Roaring drunk, in fact. Blind, stinking, puke-all-night, drunk."

The bitterness in his voice tore at Kristin. "People have gotten drunk with a lot less motivation than you had that night," she said softly.

His laugh was dry and humorless. "Maybe so, but damn few have made such a lousy job of it." Groaning, he dragged his fingers through his hair. "I hit that bar looking for trouble and I found it. The place was a dive, but it had the standard over-the-bar television set. By the time the news came on, I was whacked to the gills but not so far gone I can't remember everything that happened. I wish I could forget, but I can't."

Kristin found herself standing in front of Brodie, lacing her fingers together to keep from wrapping herself around him. "What happened then?" she asked, not wanting to know but realizing she had to hear it as much as he had to tell it. We all have our nightmares, she realized. This was Brodie's.

"Suddenly, it was all there again, on the TV screen, in bloody, living color. Martin, sprawled across the sidewalk while his mama screamed over his body, some white-toothed, slick-haired reporter trying to shove a mike in her face while they bag up her son...'' His eyes narrowed into an expression as hard as steel. "Then this fat, sluglike bastard next to me laughs and says, 'Good riddance. That's one less spick in the world.'"

"My God," Kristin whispered.

Face impassive now, Brodie's voice became an expressionless monotone. "I wanted to kill him, and I nearly did."

Neither was aware of the pressure of her fingernails digging into his arm. "Oh, Brodie." Kristin was stunned and breathless. Her chest ached, her eyes stung. "I know what it must have done to you to see that, to hear that. I'm so sorry."

Then her arms were around his waist, her face pressed against his chest. Like a statue he stood, immobile, rigid, then she felt his hand tangle in her hair, his lips touch her temple.

"I was guilty, Kris. I never denied it." His grip tightened. "I paid the man's medical bills and lost wages and got a suspended sentence. Judge Markham sealed my file because he knew that a felony conviction would be frowned upon by the powers-that-be in the juvenile investigation department. New Wave would never have gotten off the ground." Circling his index finger beneath her chin, Brodie tipped her face back. "I should have told you, honey. I'm sorry."

"It's all right." The words were choked. Tears do that. "I understand, Brodie. I really do understand."

His breath brushed her hair as he whispered, so softly she couldn't hear, then the words came again, filtering through the air like particles of dust, invisible, yet shimmering like slivered jewels when sprayed by a shower of sunlight.

"I love you, Kris." The words floated, shimmered and disappeared. "I love you."

The next three days were a whirl of daylight laughter and moonlight passion. Kristin brought more to New Wave than beauty and a feminine touch; she brought logic, innovative ideas and the ability to prepare a solid financial plan for the ranch.

Brodie was deeply, irrevocably in love. He'd finally found the woman who shared his devotion to the boys, his commitment to their future. At Brodie's request Kristin had arranged for Ernie's private art lessons. When the church needed help in its day care center, it was Kristin who had convinced Father Jonas that Jess, with his bilingual ability and instinctive leadership style, would be perfect for the job. Jess seemed to love working with the children.

Watching her through the office window, Brodie's heart swelled with a love so intense, he ached beneath its sweet burden. Each night she came to him, fiery passion, honeyed softness, giving more than she took, filling him with desire and quenching it with love.

And she *did* love him. Brodie knew it, felt it in her touch, her smile, the light in her eyes when she saw him. But she would not say it, would not admit it, even to herself. If he prodded her, she pulled back, eyes veiled against the fear she could not quite hide.

Fear—of him, of commitment, of love itself—Brodie didn't know. He knew only that he would back off, give her space. Then she would smile and his guts would twist, she would speak in that husky whisper and his breath would catch in his throat.

She was walking toward the stable now and Brodie smiled at the orange spears clasped in her hand. Carrots for Martha. A gutsy lady, Kristin Price. Every morning it was getting easier for her, but even when she'd been terrified, she'd forced herself to go into those stables. She fought her fears courageously, relentlessly and alone.

Sadness curtained his face. He loved her desperately, yet there was a small, walled part of Kristin's mind and soul that she kept secret, a part he couldn't reach. Her nightmares lived there still, and her own private dragons. She battled them alone.

Always, alone.

He watched her disappear into the stable's gaping mouth.

Kristin hesitated only slightly as she passed from the late afternoon warmth into the musky shadows. It was cooler in the stable, she noticed, almost cold. Soft snorts and wickers floated from the occupied stalls and the floorboards vibrated beneath restless hoofs. Her legs faltered, quivering, and she grasped the rail of the empty foaling stall for support. Then she wiped the clammy chill from her palms and forced herself down the hay-strewn aisle toward Martha's stall.

Would she never overcome this nauseous terror? Every day, she came here. Every day, she wanted to throw up and run screaming back into daylight. Why did she do it? She would be leaving soon—too soon.

Certainly she was making progress. The fact that she could actually walk into the stable was testimony to that. Still Kristin's brain told her, with its usual flawless logic, that this torture was unnecessary. It wasn't as though she were seriously considering Brodie's request for her to stay and work at New Wave. Even if she wanted to, she couldn't spend the rest of her life doing daily battle with shaking legs, icy skin, gnawing terror.

Kristin wasn't cut out for ranch life. She knew that, even if Brodie didn't. She would be a liability to him, to New Wave, and eventually, he would hate her for it.

A career path was already carved for Kristin Price, a path that led away from Mariposa County and ended amid steel and glass and concrete and asphalt. Her life was in the city, protecting its children from reliving the horror of her own childhood.

And Brodie, a man of vision and integrity, well, he would save those same children from the city itself.

Impatient snuffles, louder than the rest, urged Kristin onward. Martha stretched her sleek neck over the stall door and Kristin ignored the other stable residents, fixing her eyes on the mare. The mare's eyes were fixed on the carrots.

Finally, Kristin held them out. "Bet you thought I'd never get here, didn't you?" she whispered. Martha lipped at one of the fat spears, then delicately lifted it from Kristin's palm and crunched it with relish.

"Didn't expect to see you in here."

With a gasp of surprise, Kristin whirled around to see Jess hanging loosely over the gate of a stall across the aisle. He gave her a knowing look and a smug grin. A large black stallion minced anxiously in the stall, snorting loudly. Jess seemed oblivious to the power of the huge animal flexing its muscles beside him.

"You startled me." An obvious and unnecessary announcement. Kristin had paled to a sick, chalky color.

"Sorry." He was obviously not sorry at all. "Just cooling down Thunder. Gus usually does it, but..." Leaving the sentence unfinished, Jess rolled his shoulder in a careless shrug. Thunder pitched his head, arching his massive neck.

"Oh." Swallowing a retort to the amused glint in the boy's dark eyes, Kristin managed a feeble smile. "How's it going with the kids?"

The expression in his brown eyes softened. "Okay," he said almost tenderly. "They're real cool little dudes."

An amazing change, Kristin noted, from city savage to doting guardian. "Father Jonas is very pleased."

"Yeah? He's an all-right guy, you know? I thought he'd be...I don't know, stuffy or something, but he's mellow. We get on."

"Umm. Wait a minute." Kristin laughed as Martha pushed her shoulder with her soft muzzle. "Here, you greedy girl."

"Ms. Price?" Jess lowered his eyes. "I just wanted to...thank you for telling Father I could handle it."

"It was the truth, Jess. You're very good with the other boys." A red flush crept up Jess's neck and stained his cheeks as Kristin added softly, "Brodie and I are both very proud of you."

"Yeah, well..." He coughed nervously, then mumbled, "Got to finish," and disappeared into the shadows.

Thunder, however, did not disappear. He eyed the carrot in Kristin's hand and rumbled, bobbing his head irritably. Since Jess was inside the stall with the horse, the latch on the stall gate was unfastened. Kristin saw the unhooked clasp at the same moment Thunder made his move on the coveted carrot. The gate swung open and nothing but air stood between Kristin and the huge, black stallion.

She froze. Then, to her own amazement, she extended the carrot. Thunder took it. In mere seconds, Jess pulled the horse away, locking it safely in the stall, then escorted Kristin from the stable.

When Brodie saw Kristin's white expression, he ran to gather her in his arms. "Kristin, what is it?" A pale strand of hair stuck to her cheeks and he pushed it gently away. "What happened, honey?"

Jess answered. "Man, I'm sorry, Brodie. It's my fault."

Brodie set his teeth. "What happened, Jess?"

"Thunder got out of his stall and scared the sh—scared her half to death."

"Just *happened* to get out of his stall." Brodie's voice was as cold and disbelieving as his eyes. "Like the snake just *happened* to crawl into the drawer and the radiator just *happened* to be slashed."

Wincing only slightly under Brodie's blue steel stare, Jess's chin lifted. "Like I said, man. It was my fault."

"No." Kristin's voice was muffled against Brodie's chest. "It was an accident. I'm fine, really."

"Then why are you crying?"

She was startled, then embarrassed. "Relief, probably. Honestly, it's no big deal. The horse wanted Martha's carrot and I gave it to him."

"You actually gave it to him? That was a big step for you, Kris." Eyes narrowed, Brodie's gaze anchored on Jess. "Still, it shouldn't have happened." Brodie's voice was soft, deceptively so. Kristin couldn't see the hard, angry set of his expression, a cold, steel-blue warning that clearly promised considerable punishment if such an accident ever occurred again.

But Jess saw, understood and nodded.

"Go finish up your chores. We'll talk about this later."

"I'll bet," Jess mumbled sourly. Kicking at dust, he slumped back toward the stable.

Gently, Brodie guided Kristin into the house. Kristin sank gratefully into the sheltered thickness of the sofa's faded cushions.

Sitting down beside her, Brodie offered a handkerchief. She took it, smeared it across her wet face, then blew her nose with gusto.

"Thank you," she sniffed.

"Feel better?"

"No." She blew her nose again. "I feel like a fool. I'm embarrassed—make that humiliated—and I'm absolutely furious."

"With Jess or Thunder?"

"With myself."

"You should be proud of yourself. You didn't scream or run or even faint. You gave the horse a carrot and walked calmly out of the barn."

Her hand flicked impatiently. "But I'm shaking like a leaf. I seem to be making a career out of behaving like a sissy—a pantywaist in panty hose."

Blue eyes crinkled even as he struggled to smother a smile. "You've come a long way, baby."

"Don't patronize me, Nathan Brodie," she snapped. "Don't you *dare* patronize me." She leaped to her feet and paced the room, feeling Brodie's eyes follow her with silent understanding.

What was wrong with her? Why was she continually forcing herself to confront every demon that had haunted her since childhood? Kristin knew she'd made tremendous strides, maintaining at least external control, but it was pointless. This was just another assignment for heaven sake, and it was over. Why...?

Abruptly, she halted, staring out the window at the rolling Mariposa foothills. Her assignment really *was* over, she realized, and had been for days. The report was complete, her job at New Wave was done.

Yet she'd stayed on, not even admitting to herself that no deeply rooted sense of duty had kept her at New Wave. It was Nathan Brodie.

Brodie. The man who made the blood simmer in her veins, who unfurled a sense of longing that spread like tiny fingers of pain, then blossomed into incredible happiness. It was as though an empty vessel deep in her soul had been filled.

So she had challenged terror to preserve joy, to delay the inevitable loss.

The hollow pit returned. "I have to go," she whispered. "Tomorrow."

Tomorrow. The word echoed in Brodie's mind, a deafening thunder in the silent room.

"Stay with me, Kristin," Brodie said quietly. "I love you."

"I can't." She felt him behind her, like the shadow of a mountain, proud, enduring. Her heart twisted.

"You're part of New Wave now, part of me. You belong here."

Belong here? No. She belonged in her own home with the ocean at her door, salt breeze in her face. Closing her eyes, she tried to picture the surf, remember the comfort of her home, but the images blurred into jagged hills, a lean, angular face, midnight eyes.

"Life isn't a Disney movie, Brodie. 'Happily ever after' is a bunch of romantic nonsense." Her voice softened. "This is reality, and reality isn't always pretty."

"Don't you think I've seen a bit of that 'reality'?"

Kristin cringed. Of course he had. Brodie had lived with the world's cruelty and ugliness, seen more of it than Kristin could even imagine.

Brodie's eyes pierced like laser beams. "I saw my father drunk more often than sober and can remember his fists more clearly than his face." He slipped his palm beneath her chin, lifting her face to meet his intense gaze. "There's hope for something better, Kris. It takes work, commitment, but the rewards are worth it."

Commitment. She panicked at the word. "The risks are too high."

"Risks? What risks, Kris?"

"Failure, rejection, loss—all of the above."

"Are you waiting for a guarantee?"

"Of course not."

"What, then?"

Helpless, she shrugged. He was confusing her and she was already confused enough. Her life was planned, meticulously organized to avoid the mistakes of the past. She simply had to focus on that plan and ignore the gnawing ache, the intuitive little voice that kept telling her to believe that fairy tales really *could* come true.

A quiet desperation tinted Brodie's voice. "Listen to me— please. Think of the boys, Kris. They need you, they need your concern, your love. This is the perfect place for you to continue your work, your research." Her hands lay stiffly knotted in her lap and he covered them with his own. "You'll have the opportunity here to really contribute to their lives, not just flit through like a spray of moon dust. It will give real meaning to your work."

She became rigid. "I like to think my work already *has* real meaning." Her voice was low, husky, controlled. "All my life I've been shuffled through other people's homes, been part of other people's dreams. Sometimes, they pretended I belonged, but it wasn't real. It wasn't ever real." She faced him squarely. "I have my own home, my own dreams. I've made a life for myself and it's quite real because I control it."

He saw the truth in her eyes but couldn't accept it. Desperation rang in his words. "What we have is real. You love me too, Kris. For pity's sake, can't you even admit that?"

"Love is just a word, Brodie, a soft and pretty word." Her voice was flat, emotionless. "My husband 'loved' me but he rejected me and he betrayed me. Eventually, so would you."

"Do you think so little of what we have, so little of me?" Anger sharpened his tone. "Poor little Kristin, everyone's out to give her the shaft." Catching her arm as she tried to push past him, Brodie spun her around. "You're right about one thing, though. You *are* a coward. You won't give even a tiny piece of yourself to anyone because you're afraid you won't get enough back to make it worth your while."

She paled. "Let me go."

"That's the most cowardly, selfish kind of fear. Horses and dogs are just your excuse for running away from real commitment."

She stood rigid, unwavering, privately swallowing the pain of his words behind a taut, impassive expression. "You're right, of course. If I wasn't a selfish coward, I would most certainly trade my dreams for yours."

Stunned, Brodie released her, the quiet power of her words reaching him. Dragging his fingers through his hair, he turned away. She was right. Brodie realized he was asking her to give up everything while he gave up nothing.

He groaned as his own words haunted him.

Cowardly. Yeah. Sure. A coward would hardly swallow her terror to leap into the branding corral to comfort an injured cowboy or ignore her own fear to console a grieving boy the night his foal died.

Selfish. Was it selfish of her to convince Dr. Amatti to allow Todd to work at the clinic or to line up Jess's job with Father Jonas? Enrolling Ernie in art class, buying his art supplies as a gift, could that be considered an act of self-indulgence?

And when they made love, she gave herself totally, completely, asking nothing, yielding all. In return, he'd demanded everything and offered nothing, all in the holy name of love.

The realization shattered him. She could never be happy at New Wave and, as much as he loved her, Brodie knew he could never be happy anywhere else.

Kristin's chin was still hiked defiantly, yet it quivered beneath his fingertips. "Forgive me, Kris," he said, and silently prayed for the strength to let her go.

In the hallway outside the living room, Brodie heard a loud thump, as though someone had bumped into the telephone stand by the stairwell. The noise was quickly followed by the sound of sneakered feet and the slamming of the front door.

It was the last straw for Kristin. "I feel like a bug in a bottle. Someone is constantly watching me, spying on me."

"Calm down, honey. It was probably just one of the boys coming from the kitchen with a snack." Brodie's words were soothing, but unconvincing, even to himself. He remembered the crunch of shoes outside the barn and he, too, frequently had the uneasy sense of being surveyed.

Kristin was tired, too tired to worry about a juvenile game of spy and sneak. She had to get away, find the space to think. Brodie had a way of jumbling her thoughts until she couldn't remember who she was, what she'd planned for her life. Without a backward glance, she strode out the front door, breathed deeply of the pure air, then trudged toward the knoll and stretched out on the soft grass. Somehow, she couldn't face going to the tiny guest room, lying on the bed where she and Brodie had shared such beauty and wonder. Tonight, she would pack and tomorrow, well, tomorrow always has to come, doesn't it?

Exhaustion took over and she fell into a deep, dreamless sleep.

It was dark when she awoke. In the house, Oaf was humming into the dishwater. Obviously, she'd missed dinner again, but she really didn't care. The last thing on her mind was food.

As she started up the stairs, she saw the golden glow cracking beneath the door to Brodie's office and had to swallow an almost overwhelming urge to go to him. One last night, one last memory.

Forcing herself forward, she went up the stairs to her room. When she flicked the light switch, she froze. It was there, on the bed.

Lock broken, her briefcase lay open and empty like a great, gaping wound. The manuscript was gone.

Kristin panicked. It had been nearly two weeks since the last incident. She'd been confident that the boys' animosity, if not totally absent, had dwindled to safe proportions. Had one of them broken into her briefcase and taken her manuscript?

Her blood froze. The outline was gone, too, those distorted, speculating notes on the New Wave operation. If those pages ever got back to the Social Service Agency in their present form, Brodie would be ruined.

No. No, he wouldn't be ruined, because she would admit that it was all a pack of lies, speculation, totally unprofessional libelous garbage.

And the rest of the pages would be labeled as garbage, too. They wouldn't sell as bird cage liner, let alone be published as a respected research paper. The bureaucracy would belch along, business as usual, spewing neglect instead of care, hurting instead of healing.

Knowing it was probably useless, Kristin still ravaged the small room searching for the manuscript. She worked grimly, quietly, not wanting the noise of her search to draw unwanted attention. Drawers were carefully emptied in the middle of the floor, the contents of the closet were laid across the mattress. She crawled under the bed, stretched her hand under the dresser and finally sat in the midst of the chaos, accepting the inevitable.

She had to tell Brodie. Everything.

She would have rather swallowed gasoline, but Kristin dragged herself to her feet and pushed herself down the stairs. Stopping in front of the closed office door, Kristin took a deep breath, flexing her fingers before she knotted them into a fist, and knocked.

There was a long pause before she heard his response and her upper lip was beaded with nervous moisture as she twisted the knob.

He sat behind the desk, head lowered as he studied the stack of papers scattered in front of him.

"Brodie, I . . ."

His eyes snapped up, cold as frozen granite. His lips curled into a dry, frightening smile. She felt stinging gooseflesh slide down her spine as her gaze dropped to the papers piled in front of him. Her manuscript.

"You." The breath caught in her throat. "Oh my God, Brodie. It was you."

Chapter Twelve

Had it been Brodie all along?

Had Brodie systematically searched her room? Had he left the threatening note and sabotaged her car? Nausea overwhelmed her at the thought.

The tender words of love, the sweetness of their joining—was it all part of his deception? It would be the ultimate betrayal.

Sweat iced her brow and palms. Clutching the door frame, Kristin tried in vain to stop the sickening sway of the room. The words choked her. "I...trusted you." They came out in a weak whisper, filled with pain. She felt as though something vital in the very pit of her had been surgically removed.

Slowly, Brodie stood, regarding her with a cold indifference that sliced her to the core. Then he raised his hands, clapping his rough palms together in mocking, slow-motion applause.

"Very good, Kristin. You really could have made a career in the theater." He stopped, dropping his hands to his sides in balled knots. "But then, all the world is your stage, isn't it?" He glanced down at the stack of sheets on the desk and absently flipped the pages. "I have to hand it to you, though. You're good." His eyes froze her. "Damn good."

Kristin stared, motionless, unable to comprehend his cruel derision. It was he, not she, who'd given the performance of his life and, like a gullible adolescent, she'd been too blind, too naive to see through the brutal ruse.

He gestured sharply toward the neatly typed pages. "Should be a best seller," he said bitterly. "It's got it all—mystery, intrigue, greed and abuse of power—" He interrupted himself with a vile curse. "The royalties alone should keep you in real style."

Knuckles whitened by her grip on the door jamb, Kristin's mind whirled in bewilderment. "What are you talking about? I don't understand . . ."

"Drop the act, Kristin," he growled. "The lights are off, the curtain's gone down. You've had your applause."

Gray eyes widened, then narrowed darkly as Brodie's meaning became clear. Anger began to simmer, boiling up to fill her hollowness with fury. "How dare you accuse me? You lied to me, pretended to be this . . . this wonderful, loving, all-American guy. I must have given you some great laughs." Insecurity overshadowed logic. "Did you share the laughs with your men, Brodie? Did you and Gus and Merle all sit around and chuckle over the gullible woman who believed your sweet words and took you into her bed?" Tears of humiliation and anger hovered on her lashes, but she blinked them away. "How about the boys? Did you tell them all about it . . . all about the pitiful, scarred woman who honestly believed that you found her beautiful? Did you describe everything we did in colorful detail or just give them a few lewd generalities?"

"Stop it."

"Stop what? The truth?" Two strides to the desk and papers flew as she slapped the stack onto the floor. "Tell me, Brodie, was it you who sabotaged my car?" Deny it, she begged silently. He didn't. She sucked in a ragged gulp of air. "The anonymous note was beneath you. A bit childish, but still quite effective."

Brodie's eyes darkened dangerously, his lips drawn into tight, whitened lines.

"Good battlefield strategy," he said quietly. "When your back's against the wall, attack." He thrust out a fistful of papers. "The show's over, lady, and the audience has gone home." He opened his fingers violently and wrinkled sheets fluttered softly downward. "It's time for you to do the same. Go home, Kristin." God, he was tired. *"Go home."*

The mask of anger was gone now, his expression was a raw, throbbing wound. He seemed to age ten years in ten seconds and Kristin watched the rigid curtain shatter, exposing hurt, disillusionment, defeat. It tore at her heart and her own fury dissipated as the hollowness she'd arrived with returned. Kristin felt empty.

Brodie had betrayed her, perhaps even tried to destroy her and yet her instinct had been to go to him offering comfort. She could understand now why battered women returned time and time again to the very men who had abused them. Something deep inside her ached at his suffering, as though easing his anguish was the only thing that could possibly alleviate her own.

With a deep, shaking breath, Kristin turned to the one part of her she could trust, the single segment of Kristin Michaels Price that could be depended upon to get her through—her logical mind. Like a computer eliminating bad sectors of a flawed disk, her brain whirred, isolating her emotions, sorting facts in a mental data base.

Facts, not instincts, would insure her survival and the facts showed that Nathan Brodie was not what he seemed. People, she noted impassively, never are.

"I will, of course, be leaving tomorrow morning." Her best professional tone. Good. "I'll need to tie up a few loose ends first. The report is completed, as you're well aware." She saw surprise flicker across Brodie's face but disregarded it. "There is a copy for you and one for the Agency. I've already signed them both, but they require your signature as well."

As she spoke, she automatically straightened the scattered pages. "I assume the report meets with your approval. If not, you have the option of adding any comments you wish."

Bending, she gathered the last of the sheets strewn across the floor. When she straightened, she met Brodie's stare. "Will you be adding anything to the report as written?"

Brodie frowned in annoyance. "How should I know? I haven't even seen the report."

Impatience sharpened her tone. "Oh come on now, Brodie. The report was in my briefcase, which you emptied to get to the manuscript." Pages thumped brusquely on the desk as she squared the stack. "Pretending you didn't even peruse it is, under the circumstances, rather absurd, wouldn't you say?"

"What briefcase?" He emitted a frustrated grunt followed by a muttered oath. "What are you talking about? I found this little pile of dynamite sitting in the middle of my desk, just where you put it." His jaw clamped. "I figured you wanted to surprise me." He jammed his hands into his pockets. "You did."

"Do you really expect me to believe that? Give me a break, Brodie. I may learn slow, but I *do* learn."

"I don't give a flying fig what you believe. I found the manuscript on my desk." He lifted an eyebrow speculatively. "Are you trying to tell me you didn't put it there?"

She sighed, suddenly exhausted. "Give it up, Brodie. If you get your kicks out of ransacking my things, fine, but give me credit for at least a shred of intelligence." Clutching the stack of wrinkled papers, she marched to the door, then hesitated. "I'll bring the report down and I'd appreciate any written comments as soon as possible. If they're not ready by dawn, mail them."

Brodie watched her disappear, heard her soft, slow footsteps on the stairs. Dropping heavily into his chair, he focused sightlessly into space, the events of the past hour billowing through his mind like a technicolor filmstrip. When he'd read those notes filled with ugly innuendo, searing suspicion, he'd felt sick. It had winded him like a fist in the gut.

He'd honestly thought Kristin believed in him, believed in his ideas but when he'd read her damning words, he'd realized that he had been royally duped.

Still, doubt gnawed at him. Kristin had looked so shattered, so utterly spent when she'd come into the office. When she'd seen the manuscript, she'd appeared stunned, almost in a state of shock.

An act, he reminded himself. She's a good—make that great—little actress.

Still, how *had* the manuscript appeared on his desk? Why would she have put it there, only to deny her actions? And if she hadn't, who had . . . and why?

She'd done it, he decided bitterly. A big scene created to make a clean break. After all, she couldn't have some lovesick fool following her back to the city and making a nuisance of himself.

Brodie slammed his fist into the desk in disgust. He would have, too. He would have trailed after her like a trained puppy. Even now, even after everything he'd discovered, he burned to haul her off to bed and make love with her until she threw the book out a window, declaring her undying love and promising never to leave him.

Fool. Idiot. Sucker.

No matter what she'd done, Brodie knew he still loved her.

A folder slapped the desk. Startled, Brodie blinked up to see Kristin's rigid back as she stiffly left the room. He'd been so engrossed in his own misery, he hadn't even heard her return.

Cautiously, Brodie fingered the manila folder briefly, then flipped it open. "Why not?" he muttered. "It couldn't get much worse."

Thirty minutes later, he turned the final page and quietly closed the report, wondering if he'd completely lost his mind or was merely caught in some kind of sixth-dimensional nightmare.

The report was, by any interpretation, a glowing narrative of New Wave's theory and operation. Kristin had praised Brodie to the hilt, commenting on his commitment to the boys, his personal devotion to their future and his deeply rooted sense of integrity. She'd nearly deified him and there was not even a hint of his drunken brawl two years ago.

The analysis of financial aspects was thorough, objective and complete. She'd obviously done her homework, quoting several legal sources to indicate that neither his trust fund concept nor the wages that had been set aside were against any laws. Brodie had breathed a massive sigh of relief at that paragraph.

There were also weaknesses noted, along with recommendations for improving the efficiency and effectiveness of several operational functions. Although the report expressed concern over exposing the boys to certain hazards inherent to the ranch environment, Kristin had also pointed out the precautions that had been established for the boys' safety. In spite of himself, Brodie had had to smile when he'd read the rather lengthy list of additional safety measures she was recommending. Obviously, she hadn't entirely overcome her prejudice about working with animals.

All in all, Brodie decided the report couldn't have been more favorable if he'd written it himself. In fact, he was impressed by most of the recommendations she'd offered and could see immediately how their implementation would cut costs and improve safety. Grudgingly, he had to admit that he would never have thought of any of them on his own. Kristin had a real knack for slicing through the superficial skin of a problem and analyzing its underlying obstacles.

Thorough, objective and a top-notch, professional piece of work. Obviously, the report and the scathing manuscript notes had not been prepared by the same person. Something strange was going on here and Brodie didn't like it one bit.

Grabbing the report folder, Brodie stomped up the stairs, flinging the guest room door open with a resounding slam. Kristin jumped, dropping the peach sweater she'd been folding into a furry pool on the carpet.

"Ever hear of knocking?" she snapped. "It's a rather quaint custom practiced by the more civilized cultures."

Brodie's gaze swung once around the room. "Ever hear of the truth?" He saw the bare dresser, empty drawers hanging open like dead limbs, then settled his attention on the open suitcase sprawled across the bed. "You know what the truth is, don't you, honey? That's the middle ground between what goes on in your pretty little head and what rolls off your sweet tongue." With a deft wrist movement, the folder soared briefly before colliding with the suitcase's open mouth. "Reality, sweetheart. Let's try it. I guarantee it won't hurt a bit."

Kristin gaped at him. "You're mad."

"Angry," he corrected. "I'm angry and I'm confused and I'm sick to death of your lies."

"Lies? *My* lies?"

"If I wanted a parrot, I'd buy one. Now, who wrote this report?"

Her gaze automatically slanted toward the folder. "Since I signed it, I guess I must have written it. What kind of fool quest—"

"Then who wrote that lousy outline that made New Wave sound like a mafia stronghold and set me up as some kind of diabolic godfather?"

Unable to meet his hard stare, Kristin bent to retrieve her sweater. "I did," she mumbled, folding the garment furiously. "It's trash and I apologize. I should have thrown it out weeks ago."

Now it was Brodie's turn to gape. "Weeks ago? What about all that 'opportunity for unscrupulous activities' garbage? And the 'abuse of county funds'? How about the part accusing me of 'enslaving teenaged wards to perform hazardous ranch functions'? You wrote those notes as soon as you got here?"

Nodding miserably, she dropped the folded sweater into the suitcase with a helpless shrug. "I made some . . . rather unfortunate snap judgments when I first arrived. My initial impression was somewhat biased, if you'll recall." She slid him a wry look. "When I realized that my own, er, concerns were impairing my conclusions, I locked the manuscript away and refused to work on it until the assignment was complete." Two loud clicks punctuated her statement and the luggage was closed. Straightening, she faced him. "I kept those notes to remind myself what happens when I lose sight of the facts. If I'd known it was you prowling my room like a thief in the night—"

"Blast it, Kris!" The words exploded. "I told you I've never been in this room." His eyes softened, remembering. "Unless you were here with me."

Flushing, she turned away. "Don't. It's not going to do either of us any good."

"Yeah. Well, I guess that's it, then." He turned, hesitating. "Kris?"

"Yes?"

"You can't really believe I sabotaged your car." It was a flat statement, yet he awaited her response.

"I honestly don't know what to believe. You didn't deny it." Kristin was suddenly unbearably weary. Her arms pulled like lead weights on her aching shoulders, and something that had crawled into her brain was now pounding to get out. "It really doesn't matter at this point. The car, the note—it's over."

The note again. "What's this note you keep talking about?" Brodie was frustrated and irritated.

"Just forget it." And go away, she mentally amended.

"Not until I find out what you've been babbling about." He took two lean steps into the room and took hold of her arms firmly. "Now, what note?"

She gasped at his touch. It was not pain causing her to flinch, it was a sharp jolt, the familiar burning sensation that still took her breath away. Tugging against his grip, she said, "The one you left in my typewriter." She jerked away. "The cute one telling me to get out or else."

Brodie's face hardened into a white mask. "When?"

"Oh, stop it. You know wh—"

"*When?*" With a convulsive jerk, he hauled her against him.

Stunned, Kristin examined his shocked expression, absorbed the confusion and fury twisting in his eyes. Her breath whooshed out in relief.

"You really don't know, do you?" she murmured before her body slackened under his fingers. "Thank heaven."

He took her into the embrace of his strong arms. "I'd never hurt you, Kris. Never. Tell me, honey. Please."

His softness, his concern nearly unraveled her and Kristin's voice cracked. "I-It was after the barbecue. When I got back to my room, the note was in the typewriter. It said 'get out while you can.'"

"Why didn't you tell me?"

"You were so distraught over the radiator thing—it was as though one of the boys had betrayed your trust. I just couldn't tell you. It . . . would have hurt you too much."

A groan shuddered through him. "My God, Kris. You kept a threat like that to yourself just to protect my feelings? You little fool, you still don't get it, do you?"

Finding his answer in her bewildered expression, he whispered, "I love you, Kristin Price. I care about you."

Gently, she eased from his embrace. "You love New Wave, too," she said quietly. "And the boys. How could I ask you to choose?"

Brodie couldn't deny it. The ranch and the boys had meant everything to him. Now he felt as though he'd been given that choice between New Wave, his dream for the future, and a life with Kristin. She'd read him like a giant billboard, he realized, and was taking that choice away by leaving.

Cursing himself, Brodie knew he was going to let her go. In effect, he'd made that choice already.

And Kristin had known he would. She'd known it all along.

She turned, walking away from him.

One last look, thought Kristin, as she stared out the window, absorbing the silhouetted hills blanketed by trees tipped silver with sprays of moonlight. So beautiful, she mused, surprised to realize how very much she would miss it. She would miss the quiet beauty, the crickets' song, the scented air—she would miss the boys and Oaf and, yes, she'd even miss Gus's crusty complaints.

Nathan Brodie? Her chest tightened spasmodically. Oh, yes. Most of all, she would miss him.

Sadness clogged her throat and she tried to swallow. For heaven's sake, it wasn't as if she'd never had to leave someplace she cared about. Kristin had spent much of her life packing, moving on and never looking back. Only once before had she felt sorrow this deep, like a part of her was being left behind. Mama Lu . . .

Wiping at her cheek, she heard Brodie cough hoarsely, then clear his throat as though testing its function.

"So, you'll be leaving in the morning." It was a flat, dull statement. "We still have a bit of a problem."

Surprised, she swiveled to face him.

"Someone broke into your room tonight." He walked to the foot of her bed, hoisting the broken briefcase. "I can't just leave it at that."

"What are we supposed to do, call out the dogs and dust for prints?"

"No, but I can sure make a few waves."

Kristin recognized the determined set of his jaw. Argument was useless at this point. He would line the boys up like convicted felons and interrogate them until someone broke.

Only it would be Brodie who would break first. He would be defeated by the knowledge that his trust had again been violated. It would destroy him and, eventually, it would destroy New Wave as well.

Kristin would give anything she owned to prevent that from happening, but she was helpless. One of those kids had lied, stolen, sabotaged, threatened—the whole ball of wax. Maybe even all of them, joined in an adolescent conspiracy.

Something was nagging at her, a niggling, mind-teasing tidbit that she couldn't quite put her finger on. A clue, so fragile her brain wasn't able to bring it into focus and yet it was there, faint, fuzzy around the edges, but definitely buried somewhere deep in her subconscious.

Think, Kristin.

When did the little brain light first begin to flicker?

"Kris? What's wrong?" Brodie was examining her somber expression with growing concern.

"I don't know. Something has been, well, bothering me."

Perplexed, he pursed his lips. "Bothering you?"

"Umm. A few minutes ago, you said something that reminded me..." Her voice trailed off, forehead screwing into tiny furrows. "The notes, you said something about..." Eyes rounding in shock, the words scattered into the air sharply.

"Oh no." She shook her head as though to deny her own thoughts.

In a flash, Brodie crossed the room, grasping her shoulders to support her folding legs.

"Brodie." A hoarse croak. "Oh, Lord, Brodie. I know who did it."

The bunkhouse door crashed open and Brodie roared into the room like an armored tank.

Ranch hands gathered at the table playing cards were startled by the unannounced invasion as the entire deck flew into the air. Kristin panted into the doorway, halting as thick tension vibrated from the room.

Gus, who'd been dealing the cards, exploded with a string of explicit oaths. "Just what put the burr under your saddle, I'd like to know?"

Ignoring his foreman, Brodie's eyes coldly swept the room. Jess and Ernie sat on the couch, eyes wide and motionless. In front of them, the television set mumbled and flickered.

"Where's Todd?" Brodie's words rumbled through the room.

"Well, now, I don't rightly know." Gus squinted at the man he'd known for twenty years and recognized Brodie's tightly leashed temper was dangerously close to unwinding. "Might be in his room, might be down to the stable."

"Get him."

No argument was offered. Gus nodded somberly and ambled down the hallway toward Todd's room. He returned moments later with the boy in tow.

The boy's round face was sober. He looked frightened, but then, so did every other man and boy in the room.

Brodie iced a look toward Todd, then snapped his head toward the sofa. Todd obeyed the curt gesture, quickly joining Jess and Ernie. Three pairs of eyes followed Brodie's movement from the doorway until he towered in front of them.

Kristin's heart sank to her knees. They all looked so young, so frightened, so vulnerable and Brodie seemed as cold as a programmed android. She wrung her hands, analyzing the wisdom of throwing herself between Brodie's murderous fury and the terrified youngsters.

Gus cleared his throat. "You be a'wantin' some time alone with these younguns?" Worry puckered his bushy eyebrows.

Brodie's voice was dangerously soft. "This isn't a private matter. It concerns all of you." His eyes never left the three rigid bodies perched on the edge of the sofa. "Let's just kind of run down the situation here. Ms. Price has been the victim of some pretty nasty pranks, only I didn't know the half of it until tonight." Impaling each boy with a frigid stare, he continued. "You were all in on the snake business but nobody's leaving this room until I find out exactly who's responsible for the rest of it. I want to know which one of you put the threatening note in Ms. Price's typewriter and I want to know which one of you slashed her car's radiator." His eyes dulled. "I already know which one of you broke into her briefcase and stole her manuscript." Sadness loosened his expression as he fixed his eyes on Ernie's white face. "But I would like to know why."

The boy's thin cheeks seemed to pinch and pale under Brodie's intense scrutiny. Skinny fingers plucked absently at the knee of his jeans. "I didn't do nothing," Ernie whispered. "Why're you looking at me like that, man? I didn't do nothing."

"Why, Ernie? What possible reason could you have for stealing those papers and leaving them in my office for me to read?"

Dark curls bobbed violently as he shook his head. "No!" Ernie's voice cracked into a prepubescent squeak. "I told you I didn't do nothing. Maybe it was Jess . . . or Todd . . ."

Ernie's pathetic entreaty was interrupted by Jess's savage curse. With a powerful thrust, Jess reached around Todd, grabbing a fistful of Ernie's shirt. Backpedaling frantically, Ernie jerked away, digging in with heels and hands to push himself into a standing position.

"No," Ernie stammered, gulping. "It was Gus who done it." Ignoring the foreman's disgusted snort, Ernie swiveled his head feverishly, backing against the far wall as every eye in the room was trained on his every movement. "Why are you blaming me? Why does everyone always blame me?"

"Ernie, please." Kristin took a step toward the frightened boy and he cowered as she extended her hand. "I'm not going to hurt you, Ernie. I just want to know why you did it. Do you hate me so much?"

"I didn't do nothing! You can't prove it!"

With a sigh, Kristin's hand dropped. "Ernie, do you remember the day I came here to talk to you, the day you first showed me your drawings?"

His Adam's apple leaped wildly, but he managed a stiff nod.

"I asked you why Jess didn't like me, remember?" His eyes told her he remembered very well. "You told me that I had said the ranch 'provided the opportunity for unscrupulous activities and abuse of county funds'."

He sniffed. "You *did* say it."

"No." She shook her head sadly. "I never said that, Ernie, but I did write it. It was in my manuscript, the one you broke into my briefcase and stole."

Ernie may not have been the brightest person in the room, but he was defeated and he knew it. His eyelids dropped and Kristin saw the quiver of his lower lip as he fought for control. When he again met her gaze, his face was composed, the frightened child had disappeared.

"Why, Ernie?" His grim acceptance of his fate squeezed Kristin's heart.

"Because you wrote such mean things about Brodie and he liked you so much. You were always kissing him and stuff, and then you went and wrote that bad junk." Ernie angled a pitiful glance at Brodie's rigid face. "I wanted him to know you were lying to him," the boy whispered. "I didn't want you to hurt him no more."

"Oh, Ernie." Kristin couldn't stand to see the boy's pain. She turned away as the room blurred. "It was you spying on us, wasn't it?" She remembered the crunch of stones outside the stable, the muffled thuds outside the office door.

"I wasn't spying." The boy's voice was flat, defeated. "I just happened to see . . . things."

Yes, Kristin could imagine the things Ernie had seen and heard. There was no excuse for him having gone into her room in the first place, but Kristin could also imagine what the boy must have thought when he'd read those scathing pages.

She swallowed as she scanned the room, seeing the eyes of the men focused on her, narrowed, questioning. "I have already explained what I wrote to Brodie," she said quietly. "But all of you have a right to the same explanation and the same apology."

Only twice did the syllables choke in her throat as she told the men what she had written, and why she had written it. The apology seemed so futile considering the results of her unjust accusations. Shock and anger reflected from the men's faces as she spoke.

Kristin had realized weeks ago that her analysis had been impaired by her own terror, her own cowardice, yet speaking the words, admitting her weakness aloud, tore away the final shreds of self-denial.

When she'd finished, the only sound in the room was Gus's low, hissing whistle and muttered, "Well, if that don't beat all."

Finally, Brodie broke the deathly silence. "Ernie's taken responsibility for his actions and Kristin's taken responsibility for hers. Now I want the rest of the answers." From the look in his eyes, there would be no escape from the truth.

Chin high, Ernie met Brodie's unwavering gaze. "I poked the radiator with one of Oaf's steak knives. I done it all." The boy looked at Kristin, then lowered his eyes almost shyly. "Didn't mean for you to get hurt," he mumbled, staring at his own feet. "I just wanted you to go away."

Not trusting her voice, Kristin merely nodded.

"Guess this means you'll be sending me back." Ernie was still talking to the rug. "Guess I let you down pretty bad."

A tense muscle in Brodie's jaw twitched. "Yeah." It came out as more of an exhaled breath than a word. "I guess you did."

Ernie flinched as though struck as Brodie abruptly spun around, walked stiffly to the door and disappeared into the night.

Suddenly, there wasn't enough air in the bunkhouse. The room was stifling and Kristin felt disapproving stares burning into her skin. She stumbled out the bunkhouse and the cold, damp night seemed to slap her cheeks like an angry parent. She felt guilty, as though she'd caused all of this misery by her mere presence.

When she returned to the house, she saw the door to Brodie's office was closed. She hesitated, then angled past the stairway and knocked. No light spilled from beneath the door and there was no response to her soft tap, yet she knew Brodie was inside.

Standing motionless for several minutes, she finally heard a revealing creak of the battered old swivel chair.

"Brodie?" Silence. Kristin twisted the knob.

Even silhouetted in the dimness, she recognized sadness in the curve of his shoulder, the sag of his head. "Oh, Brodie, I'm so sorry."

He didn't turn, didn't speak.

Kristin stepped softly into the room. "I know how hurt you must be, how disappointed." More silence. Kristin perched on the armless wooden chair across from the desk. "What Ernie did was very wrong and I'm not defending it, but he did it because he loves you so much."

Finally, she heard his deep, almost painful sigh. "And love is just the flip side of grief, isn't it, honey?" Brodie hadn't moved, but at least he was speaking to her.

"Sometimes," she acknowledged, remembering their discussion at the barbecue. "But New Wave is for healing. You told me that, Brodie, remember? Ernie's still healing—we all are. Be patient with him. Please, give him another chance."

The shadowed head lifted. "What about next time, Kristin? What happens then?" He stood, turning to the small window. "Do I give him a third chance, then a fourth?"

"I don't think there will be a next time."

He spun to face her. "A guarantee, Kris? There are no guarantees, remember? Life isn't a Disney movie."

She grimaced as he threw her own words back at her. "Ernie needs professional help but his anger is directed only toward me. When I leave, the problem will be easier to deal with.''

His expression was obscure, as shadowy as the gray room. The waning moon's faint light offered little illumination. ''When you leave, will your problems be easier to deal with, too?'' he asked. ''Will you go back to the city and forget New Wave ever existed?'' *Will you forget me?* he added silently.

''I'll never forget New Wave.'' *I'll never forget you,* she added silently. Part of her wanted to stay, but she couldn't. The facts had proven that.

She would lose her home and a career she'd spent five years building. She'd be working with the boys' constant resentment and hostility. She would risk the inevitable loss, the vulnerability of pain and rejection. She'd spend the rest of her life surrounded by the flesh-and-blood embodiments of her childhood nightmares.

But she would be with Brodie.

''Kris . . .'' He hesitated, dragging his hand through his hair. Silence slid through the darkened room, followed by a decisive sigh of resignation. ''You're right about Ernie.''

He'd nearly asked her to stay again, almost begged, actually, but pride had stopped him. Nothing had changed. Brodie would still have been asking her to give up everything and he still had nothing to offer in return.

Nothing, except himself.

''Ernie's frightened,'' Brodie said quietly. ''And he's feeling threatened. You were right. It will be easier to handle that after you're gone.''

Kristin's mouth went dry. ''Of course.'' She licked her lips, cleared her throat and squared her shoulders. ''Perhaps I'll see you in the morning, before I leave.''

''Perhaps.''

There was nothing more to say. The invitation had been withdrawn. Since the problems caused by her presence had been so clearly and painfully illustrated, Kristin realized she'd been foolish to have believed it could possibly have been otherwise. She shouldn't have lowered her emotional wall, even for a moment.

"Good night, Brodie," she whispered, and meant goodbye.

Awakened with a start, Kristin rubbed her swollen eyes and hauled herself out of bed. It was still very early, not quite dawn, but the ranch's work day was already beginning.

Voices filtered through the hallway, capturing her attention. She was determined to avoid Brodie this morning. It would simply be easier that way. But there was an agitated quality to the mumbled sounds, a low urgency that bothered her. Something wasn't quite right.

Slipping into her robe, she cracked the door. Gus and Brodie stood at the top of the stairs. Brodie was cursing softly under his breath and Gus's grizzled face was drawn with worry.

Kristin felt cold. "What's wrong?" Her own voice was brittle and anxious. "Brodie, what is it?"

Brodie looked as though he hadn't slept in a week. Purple shadows framed reddened eyes that appeared to have sunk into his skull. Stubble roughened his jaw and his mouth stiffened into a taut, flat line.

His answer was curt and tense. "He's gone."

"Who?" A whispered word, an unnecessary question. Kristin knew, yet the answer cut her like a finely honed saber.

"Ernie's gone. He's run away."

Chapter Thirteen

Maps blanketed the kitchen table, shadowed by a circle of men bent over in solemn scrutiny. The room was still somberly tinted by dawn's gray pall.

Mute anxiety thickened the air. Voices were quiet, expressions grim. Oaf didn't hum as he refilled mugs with steaming coffee. His shiny head drooped over bulbous shoulders, tiny eyes submerged into deep purple crescents. Oaf lumbered toward Kristin, extending a huge fist from which a column of steam was wafting. Murmuring her thanks, Kristin accepted the coffee.

The mug quivered as she raised it to her lips and Oaf frowned briefly before offering a weak smile. "You will not have the worry, ja?" His hand tented her shoulder, embracing it with surprising delicacy. "Mr. Brodie will find, okay?"

"Of course he will." Brodie *had* to find Ernie. He simply had to. Kristin acknowledged Oaf's gesture by stretching her lips in a tight, curving grimace. "Everything will be fine, just fine."

"Ja." Oaf's voice echoed the same lack of conviction as her own and, as though his muscles could no longer endure the effort, the synthetic smile flattened, hanging loosely against his chin. "Ja," he repeated, then rolled away.

Kristin moved toward the huddle of men, standing quietly behind Brodie as he hunched over the map.

"Are you sure?" Brodie's eyes held Jess in a steel grip.

"Yeah, man. He's got a cousin or uncle or something there."

"Did he ever mention a name?"

"Nah. Just said he had people in Fresno."

Brodie returned his attention to the map and Gus slid a crooked finger along a waving red line.

"Well, he ain't a'plannin' to walk sixty miles across a dang wilderness," Gus mumbled. "Even a brainless toad like Ernie's got more sense than that."

"Maybe." Brodie scanned the map grimly. "If he was going to hitch a ride, though, he'd have to get out of the valley first. Everyone here knows where he belongs and would haul him right back here."

"Yep," agreed Gus sagely. "So he'd most likely stay away from 140—" the bent finger edged from one highway junction on the map to another "—and try to come out on Highway 49 the other side of Mariposa." Gus issued a disgusted grunt as he eyed the map, noting a ten-mile stretch of forest and barren hills covering the route. "Dang fool youngun."

The back door clamored open and Merle Deever shifted into the room. "Ma'am," he intoned, touching his hat as he glanced at Kristin, then turned his attention to Brodie. "He's heading southeast. His trail is veering off toward Scott Canyon." Deever reached over Brodie's shoulder and poked at the map. "He'll probably skirt the base of Buckingham Mountain, here . . ." Merle paused to allow Brodie's muffled curse. "My guess is that he'll try to hit either this logging trail or that firebreak road and follow one of them down to the Harris Cutoff."

Brodie nodded. "Which takes him around the valley and dumps him a half mile from the main highway."

"That's rough terrain, though. He's not likely to make the cutoff much before dark." Deever pushed his hat back and flattened his lips. "*If* he makes it that far."

Kristin sucked in her breath at Deever's ominous tone, one hand automatically going to her throat while the other whitened its grip on the edge of the table. Brodie tilted his head, observing her concern. "We'll find him before he gets that far," he explained. "That's all Merle meant."

"Yes'm." Deever quickly followed Brodie's lead. "We'll find him first, no need to fret."

She didn't believe either one of them. "What about the sheriff? He has more men, more equipment. Don't they use helicopters or something?"

"The sheriff's been notified, but this isn't Los Angeles," Brodie pointed out. "He has five deputies to cover an area the size of L.A. County. Teenaged runaways are not their biggest priority, but if they spot him, they'll let us know." Brodie saw the indignant anger bubbling in Kristin's eyes. "If we don't find him in twenty-four hours, they'll take a missing person's report and put it on the wire."

The tight clamp of her jawline told Brodie that she wasn't particularly pacified. He understood that. He wasn't, either.

Brodie stood, the huddle dispersed and the kitchen vibrated as bench legs scraped the wooden floor. "Listen up. Merle, Tug and Jess will spread across these hills east to..." Brodie paused, then ran his fingers across the undulating circles radiating across the detailed topographic map. "To where the creek cuts through. By then you'll be in radio range. Check in, leave the horses there and fan out on foot. The rest of us will head directly to the cutoff, spread out along this ridge and swing back up along both of the trails he might use." Brodie straightened, stress lines slashing his face from temple to jaw, deep-set eyes completely shadowed by a thick furrow of dark brows. "We'll be moving toward each other with Ernie in the middle."

One chance in a hundred, he told himself. It was a big forest, hard enough to find someone who wanted to be found, let alone a boy who was moving fast and hiding quiet. If the kid got hungry enough, or scared enough...maybe.

With stiff, angry motions, Brodie folded the map. "Gus, break out the squawk boxes. Dwayne'll handle the base station."

As the room emptied, Kristin snagged Brodie's arm. "I'm going with you."

He shot her a brief glance, neutral and slightly cool. "No."

She squared, feet planted firmly. "I'll go alone."

Appraising her carefully, Brodie knew that she was stubborn enough to do it and then he'd have two lost souls on his hands. He clamped his teeth. "It's too dangerous."

"Then why are the boys going?"

"They know the area, they know how to follow orders."

"I can follow orders."

"Sure."

"I'll keep up and do whatever you say, but I'll go crazy if I stay here." The wobble of her chin gave her away and her voice cracked with emotion. "Please."

Brodie strained against the desire to gather her in his arms. "There's no reason for you to change your plans." If she didn't stop looking at him like that… "Go home," he grated. "We'll handle this."

Before she lowered her eyes, he saw the hurt his words had inflicted. Then her chin came up and she met his gaze with control and determination. "I won't leave until Ernie is safe."

Rubbing his knuckles lightly across Kristin's cheek, Brodie sighed. "All right." He saw her subtle flinch at his harsh voice. Damn the woman. She was unraveling him. "You'll do what I tell you or you'll find yourself hog-tied in the truck bed."

She nodded and followed him out into the yard, where three horses stood saddled and ready. Merle, Tug and Jess mounted, holstered the walkie-talkies and received last minute instructions from Gus before reining their horses and then spurring them into a flat-out run toward the eastern knoll.

In five more minutes, the pickup launched across the dirt road with Kristin sandwiched in the cab between Brodie and Todd while Gus and Billy took their chances bouncing in the truck bed. Except for the tortured creaking of springs as the battered vehicle hit each rut and pothole, the ride was a silent one.

They turned left onto Highway 140, then picked up Highway 49 in Mariposa. Kristin found herself squinting at everyone they passed, praying to see a familiar, lanky form, a shocky brush of tightly wound curls. She saw only a large dog loping loosely along the shoulder of the road. It glanced up curiously as they passed.

Outside of Usona, Brodie swerved the truck to the left and rattled across a narrow gravel road. Gus swore grumpily, pounded on the back window and offered a rather explicit opinion of the driver's skill. Behind the wheel, Brodie's eyes remained fixed on the road and Kristin guessed that his mind had wandered several miles ahead.

Timber was thicker now and the stinging gravel was replaced by packed red dust. They'd been climbing steadily, though not sharply, Kristin realized and the road thinned into twin grooves.

A pull-off appeared to their left and Brodie angled the truck into it, pushing open the driver's door almost before the vehicle had jerked to a complete stop. By the time Kristin slid out, Brodie and Gus had spread identical maps over the hood and were quietly finalizing their plan. Nodding, Gus tucked the folded sheet into the breast pocket of his plaid shirt, accepted the rifle Billy held out toward him and slipped on a small backpack. Continuing to unload the equipment, Billy handed one pair of binoculars to Gus and another pair to Brodie, along with packs, rifles and canteens suspended by long straps.

Brodie shouldered his gear and looked at Kristin. "It'd be better for you to stay with the truck," he said.

"I'm going with you."

"Yeah." He'd expected that. Stubborn woman. "Let's go." Kristin followed him into the forest.

They walked in silence until they crested a wooded ridge. Brodie lifted the binoculars that hung around his neck, scanning the canyon below and the slopes beyond. Dropping them, he pulled the walkie-talkie from his belt and signaled Gus. The instrument crackled and hissed.

"Whatcha got?" Gus's unmistakable rasp filtered back.

"We're at the crest of the ridge about fifty yards across from a bedrock sheer. What's your location?"

A broken noise that Kristin determined was a grunt. "'Bout halfway down the canyon." Crackle. "Ain't seen squat."

Brodie squinted at midsky. "Unless he sprouted wings, it'll take him another four hours to get this far. With any luck, we'll meet up with him in two."

"Well, now luck just ain't something we've had us a whole lot of." Garbled, but the gist of Gus's sentiment was loud and clear. Kristin's heart dropped a bit lower.

Brodie's reply was curt and tense. "Call-check in thirty minutes. Out." The bulky black radio slid smoothly into its sheath.

"Maybe the other group has seen something," Kristin offered hopefully. "Why don't you call them, too?"

"They're still out of range." He skimmed a shrewd glance across the rugged horizon. "Terrain like this, radio waves might reach two miles, maybe less."

"But the base station back at the ranch is at least ten miles from here." The trip by truck had taken nearly an hour, but the highway they'd followed circled several miles around the search area in a wide, rambling arc. Ernie would be cutting straight through the foothills, hopefully, from the ranch to the road behind them. "What good is a base station if you only have a two-mile range?"

"The base station has a linear," Brodie told her. "The range is indefinite, depending on the weather. Dwayne can relay information to us." Brodie saw Kristin nervously chewing her lower lip and automatically reached out to massage the base of her skull. "Don't worry, honey. We'll find him."

Kristin looked at the wild, rugged wilderness stretching into the jagged horizon. "If I hadn't come to the ranch, none of this would have happened."

Her unhappiness was as palpable as a living thing. Brodie wanted to hold her, reassure her. Todd had broken out of his shell of mistrust and deception because of Kristin's patient counsel; she'd found an outlet for Jess's protective nature, his ability to guide and nurture; she'd even unlocked Ernie's talent, his hidden potential.

And she'd shown Nathan Brodie how to love someone enough to let go.

He wanted to tell her all that, but said simply, "Come on, Kris. It's time to move out."

The canyon was fairly steep, but they found a winding deer path and followed it into the gorge. Using tree limbs to steady herself, Kristin stared relentlessly at the ground, feeling awkward and clumsy. Slick pine needles were strewn thickly across the forest floor and twice she lost her footing, finally skidding on her bottom until Brodie snagged her arm, hauling her upright.

"You okay?"

"Sure." She provided a bright smile as proof. "Clumsy, but fine."

"Mind the rocks," he warned. "It'll get a bit steep later on."

Later on? Good grief, what did Brodie consider this tree-lined cliff they were scaling now? Kristin craned her neck, squinting up at the ridge from which they'd just descended, then angled a glance down. "Forget the stairs," she mumbled. "Let's head for the elevator."

"Just a few more feet," he assured her. "The firebreak road is the other side of that little hill over there."

Little hill? Right.

Gamely, she pushed on. Eventually the steep slope flattened into the canyon floor. Soon, too soon, they were facing the climb up the other side. A rock cliff faced them—ten, perhaps fifteen feet high. Using jagged ruts as footholds, they scaled it. Although the grade was becoming more gradual, Kirstin's legs soon began to cramp, quivering from strain.

The radio squawked and hissed. Gus issued a terse check-in and Brodie fiddled with the rectangular contraption briefly, trying to reach Merle's group. Apparently they were still out of range and Kristin noted the discouraged slump of Brodie's shoulders as he put the walkie-talkie away. Before she could think of a way to console him, he had crested the hill and was waiting for her.

"There's the road," he said as she dropped, panting, onto the ground. A narrow dirt path ribboned the side of the grade, near the base. "We should be hearing something soon."

Brodie didn't mention that if they didn't find Ernie in the next hour or so, they would have to turn back in order to get out of the canyon by dark. It would also mean that they had miscalculated the boy's route and Ernie could be anywhere in the two hundred square miles of wilderness area. As soon as the sun dropped, these canyons would be black as tar and unnavigable. Moonlight was trapped by towering treetops and the floor of the forest got so dark that a man couldn't see the movement of his own hand in front of his face.

Stopping suddenly, Brodie sank to his haunches and scanned something that had caught his eye. Rather large animal tracks had recently been made in the soft dirt.

A man couldn't see in the dark, he thought grimly, and a boy couldn't, but the forest beasts prowled the inky slopes at midnight, yellow eyes slicing like radar through the blackness in search of prey.

Straightening, Brodie studied the tree-lined slope. Signaling Kristin to stay close, he took the lead. They weren't alone, he realized, but then, Ernie wasn't either.

They had been following the road for about thirty minutes when the walkie-talkie cracked to life. It was Merle.

"Picked up his trail about an hour ago." Merle's voice was thin and broken, barely within range. "Looks like he's moving fairly slow." A popping sound, then a pause. "He took the logging road. If he don't turn off, Gus should be saying howdy any time now."

Kristin realized she'd been holding her breath and exhaled, relaxing her lungs, allowing air to rush out. Brodie had been right, she realized, and felt a tremendous sense of pride that he'd been so clever and that Merle's tracking skills had been so good. She saw Brodie's eyes flutter closed in relief, his stiff shoulders soften. Kristin went to him, sliding her arms around his waist as she nuzzled her cheek to his chest. She felt him stiffen briefly, then he wrapped a strong arm around her. With his free hand, he raised the radio. "Gus, did you get that?"

"Yep." Pop. Hiss. "Hold on a minute. Could just be we got company."

Knuckles whitening around the walkie-talkie, Brodie tensed. The receiver was silent, seconds stretching into minutes, and Brodie tightened his grip as though trying to squeeze the contraption back to life. It seemed that hours had passed, but it had only been ten minutes or so.

Crackle. "We just plucked us a tadpole."

Brodie stabbed the "send" button with his thumb. "Is he all right?"

"Yep. Mite tired and a mite dirty, but I reckon he'll live."

"Thank God," Kristin mumbled. Brodie tightened his arm around her shoulders.

"Merle, you got a copy on that?" Relief poured from Brodie's voice into the walkie-talkie.

"Loud and clear. Turning back now," came Merle's reply.

"Roger to that, Merle. Gus, we'll meet you at the truck in about..." Brodie squinted at his watch. "Two, two-and-a-half hours. Continue thirty-minute check-in."

"Yep." An exceptionally gross noise cracked through the air, as though someone had spit into the receiver. "Might take our time, though. The youngun seems a bit peaked."

"Understood. Out." Brodie sheathed the walkie-talkie and hugged Kristin in one smooth movement. "Everything's fine now, honey," he murmured, inhaling the soft fragrance of her silken hair. "Let's go on home."

Tears sprang to her eyes and, not trusting her voice, she nodded. As Brodie laced his fingers with hers, she walked silently beside him, realizing the tears of relief were mingled with pain. She would have one last night at New Wave, one last night with Brodie before she would have to leave.

Ernie was safe, thank heaven, but nothing else had changed. This was a wild country, filled with terrors. Brodie had touched her heart and her mind more deeply than anyone ever had, but Kristin was afraid he would never forgive her for what she had written. She'd lost sight of the facts and followed her instincts, instincts warped by fear, distorted by arrogance.

Yet, he'd said that he loved her. Love. A fragile thing, if it really exists, elusive and breakable. So many trusts are betrayed in the name of love. Then comes the pain, the loneliness of desertion. So few people in Kristin's life had said they loved her and now they were gone. Her parents, her husband, Mama Lu, all had left her. God, how it had hurt. But then, she'd loved them, too. If she hadn't, it might not have hurt so badly when they left.

As though swirling from a faraway place, Kristin's mind began to focus on a soft voice nearby. Blinking, she looked up at Brodie's concerned face.

"Hi," she mumbled, feeling incredibly stupid.

His smile extended to his eyes. "Hi, yourself. Nice to have you back."

"I, uh, I've been right here."

"Well, part of you, anyway." He brought his hand upward, pointing to the slope in front of them. "This is where we came in."

"Swell." Her head toppled back as she squinted toward the apex and she heard him laugh as he climbed to a small root, tugging at her hand.

"Two hills and one canyon," he reminded her. "Then we can hitch a ride."

"All right," Kristin muttered, allowing him to help her up the first steep steps. "But I'll be counting."

With a gentle pat on her bottom, Brodie pushed her ahead of him. During the entire hike, he'd positioned himself on the downhill side of Kristin so he could catch her if she slipped. It was a bit old-fashioned and quaintly chivalrous but Kristin recognized and appreciated the gesture.

She grabbed at a snaking tree root, stinging her palms on the rough bark as she pulled herself up a three-foot embankment. There was a small, flat area before the slope accelerated and Kristin collapsed into it, puffing. This hiking business was tough.

With a single stretch of his lean legs, Brodie was beside her, silhouetted by the sun hanging low at his back. He crossed his boots at the ankles as he sat smoothly beside her.

"Tired?" he asked.

Gasping, she scowled at him. "Not at all. I enjoy torture."

"I'll remember that," he said with a wicked grin. But the grin faded into an expression of intense concentration.

"What . . . ?"

"Ssshhh."

Listening, he turned his head. Kristin heard it, too. First a sharp crack, like a twig snapping, then the methodical rustle of leaves.

"Squirrels?" she asked hopefully.

"Maybe." His expression, however, was doubtful. Scanning the surroundings, Brodie stood quickly, a fluid reverse of the same motion with which he had seated himself. "Wait here."

Kristin watched him slide soundlessly into the forest, his rifle gripped at ready. She waited, restless, ears tuned in on every leaf fluttering in the cooling breeze. Picking up a twig, she absently broke it in two and the sound startled her, seeming to reverberate from each surrounding tree trunk. Hastily, she discarded the twig, wrapping her arms around herself to still her restless hands.

Suddenly, Brodie was looming above her. "Come on." The order was quiet, demanding.

"What is it?" she whispered, frightened by his expression.

He answered by pulling her to her feet, urging her forward with the continuous pressure of his hand on her back. Eventually, they crested the first rise and Kristin sank, moaning into the soft dirt.

"Wait," she gasped as Brodie pulled on her arm.

Brodie's eyes darted, scanning the slope they'd just ascended, then angling down toward the canyon below them. "It's downhill now, Kris, then up the other side and we're home free." The sun was half hidden behind the hills and the air was chilled by the impending darkness. Brodie knew the flashlight tucked in his backpack wouldn't be much help when night dropped its velvety black blanket over them.

And there was the little matter of the fresh tracks that had appeared on the path since they'd first passed this way.

"Come on, Kris."

She responded to the urgency in his voice, standing and dusting herself, then slowly following him as he descended into the gorge. They worked downward methodically, bracing themselves on sturdy tree trunks and massive boulders, then turning toward the earth as it steepened, as though climbing down a ladder. The last ten feet was a sheer drop with sharp, slick dikes of bedrock thrusting from the canyon floor like a vertical wall of stone. They'd climbed up using cracks and jutting shards as footholds, a technique that would be far trickier to master in reverse. The lengthening shadows distorted the surface of the cliff, concealing dangerous areas of loose gravel.

Brodie decided the descent would be too risky, opting instead to follow the rocky ridge to where the cliff dipped closer to the canyon floor, about fifty feet away. Edging carefully along the roughened ledge, they had nearly made it to their goal when a sound rumbled through the forest.

Kristin froze, her body stiffened against the harsh pressure of Brodie's hand pushing on her shoulder. "Get down," he ordered and her body finally buckled, dropping onto the hard, cold rock as another snarl reverberated the air, louder, closer, terrifying.

Oh, God. She knew that sound. It was the voice of the beast from her childhood, from her nightmares. Panic sliced through her, severing rational thought as a bubbling noise rose from her throat and she fought to get away, thrashing wildly against Brodie's tightening fingers.

"Stop it, Kristin!" His voice rasped urgently in her ear, but it seemed so far away.

Her breath came in shallow, panting grunts, then stopped altogether as the low, snarling growl echoed again in her ears. "It's here! It's going to kill us!" Someone was screaming, Kristin didn't know who it was as she wildly jerked against Brodie's iron grip.

He released her so suddenly, she fell backward against a jagged dike jutting from the ragged surface of rock. Pain stung her shoulder as the sharp edge of stone scraped her skin. She moaned, crumpling forward.

The snarling surrounded her. It was above her, below her, behind her—it was everywhere. With a sob, she covered her ears, curling into a shaking, fetal ball.

She heard the sharp click as Brodie cocked the rifle.

Brodie. It would get Brodie.

The realization that he, too, was in danger washed away the fear-induced mist fogging her brain and she scrambled to her knees. She saw Brodie, rifle stock pressing his shoulder, aiming downward into the canyon. He moved the barrel slowly from right to left, searching, his eye never leaving the V-shaped sight.

A shadow moved below, followed by a thundering snarl.

The dark outline slunk farther, as though flanking its prey, cloaked by a clump of evergreen spreaders rooted along the base of the slope.

Anticipating where the animal would emerge, Brodie shifted to his left. His eyes were locked on his target, his foot moved into thin air.

It happened too fast.

The rifle clattered to the ground as Brodie lurched forward, grunting in pain as he fell against the blunted edge of a broken limb. Then he was rolling, bouncing over jagged rock, until he lay motionless on the canyon floor, sprawled like a discarded rag doll.

Stunned, Kristin stared at his limp form. "No." It was a whisper. *"No!"* It was a scream.

She crawled, because her legs wouldn't support her, feeling her way down the darkening slope because tears blurred her vision. Someone kept calling Brodie's name, a broken, sobbing sound, and she realized it was coming from her.

Not feeling the slice of sharp rocks on her palms, the stab of barbed thorns and slivers of bark, she crawled and slid until Brodie lay less than six feet below her. He moaned and Kristin wanted to scream with joy. He was alive.

Again, Brodie moaned, but the sound was joined by a low rumble that froze Kristin's blood. The shadowed shape stood just beyond Brodie, its head lowered, yellow eyes refracting the waning light. The wolf bared its teeth, shards of white gleaming against the mottled gray fur as it arched lower, until its belly seemed to brush the ground.

Between Kristin and the beast was Brodie, crumpled and broken, groaning under the painful pall of semiconsciousness. The wolf watched Kristin, then snarled, slinking even closer to Brodie, seeming to make his choice between two possible victims.

Mesmerized, Kristin stared at the animal, unable to move, unable to breathe. She could run now, she knew, and it wouldn't follow her. But Brodie...it would...

She couldn't finish the thought.

Rifle. Where was the rifle? Her panicked gaze raked the steep incline. It was getting dark and there were too many shadows. *No time to look.* Brodie...the animal was moving toward Brodie. She had to stop it, had to keep it away from him.

Her fist closed over something hard and cool. It felt heavy in her palm as she raised her arm slowly. With every ounce of strength she could muster, she flung the rock. It missed, but startled the beast enough to deflect its attention.

Snarling viciously, it snapped at the air, eyes flashing like hot embers in a glowing campfire. It circled toward her. Suddenly, she leaped down the final slope, barricading Brodie with her own body, placing herself between his prone form and the snarling shadow.

The wolf was close, so close she could have reached out to touch it. She tasted the metallic sting of fear in her mouth, felt the nausea rise in her throat. The beast snapped again, teasing, testing for strength or weakness. She heard the sharp crack of his jaw, saw the wrinkled muzzle as its jowls receded to display sharp, white weapons.

Teeth. In her face.

Run. The voice echoed in her brain. She heard it again, hoarse, low. It was Brodie's voice. He was telling her to run, to save herself. Tears stung her eyes as the animal began to crouch.

Instinctively she knew it was going to attack.

Oh dear God, help me.

A sharp yelp of pain split the air and the animal backed up slowly, still growling furiously, but obviously confused.

Brodie had tossed the rock weakly, but accurately, before he fell back, his face contorted in an effort to bite back a groan.

Kristin took advantage of the animal's slight retreat, dropping to her knees, her hands desperately searching for, then finding, more ammunition. Sobbing, she threw rock after rock at the snarling animal, flinging each stone without aiming, until she could find no more, then continued to flail wildly, hurling twigs and leaves until she felt Brodie tugging at her shirt.

Whirling, she gasped his name, cupping his face in her hands. "Oh, Brodie," she sobbed. "Are you all right?"

"Leg," he muttered, wincing.

His leg was twisted under him at an awkward angle. Kristin felt sick. "Oh my God." She began to shake, a sharp, jolting shudder that enveloped her in waves.

"Where's the rifle?" he croaked.

"Rifle?" She stared stupidly, as if she'd never heard the word before.

"Where is it, Kris?" he asked quietly, urgently.

The realization was sobering. "Up there." She saw Brodie's eyes skim up the sheer bedrock. "It's still up there."

"Get it." Jerking as a spasm of pain shot through him, Brodie whispered through clamped teeth. "Climb up there, get it and get out of here."

"I'm not leaving you." Her voice was amazingly steady and strong.

"Kris . . . Kris, it's coming back." He pushed her weakly. "Go."

"No." Fear clogged her throat, but she wouldn't give in to it. Not this time. Brodie depended on her. She scanned the wolf's position as it circled, ever closer, and knew that by climbing up to retrieve the rifle, Brodie would be left helpless.

Kristin's jaw tightened with determination. Brodie saw the slight gesture and knew she wasn't going to leave. He also knew that their situation was serious. This animal could be the rogue wolf that had been attacking New Wave's herd. It could be injured or starving or it could even be rabid. It was definitely deadly.

Painfully, Brodie turned on his side, allowing her access to the backpack. "Flashlight," he whispered. "In the pack."

Hesitating only a moment, Kristin dug through the pack until she felt the smooth metallic column. It was a huge flashlight, solid metal and nearly eighteen inches long, the kind she'd seen hanging from a policeman's belt. With trembling fingers, she located the side switch and turned the bright beam directly into the wolf's eyes.

It growled, a kind of half bark, half gurgling sound, and crouched. Kristin could see it clearly in the harsh spray of light. The beast was huge, probably weighing almost as much as she herself did. Its coat was rangy, with ugly tufts of hair hanging from back and ribs, and saliva dripped from exposed fangs, glistening like wet spider webs. Its pleated muzzle was streaked with dirty gouges and the tip of one ear was missing, giving it a lopsided, almost ridiculous pitch.

Kristin realized the animal was as chewed up as she was, and the thought was suddenly incredibly amusing. She giggled, a wild, hysterical sound.

"The rifle, Kris." Brodie's whispered plea caught the edge of her mind. "Get the rifle before he figures out what to do."

Backing slowly toward the incline, Kristin kept the blinding light trained on the wolf's face. She used her free hand to pull slowly up the embankment, digging her heels into dirt, rock, whatever she could find to propel herself. After she'd climbed about five feet, silence shrouded the forest and she froze, listening. It was dark now, not yet pitch black, but dark enough to obscure everything not lit by the flashlight's beam. No growling, no snarling . . . the air was deadly quiet.

It attacked with incredible speed, screeching as it leaped on Brodie, rending the air with a snarling pandemonium of vicious, beastly growls mingled with grunting sounds of struggle.

Screaming, Kristin jumped from her perch as flashes of mottled gray blurred against Brodie's muted blue shirt. Fear left in a wave of fury. Her fingers touched fur and she arched the flashlight into a crashing blow aimed only at the whirling pelt. A sickening thud was followed by a sharp yelp, then vibrating snarl as it turned on her. Kristin felt teeth graze her wrist, then a knifing pain that was followed by numbness. Without thinking she brought the heavy metal flashlight crashing down into the wolf's skull.

It fell away, staggering.

Stumbling backward, she felt Brodie's hand on her ankle and collapsed beside him. She felt his body and gasped at the sticky dampness on his shirt. "You're hurt...my God, Brodie, you're bleeding."

"Ssshhh, I'm fine, honey. All he got was a mouthful of backpack." A sharp sting hit his shoulder and he sucked in a quick breath. "Well, he might've gotten a taste of me, after all."

"But the blood..."

"It's not as bad as it looks." Brodie eased the flashlight out of her impossibly tight grip, and turned the beam on Kristin and saw the red furrows slashing her forearm.

Then he looked into her empty eyes and was terrified by what he saw.

Brodie saw her eyes empty as her mind began its retreat from a reality she was unable to accept. It was, he realized, the beast of her nightmares that she had faced for him. She'd confronted it and won, only to withdraw behind a wall of self-protection.

He'd seen that look before, a kind of shell that enveloped those whose bodies had survived a trauma that the mind couldn't endure. Sometimes they came back to the world. Sometimes, escape was permanent.

Seeing Kristin's ghostly pallor, Brodie tasted fear, a bitter, metallic bile rising from his stomach, a surge of adrenalin that numbed his own pain as every fibre of his body focused on saving Kristin.

She had risked her life for him, confronting and overcoming her own nightmares. It had cost her dearly. Brodie loved her courage as much as he loved her compassion.

So if he loved her so much, how could he simply let her walk out of his life?

Silently, he answered his own question—it was because he had been so obsessed with his own dreams that he had no room to share hers. Every minute she'd spent on the ranch had been torture for her, yet he'd expected her to stay because he had selfishly refused to leave the ranch. Kristin was the woman he wanted to spend his life with, yet he allowed his own vain vision of single-handedly saving the world to sabotage their future in the same way as it had sabotaged all of his previous relationships.

Without Kristin, the dream had lost its meaning.

Brodie crawled to her, teeth set against the pain as he dragged his useless leg. Pushing himself into a sitting position, he gathered her into his arms. She was coiled into a tight ball, knees bent against her chest, fists tucked beneath her chin.

Brodie warmed her face with his hands, soothing with soft, incoherent words, much as one would comfort a frightened child. Then he briskly rubbed her bloodless limbs, massaging tense muscles until he felt the violent trembling recede. Her head rested against his chest, but she gave no indication that she was aware of his presence.

And her vacant stare remained fixed on the body of the wolf.

Kristin didn't respond as he softly called her name, so he called to her again, changing his tone to a sharp command. He felt a small convulsive jerk and was pleased.

"Get the rifle, Kris." His voice was stern, harsh, punctuated by a light shake of her shoulders. "Now, honey, get the rifle *now*."

As Brodie turned her face toward him, she twisted away, maintaining a visual vigil on the twisted lump of fur. Gently, he blocked her view with his hand, urging until she blinked up at him. "It's dead, honey. It can't hurt you now."

She appeared lost and her voice had a childlike quality. "It might wake up. I'm afraid."

His heart lurched. "I know, honey, but you're safe now." For the moment, anyway. Fumbling with the leather strap, Brodie unsheathed the walkie-talkie. It made a strange rattling sound and his heart sank. He pressed the transmitter, called for Gus, then listened. Nothing. No hissing, no crackling, nothing. Useless, apparently smashed when he'd rolled down the embankment.

If he could only get to the rifle, he could fire a couple of rounds as a distress signal. He grabbed the flashlight, sweeping the beam across the slope down which he'd fallen. The rifle was wedged behind a tree nearly at the bottom of the slope.

If he could crawl the ten feet or so to the bottom of the hill, he might be able to pull himself far enough up to reach it.

And he *had* to reach it. Those fresh tracks he'd found had belonged to more than one wolf.

Using his good leg, Brodie pushed himself to the base of the slope. Ignoring the searing pain, he groped above his head until he found a sturdy root. He pulled, straining to move upward, fighting a blinding blast of agony, a wall of red that suddenly painted the night.

Then his hand gripped air and he cried out before his mind emptied.

Somewhere in Kristin's fogged subconscious, Brodie's voice registered.

I need you.

Eyelids fluttered down, then opened as clear, silver eyes blinked into the darkness. She was disoriented, like a sleepwalker awakened in a strange place.

"Brodie?"

Had she really heard him or was it a dream?

A soft groan echoed from behind her. She turned toward the sound and called his name again. The flashlight lay on the ground, its cold beam illuminating the fallen wolf.

Kristin remembered—snarls, teeth, sticky fur beneath her fingers and Brodie, broken and hurt. She stumbled toward him, cupping his face in her hands. Brodie was lying against the embankment, half vertically, a though he'd tried to pull himself up. He was unconscious, his face the color of bleached egg shells. She eased the backpack off to make him more comfortable. Matchbooks and a small compass fell through the gashed fabric, clattering to the ground. She shuddered, staring at the torn pack. Rooting through the pack, she found a cloth and wet it, grateful they hadn't depleted the canteen's water supply. The cool dampness seemed to revive him slightly and he smiled weakly, as the eyelids barely lifted.

"You're back," he murmured groggily.

"I never left you." She continued to sponge his face. His skin was hot and dry. Fiddling with the leather case on his belt, she said, "I'm going to call for help."

"Broken." Brodie's head rocked slowly, motioning weakly upward. "Rifle." God, he was tired. If he could just sleep for a couple of minutes....

Kristin's hands still trembled as she wrapped her fingers around the cool metal shaft of the flashlight, brushing the beam over the slope. She spotted the weapon, slanting awkwardly against a tree just a few feet above her and scrambled up to retrieve it.

"I've got it, Brodie...Brodie?" His head lolled. She pressed the cold cloth to his forehead until he responded. "I've got the rifle," she repeated.

A low groan rolled from his throat.

Kristin stared at the unfamiliar length of wood and metal. Biting her lower lip, she aimed into the blackness and fired. The stock recoiled into her stomach and she grunted. Aiming again, she fired once more, this time absorbing the shock with her shoulder.

"Good girl," he whispered, then his face contorted and he moaned briefly before his head toppled backward.

"Oh, Brodie," she whispered, her heart wrenching for his pain. She loved him so much it hurt. Kristin could admit that now, in the solitude of her own mind. Seeing him in danger, knowing he could have been killed, had driven her to act far beyond the realm of her own capability. It was like the stories she'd heard of people lifting an entire car with their bare hands in order to save someone they loved.

Stroking his face, she whispered, "I love you, Nathan Brodie." His eyelids fluttered, but remained closed and she knew he couldn't hear. "God only knows how much I love you." Moisture gathered across her lashes and she brushed it away.

Get a hold of yourself.

Even if Gus had heard the shots, it was a big canyon and, at the moment, a very, very dark one.

Forcing her mind to activate, she remembered that they hadn't descended the slope at exactly the same spot they'd climbed up this morning. Brodie had wanted to skirt the bedrock cliff, so they'd gone to the left—let's see, that would be east—about fifty feet. Gus would have to come from the west. He would be back at the truck by now, so he would come through the woods to the first rise, somewhere in that direction. She stared down the canyon and upward into the inky darkness.

A signal, that's what she needed, one Gus could see from the top of that far hill. The flashlight might do it, but a fire would be far better.

Gathering the matches that had fallen from Brodie's pack, Kristin searched for small twigs and branches. Within five minutes, she'd ringed a small, cleared patch with rocks and had a roaring campfire in the middle of the canyon floor that should be visible for half a mile.

She'd just placed a large branch across the flames and was anxiously scanning the canyon's western cleft when a mournful wail filled the night.

"No." It was more a whimper than a word. She whirled, staring at the rumpled lump of fur. "It's all in my mind," she whispered, trying to believe it. "There's nothing out there."

But it came again, a series of sharp howls ending in a blood-chilling cry.

Panic shrieked through her and she jammed her fist against her lips so she wouldn't scream.

I can't control it.

Her legs begged for the freedom to run, to career wildly into the darkness seeking safety. Her throat filled with a silent scream as her pulse leaped into frantic cadence.

I'm a weak, sniveling coward.

Her own words taunted her. She couldn't handle the fear, couldn't control the terror.

Then she saw Brodie leaning weakly against the slope, helpless. She wouldn't leave him.

Again, the wolf's call sliced the thick night air and she sobbed out loud.

"Stop it!" Startled, she heard her own voice, clear and strong. She listened to it. "Think, Kristin. *Think!*"

Oh yes, she could think. She could clear her mind—she *could* control it—for Brodie. Tomorrow, she could go crazy, but tonight she would stay sane. She had to.

The fire. Animals didn't like fire. She'd read that somewhere. Brodie would be safe by the fire.

Stumbling to Brodie, she pulled his arm around her neck and circled his waist. "Lean on me." Her voice was low, urgent. Brodie mumbled and his eyes opened slowly. "We have to get to the fire." He hesitated, not wanting to move. "Hurry." She hauled him against her as the wolf's wail again cut the night, closer, louder. It got his attention. Muttering a sharp epithet, he painfully shifted his weight against her and she half carried, half dragged him to the fire. As she lowered him to the ground, Brodie's face dripped with exertion and pain.

Jaw clamped in grim determination, Kristin placed the rifle in her lap, stared into the darkness, and waited.

Finally she saw the small row of flashlights in the distance, and soon Gus was standing over her assessing the situation. He issued a low, hissing whistle.

"Well, now, if that don't just beat all," Gus muttered, poking the limp pile of fur with the toe of his boot. "Why didn't you just shoot the dang thing?"

Kristin slid him a tired look. "The thought never crossed my mind." She held Brodie's head in her lap and felt him stiffen as pain washed over him. "We have to get Brodie to the hospital."

Squatting, Gus examined Brodie's leg with a shrewd, practiced eye. "Yep," he agreed. "But his leg's clean broke and he ain't gonna like the trip much." Gus saw the convulsive tightening of Kristin's arms around Brodie and hastened to reassure her. "Don't you fret, missy. It'd take more'n a cracked leg to stop this ornery cuss."

Before she could reply, Gus was barking orders and Billy was hacking limbs from a nearby scrub oak. A crude splint was fashioned and Kristin wept as Brodie endured the agony of having his leg immobilized. Using leather belts donated by Todd and Billy, the wooden braces were strapped securely before Brodie was lifted onto a sling constructed from a woolen blanket.

Ernie dropped to his knees beside the blanket, cheeks wet, eyes filled with guilt and remorse. "Brodie," he said, the words seeming to choke him. "I—I . . ."

"It's okay, Ernie." Brodie's face was pale and damp, his voice weak. "Everything will be fine."

"Grab a corner, younguns," Gus directed. "And take care not to drop him, or he'll be a mite peeved."

* * *

Hours later, Kristin sat in the hospital emergency room while a pink-faced resident dabbed antiseptic on the gouges in her arm. "You're fortunate the wounds are superficial. I think we can get by without stitches." The young physician frowned at the white scars extending from wrist to elbow. "It appears you've had a similar experience."

"Yes." She didn't elaborate. "How's Brodie?"

"Umm? Oh, he's in X ray, I believe." The doctor pulled a small penlight from his pocket. His hands smelled of antiseptic and were cool against her skin. "Look this way, please." He flashed the beam in each eye, measuring the contracting of her pupils. "Your color is a bit off, but that's to be expected. Still, it might be wise for you to stay at the hospital overnight as a precaution. You seemed a bit shocked when you arrived."

"No." Kristin hated hospitals. "Gus can drive me back to the ranch."

"Gus? Ah, Mr. Krieger." He scribbled on her chart. "He and your friends have gone to retrieve the body of the animal that attacked you." Deftly, he wrapped a length of gauze around her forearm and taped it in place. "If the lab tests are negative, we can dispense with routine rabies inoculation."

Kristin blanched. She'd forgotten about that. Noticing her distress, the doctor gave her hand an encouraging pat. "Don't worry. These cases rarely test positive."

"But it attacked us. That's unusual, isn't it?"

"Yes, but certainly not unheard of. There have been a lot of wolf and bear sightings in the valley this year, more than normal. I understand that the animals' natural habitat was destroyed by the fires last fall so they've come to the lower elevations looking for food and new territory. You see? Unusual behavior doesn't necessarily mean the animal is rabid."

Her breath slid into a smooth sigh. "Thank you, Dr...." She squinted at his name tag. "Dr. Fletcher. I'm concerned about Ernie. Is he all right?" Dr. Fletcher appeared momentarily perplexed and she added, "Ernie Fenton, the boy who was...lost."

"Oh, yes." He brightened. "The boy is fine. A bit dehydrated, of course, and rather tired, but he should suffer no substantial effects from his little adventure."

"That's a relief." Poor, confused Ernie. Kristin remembered his expression of horror when he'd seen that Brodie had been hurt. Ernie would need careful counseling and guidance to help him through this, help him understand and forgive his own behavior. Kristin wished she could work with him, help him somehow, but she couldn't. As soon as she was assured that Brodie was all right, she would have to keep her promise to leave. The thought hurt. "Dr. Fletcher, do you think Mr. Brodie is out of X ray yet? I—I'd really like to see him."

"I'm sure he's fine," the doctor said. "But I'll be glad to check for you."

She smiled gratefully and the doctor swept briskly from the room. Exhausted, Kristin sagged against the sterile white wall and began to shiver. The acrid hospital smell was stifling. She just hated hospitals. Too many memories, too much pain.

A cold dampness filmed her brow and her fingers iced as she fought a wave of nausea. It was over, she told herself, battling the delayed reaction. Brodie was safe, Ernie was safe, and it was over.

Flashbacks of the past month filled her brain with images. In her mind's eye, Brodie stood, tall and proud, watching over the ranch he'd built with sweat and courage. She saw herself, haughty, rigid, tearing at his accomplishment until his face grew haggard and desolate.

Kristin Michaels Price, and her never-ending quest for facts, figures and statistics. How ruthless she'd been in her pursuit, ignoring the gentle, guiding voice of conscience. She'd told herself that her cause was noble, that her sole purpose was to provide better lives for the children who lived in quiet desperation.

What ego, she thought sadly. Her entire career had been devoted to fluttering from one case to another, never touching or being touched, trying to save them all yet saving none. She'd drifted through their young lives like a feather on the wind, caressing softly for the moment, then floating away.

Brodie had given the boys something permanent and enduring—himself. Kristin had nearly destroyed him.

He'd nearly died because of her.

If she hadn't been so blind to her own fears, her own innate weakness, New Wave wouldn't have been threatened and Ernie wouldn't have felt driven to protect it.

Ernie loved Brodie. Kristin loved Brodie, too, and the depth of her feelings was frightening. She had, after all, spent most of her life avoiding love, armoring herself against the painful loss she knew would inevitably follow.

This loss would be worse than all the others. She would return to the city, but Kristin knew that part of her soul would be left behind.

"Uh, Ms. Price." The young doctor had returned, looking concerned.

Stiffening, Kristin whispered, "Brodie?"

"Oh, he's fine, just fine. An oblique fracture of the fibula, mild concussion and assorted abrasions and contusions. Only..." His lips pursed. "We'd like to keep him overnight for observation."

Kristin relaxed slightly. "Of course. I understand."

"Unfortunately, Mr. Brodie does not. He's, well, causing a bit of a stir in the ward and I wondered if you could, ah, talk to him."

Smiling, Kristin shook her head. She could imagine what kind of 'stir' he was causing. "I assume he wants to leave."

"Precisely."

With a sigh, Kristin slipped off the paper-wrapped cot. "My recommendation is that you hand him a pair of crutches and wave goodbye." Her lips twitched. "Unless, of course, you plan to render him unconscious." A light gleamed in the young doctor's eyes and Kristin hastened to reassure him. "But I'll talk to him, of course. Where is he?"

"Down the hall, to your right, room 114." A flash of white coat disappeared through the door.

Kristin followed, and as she walked out of the examining room, she nearly collided with Merle Deever and Jess. "What are you two doing here?"

"Billy called and told us what happened." Deever's eyes slid to her bandaged arm. "You okay?"

"Fine," she said, then relayed the doctor's message on Brodie's condition. When she finished, Deever's face cracked into a broad grin.

"Guess we'd best get to him before he starts flinging bedpans," Deever said. "Then we'll take you on back to the ranch. The car's right outside."

"What car?" Kristin asked. Gus still had the truck and the only other vehicle at the ranch was her rental car. Deever shifted uncomfortably. "My rental car?"

"Yeah, well..." Deever cleared his throat. "We didn't think you'd mind."

"But I have the keys," Kristin insisted.

Jess rocked back on his heels, stuffed his hands in his black denim pockets and smiled.

Kristin gawked at the smug teenager. "You didn't."

"The boy's got real talent," Deever mumbled, then took Kristin's elbow and propelled Kristin down the hall.

Brodie's voice filtered down the hall, angry muttering followed by a loud yelp and a rather graphic oath. As they reached the doorway, a smiling nurse was emerging with a huge hypodermic needle. "Better hurry." She appeared immensely satisfied. "He'll be asleep in two minutes."

Apparently, the young doctor had taken Kristin's remark literally.

Kristin stepped through the door, dodging the pillow that flew from Brodie's hand. He froze. "Kris?" A wan smile curved his lips. "Are you okay? They wouldn't tell me anything..." The smile slipped to a scowl as he rubbed his flank. "Sadists," he mumbled.

"You look, ah, well." She smothered a grin and added, "Considering."

His hair ruffled upward in curling sprouts and the too small hospital gown had slipped up to reveal a muscular, furred thigh that disappeared into a solid cast from knee to ankle. He glared at the plaster casing, then saw Merle and Jess sidling in the door.

"Nice threads," Jess observed.

Brodie's expression was thunderous and he turned it on Merle. "Get my clothes," he growled. "I'm getting out of here." Even as he spoke, his eyelids drooped.

"Not likely, boss," Merle said. "Doc says you can come home tomorrow, though."

Brodie's head dropped limply back. "Kris . . ."

"I'm here." She wrapped her fingers around his hand.

"Don't leave before I get back." His eyes were closing in spite of his efforts, but he managed to squeeze her hand. "Promise," he whispered hoarsely. "Promise you won't . . ."

Then he slept. Kristin touched his face, smoothing his cheek with the back of her hand. "I promise," she said softly.

Yes, she would be at the ranch when he returned. She'd be there to say good-bye.

The trunk slammed shut, entombing the pile of battered luggage.

Dusting her hands, Kristin looked toward the house. Flowers, she mused. *That's* what was missing, why the house looked so barren and lifeless. A few hanging baskets dripping with fuchsias, a colorful border of bright marigolds and stately gladiolus, that would give the loving look of a home to the plain, white-washed building.

When she got back to the city, she would pick up some seeds and send them to Oaf.

Her glance skimmed the green knoll and she remembered the faint echo of games and laughter. She saw the stable and could swear she heard Martha issue a soft, nickering farewell. The bubbling rush of a mountain waterfall, the burning touch of Brodie's fingers on her skin. A flood of memories.

During her stay at the ranch, Kristin had felt grief and pain, love and happiness, terror and triumph. For the first time in so many years, Kristin had actually allowed herself to feel, to love, to live.

She would cherish those feelings, those memories, for the rest of her life.

But now, it was time to go.

The dust cloud rising in the distance signaled the truck's return even before the soft groan of the engine wafted to her ears. The hospital had called early this morning to say that Brodie was ready for release. Actually, the harried voice of the nurse had given the impression that the hospital staff was as pleased at the news as Kristin herself was.

Gus had insisted on escort duty, and now pulled the truck into the main yard. Since Kristin had parked her rental car in front of the house to make loading easier, the truck shuddered to a stop a few feet behind the smaller vehicle.

Kristin tensed as the passenger door opened. Brodie struggled out, ineptly manipulating the awkward crutches yet refusing Gus's gesture of assistance with a silent scowl. When he maneuvered into an upright position, Brodie's eyes locked with Kristin's. Neither of them saw Gus's shrewd glance, or heard his muttered retreat into the house.

"You're leaving." Brodie's stare was as tangible as a touch and kept Kristin's feet cemented to the ground.

She nodded. "I have a four o'clock flight out of Fresno."

He swung forward until he loomed over her. "Can you postpone it? The flight, I mean."

"I...I have to get back." Her voice sounded lame. "There's really no reason to put it off. My work here is done."

His lips pursed. "It's just that I could use a little help." He wiggled a crutch for emphasis, then added, "With my luggage. The doctor said I should get away for a little while." He grinned sheepishly. "I've always kind of liked the beach. Besides, a change of scenery would be good for me—soak up some sun, breathe the ocean air. Gus can hold down the fort for a month or so."

Stunned, Kristin's brain caught up with his meaning. "You want to go back with me?"

"You've got a sun deck on that ocean condo, don't you?"

"Yes, but—"

"Great. Of course, I'll bring my own suntan oil."

Kristin's eyelids lowered. "Brodie, it will just be more difficult when it's time for you to leave."

"What makes you think I'm going to leave?" The smile was gone and his expression was deadly earnest.

Confused, Kristin scanned his face. "This is your home, Brodie. More than that, it's your dream."

He shrugged. "I've been thinking about a lot of things. New Wave can exist anywhere, even in the middle of L.A. It's the concept that counts, not the location."

"You can't be serious." Kristin's jaw slackened. "This ranch means everything to you."

"Not *everything*, Kris." His hand brushed her face. "I thought it did, until I met you. It's people that really count. This ranch is just a few acres of raw ground. People make it live, love makes it grow. I love you, Kristin Price, and I want to marry you."

"Marriage?" She was stammering. "We've never discussed...I mean, I never even thought about marriage."

"Of course we've discussed it." Brodie loosened his hand from the crutch in an impatient gesture. "I asked you to stay with me. What did you think I meant?"

Then Brodie remembered that he'd only asked her to stay, to give her work "real meaning" but not to marry him. He'd assumed she understood. Brodie moaned.

Balancing on his props, he extended his hand and brushed a fingertip across her cheek. "I guess I'm not very good at proposing, but then, I haven't had much practice."

Marriage. Kristin knew she loved him, but marriage meant commitment and commitment meant broken promises, betrayed trust. "You told me to leave." Kristin wet her lips. "After you saw the notes, found out what I'd done, you told me to go home."

"I was hurt and angry. I didn't know it was something you'd written weeks earlier." He paused, searching for words. "I thought—just for those brief moments—I thought you'd been deliberately deceiving me."

"No." She shook her head in vehement denial. "I never meant to deceive you, Brodie. I love you." Yes, she loved him and to say it out loud seemed suddenly so natural, so right.

His eyes softened. "I know that, honey, but it sure took you long enough to admit it." Lifting her chin, he caught her lips in a slow, sweet kiss. "Let's go back to L.A. together, Kris. I want us to be together always."

She was confused. "And the ranch, Brodie? What about New Wave?"

"We'll relocate anywhere you want. You choose, Kris."

She shook her head, not believing the words. "You make it sound so easy, so casual. It's not, Brodie. Happily-ever-after doesn't exist in real life. Eventually, you would hate me for everything you'd given up. I couldn't stand that."

"Listen to me, Kris. I asked you once to stay here, to give up your own dreams because I wasn't willing to compromise. Watching you risk everything for me last night, I knew I couldn't let you walk away—not without me. In the city, you can continue your career, the life you've chosen. I'm asking to share it with you, and I'm asking you to share mine."

The realization stunned her. Brodie was offering to give up the ranch and relocate, even in the city he hated, for her. Tears stung her eyes and she whispered, "No."

Brodie's expression shattered. "Just like that? You won't even think about it?"

"I don't have to think about it." Her voice trembled and she took a deep breath. "I've been running away from life, hiding from so many things. Commitment has terrified me—I can admit that, now. You could say I've chosen the easy life, never caring too much because I might get hurt, avoiding my fears instead of confronting them." She touched the face she loved so much. "And then you came along and made me face my own hypocrisy."

"You're no hypocrite, Kris. You're a loving, giving woman." Brodie covered the small hand caressing his cheek with his own larger one, turning the palm upward and kissing it softly.

"I want to be that kind of woman, for you and for myself. Brodie, I'm so frightened."

"Of what, Kris? What frightens you?"

"I don't want to be like the social worker who steps over drunks because she doesn't want to get involved. I've devoted myself to criticizing the system, congratulating myself for pursuing such a noble cause. But you've devoted yourself to the kids." Brodie started to speak and Kristin pressed a finger to his lips, silencing him. "You don't flit by the children, patting them on the head and telling them you care. You live every day with them and *show* them how much you care."

She cupped his face with her hands. "I love you, Nathan Brodie, and in my own strange way, I love New Wave, too. I can't let you give it up—not now."

"Kris, please." She was refusing him and he couldn't stand it. He reached out in a mute plea before his hand dropped helplessly to his side. "I don't want you to go."

She smiled and captured the limp hand. "But you're going with me. Soak up the sun, remember? And while your bones are mending, I'll be shifting my cases to the rest of the investigation staff." She squinted up at him. "Think Gus can hold down the fort until we get back?"

"Until *we* get back?" Brodie held his breath, hardly daring to hope as he whispered, "Define 'we.'"

"As in you and me, the both of us, together." She slid her arms around his waist. "I'm saying that I want to share your life, your commitments. I want to be a part of New Wave."

"And?"

"And . . ." She hesitated, certain of her feelings, yet still unnerved, almost overwhelmed by them. Brodie touched her face with such tenderness that waves of love engulfed her. He had been willing to give up so much for the sake of their love. Suddenly, her mind was clear and the hollowness deep inside her had been filled. Kristin Price knew exactly what she wanted. "I want to be your wife, Brodie."

"You will be, honey." His kiss sealed the promise. "You will be."

Epilogue

The soil was rich and fertile, lightly warmed by the sun's gentle spring kiss. Kristin's spade sank deeply into the earth, opening it to receive another tender young plant. She patted dark loam around the roots, then stretched, massaging a kink in her lower back. Pride surged through her as she regarded her handiwork, a colorful bed of marigolds rimming the porch with variegated hues of orange and yellow.

"Them posies is right pretty, missus, but you oughtn't be a'strainin' yourself that way." Gus dropped a stack of mail on the front porch, stubbled chin puckered in obvious disapproval.

Kristin laughed. "I'm hardly an invalid, Gus." Grabbing the porch railing, she levered herself into a standing position. Gus was beside her in a flash, clucking with concern as he helped her to her feet.

"Mebbe not," he conceded, "but you sure ain't as spry as you was and Brodie'd have my hide if'n you drop that youngun before he gets back."

Exasperated, Kristin said, "I'm not one of the mares, Gus."

"That's a fact," he acknowledged, then added, "I'd feel a mite better if'n you was."

She slid him an amused glance. "I can imagine. But the baby's not due for another month and Brodie will be back from Los Angeles any time now." Automatically, she scanned the dirt road leading into the yard as she'd done two dozen times in the last hour. A small frown pleated her forehead. "Merle went to pick him up at the airport hours ago."

"Now don't you go frettin', missus. Ain't good for the youngun." Gus scooped up the stack of mail on the porch, thumbing through the envelopes and magazines until he found what he'd been searching for. "This oughta perk you up a mite," he said, thrusting out a smudged letter.

Kristin recognized the penciled scrawl immediately and was delighted. "It's from Ernie." She snatched the envelope from Gus's hand and ripped it open. Ernie's spelling was still atrocious, but the letter was filled with pride and optimism. "The school is having a special exhibit and some of his work has been selected for the showing. Oh, Gus, this is wonderful."

Gus snorted. "If'n you say so," he said grudgingly. Ernie's acceptance at the New York Academy of Fine Arts had not sat well with Gus, who couldn't quite cotton to the idea of art being a proper way for a man to earn a living. "Dang waste of time, if'n you ask me," he muttered.

"You're such a grump," she said cheerfully. "I know you wanted Ernie to..." A rising dust cloud captured her attention. "Brodie." The whisper turned into a whoop. "It's Brodie! He's back!"

Following her excited gesture, Gus watched the pickup spill into view. "Yep," he agreed, then spat noisily.

Rushing toward the still-moving truck, Kristin ignored Gus's rasping plea for her to slow down. She only knew that Brodie was home and as he unfolded his lean, familiar body from the vehicle, her heart twisted with happiness. After two years, the sight of him still thrilled her.

Kristin launched into his arms, laughing and crying at the same time. Brodie gathered her against him as though she didn't have the equivalent of a large beachball expanding her belly, swung her around once, then buried his face in the curve of her throat.

"Oh, baby, I've missed you so much," Brodie whispered as he scattered kisses over her face.

"You've been gone so long," she moaned and knotted her fingers in his hair, pressing the substantial tummy bulge tightly against him. "I thought you'd never get back."

With a disgruntled snort, Gus ambled over. "Now ain't this just a fine sight," he grumbled. "Gone three days and you're a'maulin' her like it's been a month. Ain't fittin'."

Brodie grinned. "Haven't you ever been in love, Gus?"

"Well, now, sure I have." His mouth pinched wistfully. "Broke her leg, though, and I had to shoot her." A brown stream of tobacco juice splashed next to his boot. "Best dang cow pony I ever did see." With that, he sauntered off.

"Poor old goat doesn't know what he's missing," Brodie murmured, affectionately rubbing Kristin's stomach. "How're you feeling, honey?" His gaze shifted to the vibrant bed of marigolds and he grew serious. "You're not overdoing, are you? The boys could have done that when they were finished working in the garden."

Kristin glanced toward the huge plot of healthy green sprouts situated between the main house and the newly expanded bunkhouse. Four boys ranging in age from twelve to sixteen worked diligently among the furrows and as she watched, one of them playfully tossed a dirt clod at another. She smiled at their clowning. There were fifteen youngsters on the ranch now, and the vegetable garden was one of the boys' primary projects. Last summer, Oaf's kitchen had turned into a circus as he'd tried to supervise a half-dozen enthusiastic youngsters canning their own harvest. Unfortunately, the boys discovered that what they grew and preserved, they had to eat. Zucchini had been categorically eliminated from this year's seed purchase.

"Honey?" Brodie was concerned by her pensive expression. "Are you all right?"

"I'm wonderful," she said softly. "I've missed you so much." She hugged him tightly, then withdrew and wiggled the envelope in front of his nose.

Brodie's eyes lit. "Ernie?"

"Oh, Brodie. He's so happy. Some of his work is going on display."

"Really? That's great. When?"

"In a couple of months." Kristin saw Brodie's expression fall. "I know. The baby will be pretty tiny then, but I think we can still make it to New York for the showing."

Brodie seemed unconvinced. "I don't know . . ."

Her hand automatically moved to her stomach. "It will be fine, you'll see. After all, she'll be a Brodie, won't she? She's bound to be tough."

His eyebrow shot up. "She?"

Kristin shrugged. "The girls' bunkhouse won't be ready for another year. Martha and I are tired of being the only females."

"Don't be silly." He tweaked her nose. "We've doubled our stable and over half of the animals are mares."

"Yes," she said reasonably. "But the rest of them are merely horses." Kristin had become accustomed to the ranch's animal population, but Martha still held a very special place in her heart.

The mare had given birth to a beautiful, healthy colt a few months ago and Kristin had stayed with Martha through the entire process. Using knowledge gleaned from working with Dr. Amatti, Todd was not only allowed in the foaling stall, but the boy was actually able to assist in the delivery. At fifteen, Todd was maturing into a fine young man. He still loved animals, of course, but he'd discovered that people weren't half-bad, either.

Brodie laughed softly. "I found some acreage out by Riverside that could be the perfect location for New Wave South." His eyes took on a teasing glint. "And I got over to UCLA for a few hours."

"You saw Jess?" Kristin held her breath. "Has he decided yet?"

"He's already switched his major," he said, grinning at Kristin's excited squeak. "He'll be working here summers as sort of a crew leader for the boys. It'll be good experience for him and after he graduates, he'll come back to New Wave as a credentialed guidance counselor."

A lump formed in her throat. Kristin knew how much Jess's decision meant to Brodie. "I always knew he'd be the one to follow in your footsteps."

Brodie nodded quietly, then slid an arm around Kristin's shoulders. Together, they walked toward the house. When they reached the porch, Brodie scooped up the stack of mail Gus had tossed on the top step. He perused it briefly. "Have you seen this, honey? It's from your publisher."

"Umm?" Kristin took the fat manila envelope he handed her. "It must be the galleys. My editor called last week and said they'd be arriving soon. The book should be out by the end of summer."

Dropping a kiss on her forehead, he said, "My wife, the famous author. I knew you could do it."

"I couldn't have done it without you, my love."

That was true enough. Kristin had wanted to scrap the entire project, but Brodie had talked her out of it. He'd convinced her that there was a real need for the information she could share with the world and it was possible for her to accomplish her original goals.

Kristin had spent over a year rewriting the manuscript. Oh, it still pointed out the system's problems, its inequities, but this time she offered solutions and alternatives. The New Wave concept had become more than a mere chapter—it was the core and conscience of the book. Bob Sherwood had read the draft and been convinced that the book would encourage major renovations in foster home programs throughout the nation.

Brodie's ideas would find root and grow in the establishment of hundreds of similar programs. His dream would be fulfilled and Kristin would be part of it.

The baby shifted in her womb and Brodie chuckled as he felt the restless movement of his child. Miracles really do exist, Kristin mused, nestling against her husband's chest. So many wondrous miracles.

After all...a man so blessed that he can share a true and righteous love, can make his stand on any ground, casting shadows on the sun.

* * * * *

Silhouette Special Edition

MORE SPECIAL THAN EVER, SAY THESE TOP AUTHORS:

LINDA HOWARD

"Silhouette Special Editions are indeed 'special' to me. They reflect the complexity of the modern woman's life, professionally, emotionally and, of course, romantically. They are windows through which we can see different views of life, the means by which we can experience all the depths and altitudes of the great love we want and need in our lives. Silhouette Special Editions are special dreams; we need dreams—to take us out of our everyday lives, and to give us something to reach for."

EMILIE RICHARDS

"I write stories about love and lovers because I believe we can't be reminded too often that love changes lives. I write Silhouette Special Editions because longer, in-depth stories give me the chance to explore all love's aspects, from the mad whirl to the quiet moments of contemplation. There's nothing more special than love, and there's no line more special than Silhouette Special Edition. I am proud to tell my stories in its pages."

SSE-A1

ATTRACTIVE, SPACE SAVING BOOK RACK

Display your most prized novels on this handsome and sturdy book rack. The hand-rubbed walnut finish will blend into your library decor with quiet elegance, providing a practical organizer for your favorite hard-or soft-covered books.

Only $9.95

**Approximately
16" x 8"
when assembled**

Assembles in seconds!

To order, rush your name, address and zip code, along with a check or money order for $10.70* ($9.95 plus 75¢ postage and handling) payable to *Silhouette Books*.

> Silhouette Books
> Book Rack Offer
> 901 Fuhrmann Blvd.
> P.O. Box 1396
> Buffalo, NY 14269-1396
>
> *Offer not available in Canada.*

*New York and Iowa residents add appropriate sales tax.

BKR-2A

1989
IS THE YEAR OF THE MAN!

What makes a romance? A special man, of course, and Silhouette Desire celebrates that fact with *twelve* of them! From Mr. January to Mr. December, every month has a tribute to the Silhouette Desire hero—our **MAN OF THE MONTH!**

Sexy, macho, charming, irritating . . . irresistible! Nothing can stop these men from sweeping you away. Created by some of your favorite authors, each man is custom-made for pleasure—*reading* pleasure—so don't miss a single one.

Mr. January is Blake Donavan in RELUCTANT FATHER by Diana Palmer
Mr. February is Hank Branson in THE GENTLEMAN INSISTS by Joan Hohl
Mr. March is Carson Tanner in NIGHT OF THE HUNTER by Jennifer Greene
Mr. April is Slater McCall in A DANGEROUS KIND OF MAN by Naomi Horton
Mr. May is Luke Harmon in VENGEANCE IS MINE by Lucy Gordon
Mr. June is Quinn McNamara in IRRESISTIBLE by Annette Broadrick

And that's only the half of it— so get out there and find your man!

Silhouette Desire's
MAN OF THE MONTH . . .

MOM-1

Silhouette Special Edition

COMING NEXT MONTH

#511 BEST LAID PLANS—Nora Roberts
Headstrong engineer Abra Wilson and cocky architect Cody Johnson
couldn't cooperate long enough to construct a hotel together—could
they possibly hope to build a lasting love?

#512 SKY HIGH—Tracy Sinclair
When client Jeremy Winchester insisted that pilot Meredith Collins
masquerade as his fiancée, she knew something was fishy—so why
did his pretense of passion feel so real?

#513 SMALL-TOWN SECRETS—Kate Meriwether
Their high-school reunion unveiled forbidden longings...but could
Reese finally beat the ultimate rival for Sadie's love without revealing
secrets that would tear the community—and Sadie's heart—apart?

#514 BUILD ME A DREAM—Pat Warren
Toy designer ''Casey'' Casswell created dreams for children...
and dreamed of having children. Pretty, practical Sabrina Ames
would be his ideal mate—if she weren't so terrified of marriage
and motherhood!

#515 DARK ANGEL—Pamela Toth
Julie Remington and Angel Maneros had crossed class boundaries to
fall in love, only to be thwarted by the bitterest misunderstanding.
Ten years later, they were facing temptation—and betrayal—
once again.

#516 A SUDDEN SUNLIGHT—Laurey Bright
When heiress Natalia awoke from a coma—pregnant—she didn't
remember the horrors she had survived. Nor did she remember Matt,
who claimed to be her lover, her fiancé....

AVAILABLE THIS MONTH: